ROBERT CARTER

The Collectors

LOTHROP, LEE & SHEPARD BOOKS
NEW YORK

For my daughter
Louise Carter
who has the courage to love

First Edition   1   2   3   4   5   6   7   8   9   10

Library of Congress Cataloging in Publication Data was not available in time for the publication of this book, but can be obtained from the Library of Congress. The Collectors. ISBN 0-688-13763-6. Library of Congress Catalog Card Number: 94-75333.

$\mathcal{U}$nder the circle of the moon,
the soft, lush leaves of the jasmine, the clipped
and leveled lawn, the azaleas, the wisteria, and
the English willow continued their struggle against the
lemon tree, the rosebushes, the passion-flower vine,
the morning glory, and the rhododendrons. A heady mix of
lingering perfumes that revealed the night side of themselves;
the part that has waited cautiously under the sun to begin
breathing freely; the part that is colored by the dark—and by
the pearly, platinum trail of the moon.
Between the brick edges of the garden and layers of twisted
and fallen leaves, from under small pockets in the soil and
forgotten man-made objects; from corners and caverns
and cracks came the collectors. Glancing occasionally
in reverence at the sharp circle above them,
they were the first and last of
Ootheca.

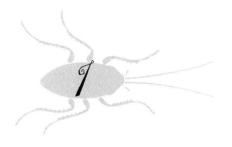

*T*he removal of the brick pile was the worst blow to the collectors in the yard. Isme and Declan were caught there, so shocked at the sudden drench of light that Declan hadn't even moved from the moment the brick rose and the Longley female screamed, and the brick descended. The male Longley kept smacking away at Isme and Declan while the scream lasted. The entire colony in the garden could feel the earth shudder with horror at each blow. A flutterer could see the two unfortunate victims were finished on the first hit, they would all say later. Afterward came the chlordane gas, falling through the air—a late-night dew, a deadly mist leaving overturned bodies with feet and legs pulsing in the air like half-mown grass in the wind.

Each night now in the garden was colder than the last and food collection in the new paved garden the Longleys liked to call a courtyard was yielding practically nothing. Some of the younger collectors were talking of a Kitchen raid—regardless of the danger. Hunger had made heroes before and everyone had heard the stories of the food in the Kitchen. Sometimes the smell of it would waft out. Stories abounded of the old Kitchen Wars and of those who had returned, never the same, bunched together at the farthest end of the yard, where their eyes and their talk skirted empty spaces as if something more than a leg or a hind wing had forever been left behind.

Under the lemon tree two young adult collectors waited impatiently for the sun to finally settle. The wind was chilling right through to their gut. They stamped a regular, marching beat into the soil to help shake the stiffness in their legs, which made tiny puffs of dust rise. Like those of most of the collectors in the yard, their stomachs were empty, and the smell of strange foods so close rushed to fill the space normally occupied by caution. In front of them in the courtyard, the Longleys clustered around in clumps eating and drinking and noisemaking. The larger of the two collectors, known as Edwud K, wanted to watch. His friend, Nolan, wanted to get well out of the way, even though they couldn't be easily seen among the shoots of new-mown buffalo grass. A baby human, dribbling and grunting, crawled up to where they stood. Edwud and Nolan dropped their antennae and crouched lower into the grass. Edwud clearly envisaged the baby picking him up and putting him into its slobbery mouth.

"Still!" he hissed to his friend. Nolan froze in an uncomfortable crouch.

The baby stopped crawling, flopped heavily back onto its padded bottom, and continued sucking on a sodden biscuit held tightly in its fist. Part of the biscuit broke off and fell to the ground less than forty leggs[1] away from Edwud and Nolan. They looked at each other.

"You're drooling," Edwud joked.

[1] A legg is a distance approximately equal to one centimeter.

6

"Ssh," Nolan whispered.

"I'm going to get that chump,"[2] Edwud said as he folded his forewings back.

"Are you mad? They can see you for . . . for thirty leggs at least," Nolan said. He sniffed at Edwud's breath and watched him for signs of unsteadiness.

"I'm going." Edwud stared at the chump. Nolan grabbed hold of Edwud's plate.[3]

"You said they can see us easier if we're moving," he said.

"Let go, damn you," Edwud called out as loudly as he dared. Nolan held on tighter, shutting his eyes for greater concentration. Edwud strained toward the sweet-smelling chump. At that moment the Longley female's arms swooped into view, scooping up the baby and the chump in one neat movement. Edwud shut his eyes and braced himself for the Longley female's infamous scream. Nothing. The baby and the chump were carried past the others and through the back door of the house. Edwud opened his eyes in time to see them disappear into the Kitchen.

For some time Edwud stared at the Kitchen door as if it might somehow invite him in.

"See!" Nolan said, still too shaken to concern himself about smugness. Edwud didn't reply. It annoyed him that Nolan was right. He looked hard at his friend and saw, beneath the fear and relief, Nolan's love for him. He raised his antennae in a kind of salute.

---

[2] A chump usually refers to an amount of forgotten, lost, or contaminated food.

[3] A shieldlike plate of armor covering the front part of the body, often including the head.

Edwud wondered why he did take such risks—was it because everything became clearer, if only for tiny moments, when he was under threat? A beautiful object is beautiful precisely because other things are not. Did danger, by contrast, and through its possibility of loss, add value to the things that he loved? He loved being alive: is that why he could risk his life? On rare moments, after collecting, deep into the tired part of the night, when groups gathered and spoke without reserve, without care of what could be thought of them—that's when he loved being alive. And he thrilled to the possibility of things he imagined, and at some moments he imagined that all things were possible.

Nolan shook his head. He had given up trying to understand Edwud. Peculiar, his father had called Edwud when they were younger. And Nolan, on one of his few excursions into thought, decided that it was probably their vast differences that held them together—like water and clay under the pressure of the sun.

The sound of an approaching collector caused Edwud to tense and direct his antennae away. The scent was Sera T's. Edwud's heart lurched. He pretended to be moonglazing,[4] and struck a pose that lined up his antennae with his hind wings, one he hoped Sera would find attractive—and Nolan would not find ridiculous.

"Ho," Nolan called.

"Ho," Sera answered.

"Sera," Edwud said, trying to sound impressively detached. Sera smiled.

[4] In deep thought. A very ancient poetic notion that the moon could be "polished" by thought.

Edwud looked at her and decided that his pose was ridiculous. She appeared calm and natural. He tried to relax his antennae but they seemed to wave around awkwardly in the air like wet stalks of grass.

"You look fierce standing there like that," Sera said.

"Do I?" Edwud tried his wise smile, nodding his head up and down, wondering whether fierce was a good thing to look. "Yes, well, I was thinking of the Kitchen . . ."

"So long as he only thinks about it," Nolan said to Sera, as if he had made a joke.

"What were you thinking about the Kitchen?" Sera asked Edwud.

"Nothing really—except that a raid might be a good idea."

"A raid!" Nolan's antennae shot into the air above his head. Sera stepped back a little from Edwud.

Edwud's thinking began to blur; he felt like a fool. He had wanted to impress Sera; once again his mouth had made words without checking with his brain. The truth was that he *had* been thinking of a Kitchen raid, but not at that moment. The truth, Edwud had decided some time ago, was like sweet food: not enough made you weak and sickly, too much would weigh you down and, eventually, perhaps kill you. The last thing he wanted if he ever did go into the Kitchen was to have to look after Nolan, who would insist on going with him.

"There's nothing in the yard," he said.

"There's nothing in your head," Nolan replied, "if you're thinking of a Kitchen raid—is there, Sera?"

Sera looked at Edwud as if he had asked the question.

9

"The Reverend Viel said that the food smells are there only to attract us in, that we should resist them . . ."

"Did he?" Edwud interrupted. Sera stopped, aware of Edwud's sour tone. "I'm sorry. Go on, what did he say?" Edwud prompted.

"It doesn't matter," Sera said.

Edwud's gaze remained fixed on her, as if by looking at her words would be drawn out of him that would say what he wanted them to say.

"I have a firm opinion of the Kitchen," Nolan said. "It doesn't exist."

Edwud turned toward him in surprise. Nolan looked at Sera.

"If it doesn't exist—I can't go in there, can I?" he said.

"What if we starve out here?" Edwud asked.

"We haven't yet," Nolan said.

"It's a bit late when your legs are waving in the air," Edwud shot back, glancing at Sera. He knew once again he was failing to impress her, yet instead of trying to retrieve the situation he heard himself push on further. "It comes down, in the end," he said, "to taking a risk."

"Yes, but risks aren't always to *do* something, are they?" Sera said. "Sometimes it's harder, even riskier, to do nothing at all."

Edwud paused to consider. He realized with dismay how his thinking deteriorated within range of Sera's scent. How could anyone smell so good?

"If you do nothing at all, that would mean you didn't want anything to change," Edwud said. Sera gave Edwud a puzzled look. He continued, "It would mean that you thought everything was fine exactly as it is."

Sera looked at Nolan, hoping for rational support. "Everything *is* fine exactly as it is," she said.

Edwud was too surprised to answer and, underneath that, too disappointed to think clearly. He wanted to explain some of the thoughts he had had about this subject, some of the things he believed he might have uncovered. "Risk is essential," he plowed on. "It's how we know what safety is—where the boundaries of our . . . our strength are. It's how we . . . we . . ."—for a moment Edwud lost the words—"we know ourselves."

The complexity of the thoughts silenced them, as if what was being said masked something that wasn't being said—like plastic wrap around a sweet chump.

As if watching a stranger, Edwud saw himself reach out with his left antenna and stroke the side of Sera's face. Sera did not make the slightest movement. Edwud felt even more ridiculous.

"I . . . I . . . it . . . I . . . was . . . ," he stuttered.

Nolan wondered how much Sera knew about Edwud. His snorting and quaffing of the soapsud foam[5] in the drains and how, when totally sotted, he insisted he was not Edwud at all but someone quite different, someone called Lennod.

"I . . . think . . . ," Edwud began.

The light coming on in the Kitchen sprang under the door and out through the windows. The breeze shifted

[5] Certain types of spume and soapsud swill passing through drains were recognized as causing a special state of intoxication, with effects varying between drunkenness and temporary psychosis.

11

direction suddenly and spread Edwud's large, delicate hind wings. As Sera moved off, she watched them lift against the last glow of the setting sun—intricate patterns of membranes crisscrossing, straining out the colors like stained glass.

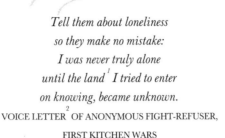

Tell them about loneliness
so they make no mistake:
I was never truly alone
until the land [1] I tried to enter
on knowing, became unknown.
VOICE LETTER [2] OF ANONYMOUS FIGHT-REFUSER,

FIRST KITCHEN WARS

$\mathcal{T}$he Director listened impassively to the charges directed against a small brown collector called Jon B. She no longer had a taste for Remedial Court with the Law Stewards and wanted to get the whole thing over with as quickly as possible. Her legs were stiffening in the cold night air. A watcher was telling how he had followed Jon B the previous night as he crossed the entire paved area and collected a chump from the Brysun family circle. [3]

[1] Use of the word *land* here is believed to refer to the *minds* of his colleagues who insisted on continuing to fight a lost war. It is also believed that the refuser was shunned by order of the Director of the time and died without ever communicating with anyone again.

[2] Formal communication passed by word of mouth on a specific topic, usually to specific person/group.

[3] A circle is territory assigned to a collector or family group for the purpose of food collection. Circles can be passed down from parent to child, or young collectors can work in the territory of wealthier families until they acquire enough votes to be allocated their own circle. Collecting in another's circle is a serious offense.

Edwud and Nolan watched the proceedings from a respectable distance. Edwud hated Remedial Courts; he knew how they ended: Jon B would have to return double the food he took illegally, and Edwud would be angry.

"I think we should go," Nolan said as he watched Edwud. "There's no point in staying until the end."

"Dung damned ridiculous! Dung damned!" Edwud cursed.

Although Nolan realized how agitated Edwud was, he was grateful Edwud was only tired from the previous night in the drains and not still sotted. Edwud's antennae alternately waved up and down as if he were teaching a young Blatta to count.

"What was Jon B supposed to do, wait until he was too starved to walk, or until a magical spill came out of the sky?"

"Ssh, you're too loud!" Nolan lifted his forewings to cover Edwud's words. Several of the Stewards looked down at them from the brick platform where they sat in neat rows.

A large black Blatta rose from the ranks of the viewers, spread his hind wings once for effect, and then settled them neatly in place.

"Director, Master Stewards, might I say something?" It was the Reverend Viel, keeper of the Fayth,[4] who was fast becoming a favorite of the Director as she moved closer to death.

---

[4] Essentially, the Fayth is considered to be a belief system based on the concept that collector life began 300 million years ago—long before all other forms of life—and that collectors were chosen to survive in the end long after all other life ceased.

"Of course." The Director beamed.

Reverend Viel climbed up onto the brick platform and smiled at each of the Stewards in turn.

"Thank you, Mem and Master Stewards." The Reverend fell silent, hanging his head as if in deep consideration of difficult and profound matters. Edwud noticed how the crowd quieted expectantly.

"I have listened with a heart filled with compassion and forgiveness for my friend here, Jon B," the Reverend began. "Driven as he was by his and his family's hunger to break the law of private circles. For all of us have known hunger— yes, haven't we?—and suffering, and sickness; and we have all been tempted—nay—even tortured toward blinding ourselves to the law and to the needs of others—to the needs and survival of the colony as a whole. *I* know how Jon B felt; *you* know how Jon B felt—perhaps some of you feel it now—the hunger, the loss of strength, the fear of death."

The Director twitched with distaste at the mention of death. Reverend Viel held the attention of everyone present as if he had pierced their minds with shaft and thread and drawn them to him.

"We have upon us a time of trial—a harsh time—a testing time. A test of our fayth, our fayth in the past and our belief and obedience to the will of the Lord Maker." The Reverend paused and turned to make eye contact with the Law Stewards. Suddenly, in a booming voice that made every antenna in the court leap back, the Reverend shouted:

"And what! I ask you! What! What will be the result if all of us—yes, all of us—listen to our weaker selves, listen to the voice that says, 'Go on, take it. Take the food from

15

your brother and your friends. Take what you want for your-self, and to damnation with the rest'?" The Reverend paused again and proceeded in a gentle voice.

"The result will be chaos. And killing. And more death."

A silence more chilling than the night settled on the session. The Reverend continued, "Jon B, for whom I have much compassion, is but one collector—one collector in a colony—a colony that is more than the sum of its parts, more than the Jon B's of this yard. He must become a les-son—an instruction for the rest of the colony. The normal punishment is not enough in these special times." The Rev-erend seemed to be nodding toward the crowd, which, Edwud realized, seemed to be nodding back in rhythm.

"He must lose the rights to his own circle," Reverend Viel said. A wave of shocked voices rose around the plat-form.

"But I would . . . I would starve to death," Jon B pleaded to the Reverend.

The Stewards raised their antennae and looked at one another, waiting for someone to commit himself to an opin-ion. The Director's head wobbled back and forth as she tried to warm her stiffening legs by shaking them one at a time. One of the younger, more ambitious Stewards, named Worik T, stepped forward.

"I think the Reverend has a point," he said. Another Steward began to move across the court toward him.[5] Worik

[5] All voting in the colony is done by eligible voters (e.g., Law Stewards in a Remedial Court) who move bodily toward the collector whose arguments they agree with. The closer they stand to the arguer, the more firmly they are in agreement.

moved closer to the Reverend, who stepped back with a grand gesture of humility.

"We could lose all control if we're not strong here," another Steward said.

Edwud felt a wave of nausea and fear start from his stomach. The fear came from the knowledge that this time his anger would take the shape of words.

"No!" Edwud shouted.

The Stewards, in the process of moving to vote, stopped in horror. The Director stopped rubbing her legs and peered into the darkness.

"Who is that?" she asked. Edwud was flooded with embarrassment.

"Mem, it is me, Edwud."

"Do I know you?"

"You knew my father, Jozef K, Mem."

"Oh, Edwud, yes, I know you. What are you shouting out 'no' for, Edwud?"

"I . . . I couldn't help it, Mem." Edwud secretly longed for even a tiny trace of the previous night's froth.

"Perhaps you should go home then, Edwud; your father wouldn't have liked your being out of control like that."

"Director?"

"Yes."

"May I say something?" Even as he spoke, Edwud was amazed at himself—speaking out at a Remedial Court. It seemed as though he were watching someone else.

"Can you say it quickly?" the Director asked.

The Reverend Viel leapt forward, antennae twitching.

17

"I think the vote is in process, Director," he said, smiling warmly toward her.

"He's going to say it quickly, Reverend. Aren't you, Jozef . . . ah . . . I mean . . . Edwud?"

Edwud coughed, hoping it would clear away his nervousness. He turned to face the large crowd of collectors who were all craning and stretching to get a view of him. It made him feel worse and he decided to speak to the Director.

"Er . . . Mem . . . er . . . perhaps the punishment . . . I mean the issue . . ." Several young Plenopteras and Blattelas nearby sniggered. "The issue . . . I mean, is not about . . . er . . . selecting the right punishment . . . er . . . but selecting . . . er . . . I mean the problem is really . . . er . . . hunger. Jon B isn't the first to collect in someone else's circle . . . and . . . perhaps the problem is more to do with . . . er . . . the fact that his circle isn't . . . very big . . . and it isn't in a very good . . . er . . . place."

An uproar arose from both the Stewards and the shuffling crowd. Edwud continued in a louder voice, his fear backing away in the face of his growing anger at the crowd reaction. "Not only do meniales[6] have smaller collecting circles, but they are . . . they are . . . stuck . . . er . . . stuck in the poorest areas of the yard."

"This is the most embarrassing effrontery I have ever

[6] It is considered extremely bad taste to speak about ranks (especially in public), although the levels are clear to everyone and maintained effectively with much decorum and many euphemistic and compassionate words. There are three ranks:

meniale—collectors with the least productive and smallest circles.
medioc—those with larger and more productive circles.
crest—those with the largest and most productive circles.

been subjected to in all my life," the Reverend Viel bellowed.

"And more often than not, they have more young to divide the circle among," Edwud said. The Reverend, puffing with anger, strode over to Edwud and glared at him.

"You are a disgrace!"

Edwud offered a silent prayer to the Lord Maker that the terror that was threatening to surface beneath his words would remain in awe of his newly acquired anger. He went on, "The meniales, and even many of the mediocs, have almost no way of improving their collection. It seems to me that they search harder and harder to return with less and less—and as the voting for circle allocation is determined by the amount collected, then they can only watch as someone else with a better and bigger circle becomes more powerful . . . as if . . . as if . . . they themselves were being . . . eaten." The crowd was silent enough for Edwud to think they were considering his words. "Perhaps we all should be more . . . generous . . . courageous . . . perhaps punishment isn't . . . right," Edwud said.

The session broke out into an excited and angry babble, although half the Stewards, including the Director, sat stunned in their places without making a sound. Some of the faces in the crowd showed they were trying to come to terms with what Edwud was saying. Was he saying that the Freeven Sistum was unfair? That the hardest-working collectors—and those who took the most risks, and whose parents had probably done the same—were not to be rewarded? Couldn't he see what would happen? Didn't he realize that crests pay the highest tariff, and in bad times, such as now, the tariff stock would be used to keep many of the poorer meniales alive? Couldn't he see that everyone had the chance to better themselves by hard work, under the Sistum?

"I think you've said enough." The Reverend Viel was even blacker with suppressed rage, his breathing rate had increased, and his forewings were folding and unfolding every few seconds. "The evil is not in the punishment, nor in the organization and distribution of circles, but within the words that come out of your mouth and the thoughts that drive them to the surface." The Reverend paced up and down the full length of the platform. "How dare you speak of courage when you have none yourself—you who have been heard to speak of a Kitchen raid." A shocked and excited murmur rose from the crowd. "Yes, a Kitchen raid that you seem to have the courage to recommend only to others," Reverend Viel said with satisfaction.

A splutter of laughter rippled through the court crowd. Edwud wondered how Reverend Viel could possibly know of his talk about the Kitchen. Viel continued:

"Your courage is in words, brave words to others—words that will end in others suffering. You, Edwud K, you are the coward!" Edwud opened his mouth to speak. "See, more words for others to act on!" The Reverend pointed his antennae at Edwud.

The crowd began shouting, "Coward, coward, coward."

Edwud felt humiliated. Was it true? Was he exhorting others to do what he wouldn't do himself? Is that what he was—a talker? Edwud knew that there had to be some truth in the thought, for it hurt so much. Had he opened his mouth and made things worse for Jon B? Should he try to apologize? His empty stomach seemed to be twisting around his heart; he wanted to get out of the Remedial Court and away from the chanting crowd. Did they believe he was a coward? He felt he might vomit, and the thought added to his fear. He *was* afraid, wasn't he? Perhaps the Reverend Viel was right.

"It is just such words that will destroy us," the Reverend bellowed to the crowd. "It is you and others that you will taint with your selfish ideas who will cause us to lose everything. It is you even more than Jon B who is the danger. It is your thoughts and words that fill the heads of . . . of those who are weaker and incite them to trample the law. The right of ownership to all of the circle that one is capable of collecting from is a right that must be protected." The Reverend turned to the Stewards. "Such thoughts of taking from those who have proven by their own strong legs and collecting labor that they have earned the right to more—such thoughts of failing to reward the greatest collectors will bring us all to the lowest level." The Reverend opened his hind wings, swung around to face Jon B, and lowered his antennae to point directly at him.

Jon B shivered where he stood in the corner of the brick platform. "I'm sorry," he said lamely.

"Sorry! Sorry! You're sorry?" Reverend Viel swung around to face the crowd. "He's sorry!"

The crowd, like a giant mouth, opened and roared with laughter. The Reverend held up his wings to silence them. He pivoted on his rear legs in a perfect circle, encompassing every collector in the court. "I call for the head of Jon B," he said quietly.

The court emptied of sound like the gasp of a single throat. The Reverend swung back to face the Stewards. "Join me—vote with me—the survival of the colony depends on it."

"His head! His head! His head!" the mob shouted.

The Stewards moved almost as one body to cluster around the Reverend. "His head, his head, his head!" they shouted in unison.

Edwud caught Jon B's look of defeat and resignation as two Stewards climbed onto his back. One lifted Jon B's plate enough to stretch his thorax. Edwud shouted so loud that the vibrations were felt throughout his body, but no one could hear him.

"*I* said it! Not him! *I* said it! *I* said it!" Edwud could see but not hear some of the words mouthed by Jon B. Something about his family. Jon B struggled with his attackers for several moments and then stopped. The court went quiet, unsure of what it was doing. Several of the Stewards looked around as if they might find the driving force of their actions, which seemed to have slumped suddenly, like a drop in the wind.

No one seemed certain of what he was doing, and Edwud would remember this moment. He would recall it later, on his own, walking the long concrete road that stretched and rolled into the distance. He would begin to question the actions of collectors—and what it was that drove them. And one of his answers would be that some, perhaps many, had no driving force of their own at all.

The first Steward to vote with the Reverend Viel, Worik T, leapt up to Jon B and bent his head sideways, exposing

Jon B's thorax. Worik looked around at the frozen figures of the court, as if their eyes might provide the necessary energy. Edwud looked directly into Worik's eyes—and Edwud would remember this moment also.

Worik turned to Jon B, covering the passive collector's eyes with his forewing, and then he lunged forward and bit off his head.

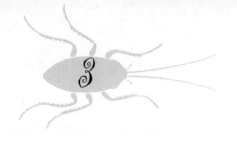

 dwud felt responsible for Jon B's death; he told himself that if he hadn't said anything, Jon B might have lost his circle only, and not his life. For some time Edwud produced enough guilt to wallow alone and half-sotted at the farthest reaches of the yard. Eventually he began to see that, like molasses, guilt was sticky and bittersweet enough to become habit-forming. He decided that his solution would be action.

Jon B's matrimate[1] had died some time ago after giving birth. Half of the eggs failed to hatch, and although the eight nimfs[2] that were left were at stage six and able to collect for themselves, there was still much for them to learn if they were to survive to adulthood. Edwud took it upon himself to teach them whenever he could and to try to answer their questions. They annoyed him greatly as they flitted and scurried in all directions as soon as it was dark.

It was a question from the smallest one, Jinni, that he had been hoping to avoid. She seemed to be taking longer

---

[1] Female sexual partner intended to remain together (in-matri) for life. Note: patrimate is a male sexual partner.

[2] Young offspring. There are twelve stages that nimfs proceed through to adulthood, and at each stage there is a molt before the new form emerges.

than anyone else to shed at each stage, and twice Edwud literally had to peel the last layers off over her head, as if she were reluctant to let go of her infancy.

"Tell us about the Orijin stories, if you are supposed to know so much," she asked Edwud twice before he responded.

"When you're older, you'll be told about them." Edwud hoped he'd dodged the question nicely.

"Reverend Viel said he would tell us."

"Did he? Good for him then."

"He said not to listen to anyone else. Why shouldn't we listen to anyone else?" Jinni asked.

"He said that, did he?"

"He doesn't like you."

"How do you know that?"

"Because I don't like you either."

Edwud tried to tell himself that she was just a nimf—a difficult one, but a nimf—yet he couldn't help how it stung him. Especially from her; she was his favorite, even though she always needed a reason to do anything and she rarely followed instructions.

"Bad-mannered nimfs don't usually get to like anyone much," Edwud tossed back at her. Jinni watched him for a moment and Edwud thought he noticed the start of a smile.

"If I make them all sit still and listen, will you tell us?" she asked.

"I would have thought that the Reverend Viel would be more to your liking."

"Are you miffed, now?" Jinni asked. "Because if you are . . . then it would be true what the Reverend said about you."

25

"What? What did he say about me?"

"That you weren't . . . weren't . . . sort of . . . like . . . like . . ."

"Yes?"

"Like everyone else . . . like . . . normal. You weren't normal."

"He said that, did he?"

"And that if you said anything strange to us, I should immediately go and tell him."

"I see. So you want something to tell him, do you?"

"No, I want to hear the Orijin stories, and I want to hear them from you."

Edwud thought about exploring why she wanted to hear the stories from him but decided that somehow she would get the better of him. "So the Reverend said not to listen to anyone else, did he? Right. Come here." With the help of Jinni, Edwud settled Jon B's nimfs around him. "I'll tell you the oldest one right now, if you all shut up and stay still long enough." Edwud twitched his antennae in annoyance at the Reverend Viel. He waited deliberately, until long after all the nimfs had stopped giggling and poking and shifting.

Just as the moon was rising and the lights of the humans bit farther into the night, he stood up portentously and began dragging one leg in the dirt behind him, tracing a large oval around the seated nimfs. They watched intently.

"In the beginning the Lord Maker drew a great circle," Edwud said.

"Why did she draw a circle?" Jinni asked.

"If you're going to interrupt—then I won't continue." Edwud stopped and stared, attempting his fierce pose again. The nimfs giggled but shut up in case Edwud became miffed and stomped off. "She drew a circle," he continued, "because the circle was sacred. The circle is the beginning, the only form that becomes itself, that is itself, that includes itself and returns to its beginning, which is its end. You won't understand that for many years—and if you don't sit still, you never will at all." Edwud was beginning to enjoy the power he now had over the nimfs.

"Anyway, the Lord Maker filled the great circle with smaller circles, and still smaller circles, and she flung the smaller ones out into the reaches of the Great Vault. You can see them spinning in the sky like lighted glass."

The nimfs looked at the stars as if Edwud had just flung them there.

"And one of the smaller ones she called Ootheca. It became the Lord Maker's favorite, and she filled it as your own mother filled the eggs that would become yourselves. Over countless ans[3] the crust of Ootheca hardened and, in time, through the crust emerged the first living thing—a small white collector with transparent wings, beautiful long antennae and a solid protective plate. The Lord Maker was delighted with what she had done and taught the collector to fill and produce her own circles, to be called eggs, from which more of her kind would emerge. Whenever necessary, the Lord Maker would drop food chumps and spills from the sky.

---

[3] One an is equal to approximately half a year.

"Soon there were large, thriving colonies of Blattelas and Periplanetas and Mitchellis and Blattas. And everyone enjoyed singing and collecting and living. The Lord Maker was so pleased that she was about to fill more small circles with the happy collectors but something stopped her.

"One beautiful day when the sun circle was warming the collector colonies of Ootheca, she noticed that one of the very largest collectors, a Blatta known as Ledi, was not collecting the chumps or spills she let drop from above. She asked the handsome Ledi, 'Why are you not collecting the food that I send?' He replied, 'I have no need, Lord Maker. I have discovered that others, smaller and less capable than myself, will do it for me, and if they refuse, I am so strong I can snap off their legs until they obey me.'

"The Lord Maker was horrified; she looked closely at the colony and immediately saw several small crippled Plenopteras struggling with food parcels toward Ledi. She was furious. Immediately she gave teeth to the crippled Plenopteras carrying Ledi's food. The Plenopteras felt their new teeth, how sharp and strong they were, and they fell on Ledi with their jaws snapping. Biting and chewing and grinding, they tore Ledi's legs and body apart and scattered them until there was almost nothing left of him.

"The Lord Maker did not enjoy this happening, and she left Ootheca for several hundred ans.

"Returning one crystal-clear morning, she discovered a different but equally distressing sight: the brown Plenopteras with teeth were flying above lines of toothless collectors who were being forced to carry food for them. When one of the line of food gatherers tried to escape, a

Plenoptera would fly down and tear at him with vicious jaw-snapping teeth. The Lord Maker groaned in dismay. At once she granted teeth to all the collectors of the colony, and she shook the vicious Plenopteras by their very wings and told them that no longer would any collector's wings enable him or her to fly, that they would flap uselessly in the air and never lift him or her from the ground.

"The Lord Maker went away by herself for a thousand ans to think about whether Ootheca was, in fact, a mistake she had made or was still something of worth. When she returned, in order to force all the collectors on Ootheca to cooperate and be kind and to share with others, she created 'love.' She made it impossible for any of them to fill the eggs of life by themselves. From that time on, the eggs of each female would require the seed from a male. And both male and female would need to show concern and caring for each other and for their own new young nimfs.

"The Lord Maker felt she had finally created the harmony she had always wanted, a place where she could share her thoughts and her wishes and gifts with collectors, who were coming more and more to resemble her. It took a very long time for the Lord Maker to begin to feel that something was wrong. Many collectors were developing strength and cleverness and single-mindedness of purpose that made them admired and successful. The more they collected, the more they wanted to collect and the more others wanted to be like them—and so they too collected harder, forcing the strong ones to strive even more obsessively to retain their positions. The Lord Maker saw that no one was giving helpful advice to anyone else without payment, no one gave any of his collection away unless he received much more in return later—and no one had time to consider the *why* of what they were doing.

"The Lord Maker became so angry and disappointed she refused to speak to the collectors at all. Finally, one dreadful evening when many of them were comparing and admiring the size of their collections, the Lord Maker, exploding in fury, cast them out of Ootheca—never to return nor hear her voice, until they had redeemed themselves and she had forgiven them."

The moon had rolled farther around the Great Vault. The strong smell of passion fruit seemed to float into the night air from the vines draped heavily along the fence palings. In the near distance the noise of crickets methodically scraping their legs in unison covered the gentler sounds of the night. Lost in the story, Jinni gazed adoringly at Edwud until she realized he was staring at her.

"Go on," one of the nimfs urged Edwud.

"I want to hear about the Monoocal," Jinni demanded, trying to regain her self-control. Edwud pretended not to hear.

It was time for all of them to begin searching for food, before the cat was sent out, before the sunlight returned to point them out to their enemies. The other important stories could wait.

"Time to stop talking and start collecting," Edwud said. The nimfs groaned in complaint and pleaded with Edwud to continue with just one more story. Edwud refused and pushed them out into the night. Only Jinni remained behind, staring intently at Edwud. "You too," Edwud said to her.

"I want to know about the Monoocal," she said calmly. Edwud raised his antennae, tilted his head and plate as threateningly as he could, and strode toward her. "Because I am going to get back to Ootheca." She turned quickly before Edwud could say anything. "But I still don't like you," she said, and disappeared into the night.

This time Edwud smiled because he saw the lie in her face.

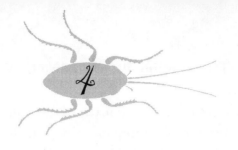

4

*E*dwud realized that Worik T had been waiting at the edge of his circle for him for some time. The same Worik T who had removed the head of Jon B.

"I won't hold you up long," Worik said. "I know you haven't quite recovered from that dreadful Jon B business. . . . Well, we all haven't, really. I think I might have been the most upset of all." Worik let his antennae fall, as he slowly waved his head from side to side. "A terrible business, Edwud, a terrible business. I wonder if you know just how painful I find the whole thing."

"Not as painful as Jon B did, I would expect," Edwud replied.

"That's not necessary, Edwud. That's not fair. I had to do what was done. You know that. For the stability of the colony—can you imagine what would happen if more of the hungry . . . ? Never mind, that's not why I wanted to talk to you."

Edwud was trying to imagine why Worik was talking to him.

"I think we need you," Worik said.

"What?"

"I think we need you. I have spoken to the Welfare

Stewards and to the Director and to the Reverend Viel."

"You need me?"

"As a Welfare Steward. Why are you laughing?"

"I couldn't raise even a third of the votes."

"With a little help, you might." Worik smiled.

"Why would you want me as a Welfare Steward?"

"Because we need someone—someone who can think."

"You didn't seem to want to hear my thinking at the Remedial Court."

Worik looked hard at Edwud and appeared as if he were swallowing a sour-tasting chump.

"There is a place for new thoughts—and it isn't in front of a huge crowd of . . . of . . ."

"Hungry collectors," Edwud supplied.

"Look, Edwud, you could do a lot more good for everyone if you joined in the running of the Sistum, instead of throwing stones at it from the outside . . . now isn't that true?"

"As a Welfare Steward, you mean?"

"Yes."

"Sort of change things from the inside."

"Yes."

"Become a part of the management of the colony?"

"Exactly. I've spoken to the Economy Stewards and they think they can allocate most of Jon B's circle to you."

"I haven't collected near enough for . . ."

"Tut tut tut, all taken care of. The Welfare Stewards will distribute Jon B's nimfs to various crest families, who will all sort of lend you a nice amount . . . that will just cover the necessary allocation votes to Jon B's circle." Worik smiled with satisfaction and sat back on his legs to allow Edwud to appreciate the cleverness of his dealing.

"I don't want the nimfs to be separated. I want to keep them together until they can take over their parents' circle."

"Edwud, everyone knows you haven't been collecting enough to keep them all together."

"There hasn't been enough time yet," Edwud said.

"That will be for the Welfare Stewards to decide, of course."

Edwud realized he had walked right into Worik's carefully prepared trap. He knew that as a Welfare Steward he would have some influence on what happened to Jon B's nimfs, but no real influence on what happened in the colony—he would forever be repairing the damage caused by the decisions of the powerful Law and Economy Stewards. He would be raised to an illustrious position of impotence.

"No," Edwud said.

Worik stood on all legs, raising his antennae stiffly.

"You think about it, Edwud. You think about it deeply." Worik turned and began walking off. "Oh, by the way, Sera sends her regards."

5

A dozen ways to die:
ten thousand ways to live.

OLD PROVERB

or the first time Edwud had lied to his friend Nolan. For Nolan's own protection Edwud had said he had no plans to enter the Kitchen; and here he was sweating and twitching outside the door. The lights had been withdrawn from inside for some time, and Edwud had counted to five hundred twice, but still he was afraid to enter. A quick swig of soapsud foam in the drains had helped, but Edwud knew that if he had taken enough to turn his fear into courage, he would never have the speed and clarity to survive.

Edwud thought of the Longleys—the new owners—of how they seemed to search for death, as if each body they crushed or poisoned would add time to their own lives. Once, just once, he would like a good rip at the female Longley's white flesh with his teeth.

He remembered his father, taken by the cat long ago, not far from where he stood. He could still remember the sound of his father's plate being cracked in the cat's jaws, and afterward the hunger of the family because they were all too afraid to collect in case the cat was out there waiting.

Even then Edwud found that imagining the cat—with its curved claws and its pointed teeth and its furry, tail-waving stink—was far worse than actually seeing it. For a while this was a puzzle to him, until he thought enough about it to realize that the cat in his mind had been feeding so well on his fear that it had grown enormous—while the real one ate only tins of tuna fish.

Jon B's nimfs reminded him of his own hungry nimf-hood, and he was beginning to suspect that Jinni's late physical development might be a result of her slow starvation. There was not enough to collect for them in his own or in Jon B's circle. All that was left was the Kitchen.

As Edwud flattened his antennae against his body for the dash to the underdoor, he heard the leaves behind him crackle. His mind produced the giant cat, as his eyes registered the sight of Nolan forging a steady path toward him.

"Nolan! Heaps of dung, I thought you were the cat!"

"I know I'm pretty ugly, but . . ."

"What are you doing here?"

"I came to talk you out of going into the Kitchen."

"I told you I wasn't going in there."

"Yes, but you kept looking over my shoulder at the Kitchen the whole time."

Edwud squinted with annoyance at Nolan. "You're not fast enough to come with me."

"Well, I'll just have to trail along behind. If you insist on having yourself killed, someone should be around to tell how you ended."

"I won't be caught. I'm going to bring back something for the nimfs."

"Yes, I know."

"Don't come with me, Nolan."

"Sorry, I have this problem with guilt."

"Well, don't you start up about the danger and every-thing, and going on and on like you do."

"I won't say a word. If you want to feed yourself to the cat, that's entirely your own business."

"See, you can't help yourself. You had to remind me about the cat."

"The cat's the least of your problems . . ."

"See, you're starting up. I'm going."

Edwud slanted his wings and antennae toward the house, shrugged his shoulders at Nolan, and took off for the Kitchen door.

*T*he first thing Edwud noticed was the blast of warm Kitchen air as he ducked through the underdoor. The second thing was the smell of food: rich, sugary cake chumps and warm grease-laden spills. This was surely a different world from the garden. He kept to the darkest edges of the room, flattening himself between the wall and a cupboard. His breath came in short, quick gulps. He stared fixedly at the underdoor, waiting to wave his position to the much slower Nolan.

Within moments the bunched and puffing Nolan was beside him. "Can you smell that smell?" Nolan whispered between breaths.

"It's coming from a heat box," Edwud replied confidently.

"A what? How do you know that?"

"They heat food in it. My grandfather told us stories of the Kitchen Wars, and he was always drawing maps in the dust of our circle. 'You might need to know one day,' he used to say. We all used to laugh behind his back." Edwud touched the side of his head. "He had a lot of injuries. I wish I'd taken more notice."

With Nolan following, Edwud began to explore the Kitchen. They moved as carefully as possible along the gap behind the cupboards. The dust and fluff were thick and pungent with grease and other strange smells. Behind the heat box the temperature was intense. Edwud kept struggling to remember his crazy grandfather's maps as they moved farther along behind the dishwasher. At the corner of the room they turned, following the baseboard behind the sink, and then suddenly Edwud stopped. There in front of him was the largest black Blattela he had ever seen. Nolan, slow to start and to stop, bumped into him and saw the huge dark shape.

"Oh, my Lord," Nolan said, and began a fevered and difficult struggle to turn around in the narrow passageway. Trapped between the panicking Nolan and the giant Blattela, Edwud could think of no sensible response, but something came out anyway.

"Arr . . . errggh . . . ayy . . ." Edwud wondered what he might have said.

The Blattela did not respond, and for a few moments Edwud thought that perhaps, subconsciously, he had come up with a devastatingly offensive new language.

Nolan had attempted a backward flip and was stuck between the cupboard and the wall, balanced painfully on his head. Edwud could see that the Blattela was unimpressed. What he knew of the Kitchen collectors was that they didn't bother with private ownership circles—it was more like "get what you can, wherever and whenever you get the chance, and tear the wings off anyone who stands in your way."

The Blattela still hadn't moved and Edwud was wondering whether he ought to stand on his head like Nolan.

Without knowing why he did it, Edwud reached out and touched the head of the giant. Immediately he withdrew his antennae. The head was cold. Edwud gave Nolan a push with his back legs and Nolan flopped back to his original position.

"He's dead."

"No!"

"There's not a mark on him."

"Is it the chlordane?"

"I don't think so. He doesn't smell like it."

"I don't think we can turn around here."

"It's okay. He won't mind if we walk over the top of him."

"I'm not walking over a dead body. I've got some standards, you know. I was brought up properly."

"You can either walk over him or stand on your head for the rest of your life." Edwud climbed onto the dead Blattela and continued along the passageway. Nolan followed, wincing and apologizing to the corpse at every step.

"I think I'm going to be sick," he moaned. "I put my foot through his hind wing, errggh."

Edwud moved up behind the refrigerator, where the passageway opened out and gave them a clear view across the Kitchen floor. The whir of the refrigerator's motor helped them feel more secure. Across the floor, near an island bench, Edwud saw the largest chump of his life. It was a sweet drop of cake that must have recently fallen, as it still smelled fresh.

"Do you see it, Nolan, do you see it, over there?" Edwud pointed both antennae and felt the juices rise in his stomach.

"It's too far in the open, Edwud. You can't stay exposed for so long—not here."

"We'll wait awhile—count to a hundred and if it's still all quiet . . ."

"Please don't do this to me, Edwud. Let's stay behind the cupboards—we'll find something here if we keep looking."

Edwud was counting.

"What about the cat? It's still in the house, isn't it?"

"Forty-two, forty-three . . ."

"How do you know what killed that black giant back there?"

"Sixty-eight, sixty-nine . . ."

"I don't know why I bother talking to you. You never listen. You just make up your own rules as you go along, and everyone else is . . . is just a fool—isn't that right, isn't that how it is?"

Faster than ever before, Edwud was running—almost skidding across the tiled floor. Nolan guessed that the chump was about 250 leggs away from where he crouched under the refrigerator. More religious than Edwud in his view of the world, Nolan prayed silently to the Lord Maker in the way that he had been taught—in the form of a letter:

Dear Lord Maker,
   Please run with my friend Edwud, who doesn't understand how things really are down here, because I can't protect him all the time myself.
                              Thank you.

The events that occurred next would replay themselves in Nolan's memory for the rest of his life as he struggled to understand the message that he felt must be encoded in them.

7

Toast, 'tato, pie;
who told a lie?

Cheese, cake, and tart;
who thinks he's smart?

Custard, mustard, jell;
who'll go to hell?

Hark! Hark! Hark!

You will, and you will;
the day you leave the dark.
NIMF PLAYGROUND RHYME

olan wasn't sure which happened first: Edwud
skidding into the cake chump or the instant,
warningless snap of the Kitchen lights.

Edwud locked his back legs onto the tiles and spun himself around in a graceful arc. The deadly light struck like a
blow across his face. The safety of the refrigerator seemed
a thousand leggs away. Nolan's look of horror appeared so
comical that Edwud would have laughed if he'd had the
time.

The human feet approaching from the doorway
belonged to the Longley child, a boy Edwud knew to be
about fourteen ans and, unlike his parents, always good for
a spill or sweet chump in the garden.

Stuck out in the middle of the Kitchen floor in full light was about as bad as it could get, Edwud calculated, and as he was there anyway, he might as well take some of the cake with him. With his front legs and teeth he tore off, in one movement, almost half the chump and began the long run back toward cover.

Nolan shut his eyes in disbelief but couldn't bear to leave them closed. When he opened them again, Edwud was about to run into the boy's shoe.

Edwud turned just in time to bump gently against the boy's shoe and to bounce off at a right angle. Nolan wanted to scream. The boy made a noise and bent down toward Edwud. Still holding the cake chump, Edwud changed direction instantly. The boy gave out a laugh and reached down with his open hand, placing it like a wall directly in Edwud's path. Edwud spun almost on the spot and raced off again in the direction of the refrigerator.

Nolan screamed out helplessly: "Run, Edwud! Run!"

Edwud was oblivious to any sound that wasn't being made by the boy. He listened with every part of his body to any noise that might help predict the boy's next movement.

Nolan was beyond fear. It seemed as if Edwud were running through a thick, sticky spill—as if each step were impossibly slow and heavy.

The boy's hand descended to form a fence between Edwud and the refrigerator. Edwud clawed at the tiles with his rear legs and reversed his course just in time for his antennae to strike the boy's hand. The boy whooped with joy. He was beginning to enjoy Edwud's frantic behavior. Edwud was gasping for air. He dropped the cake chump,

44

flattened his antennae against his body, and tried for even more speed. Each time he was about to reach cover, the boy's hand descended at the last moment and formed an impossible fleshy wall.

Edwud's whole body ached with the frenzied effort to find deliverance from the piercing light and the boy who would turn his life into a game. He was slowing, and he knew it. Several times he struck the boy's hand with the force of his whole body, unable to stop quickly enough. The boy squealed with delight each time Edwud scrambled back onto his feet and took off in another direction.

And then Edwud stopped running. Later on, Nolan would tell the others, "He just stopped, right there in the middle of the Kitchen; he just stopped and looked up at the boy—as if he weren't going to play the boy's game anymore."

The boy leaned over Edwud, reached down, and prodded Edwud's back with his finger. Edwud refused to run. The boy pushed him sideways over the tiles. Edwud still refused to run. No longer was the boy laughing. He placed a finger behind Edwud and flicked him into the air. Edwud landed on his legs a few tiles farther on. The boy said something and then blew a jet of air hard across Edwud, which lifted his forewings and briefly fluttered his hind wings.

Nolan was praying rapidly for the Lord Maker to intervene and dump darkness onto the light.

Between finger and thumb, the boy gripped Edwud's antennae and lifted him into the air. Edwud's legs automatically kicked out at the vacuum. He opened his wings and flapped them against the boy's fingers. The boy yelped in surprise and almost let go of his prisoner. Edwud flapped harder, beating his wings against the air. The weight of his body wrenched downward, stretching his thorax and tearing at the roots of his antennae. The pain was excruciating. It sliced through the spine of his body like the jagged edge of a rusted can.

The boy's free hand grasped at his left forewing. Some of the pain stopped as the wing supported part of his weight. The boy's fingers released Edwud's antennae and grabbed a firm hold on his right forewing. Edwud stopped trying to flap. He wriggled his free antennae and felt jolts of pain through his head. His weight was now pulling on the underside of both wings, which was less painful but extremely uncomfortable.

The boy carried him across the Kitchen to the far side. In the distance Edwud could just see Nolan's head under the refrigerator, and into his mind flashed a picture of Nolan's horror and panic. Edwud almost laughed, marveling at the absurdity of his own brain.

The boy stopped in front of the far Kitchen wall, let go of Edwud's right wing, and reached for something on the cork bulletin board directly in front of him. Edwud pulled his released wing into his body and strained to see what the boy was doing. In front of his face, Edwud watched the boy withdraw a steel spike almost as long as Edwud himself. The spike had a round head like a nail and a sharp point at the other end. Edwud began flapping again—something about the nail-like shaft frightened him more than the light and more than the appearance of the boy himself.

The boy plucked another shaft from the bulletin board

and slammed Edwud's back against the cork. The boy's face came closer and Edwud could feel his breath and smell his horrible fleshy smell. His eyes, Edwud noticed, were huge, wet, blue and white bulbs with a black circle in the middle. If he came a few leggs closer, Edwud would have been able almost to kick at him or bite him—right in the wet blue part.

The boy's fingers stretched Edwud's wings out wide against the board, and with his other hand he approached with the sharp end of the spike. Edwud lashed out with his legs, striking the point of the steel shaft with one of his feet. The boy held him tighter. Edwud shut his eyes and felt the pressure of the hand increase and, before passing out, heard the sound of the nail-like shaft squeaking its way through him and into the cork.

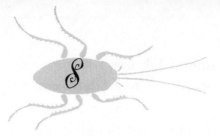

olan had decided never to move from his place under the refrigerator, ever. The boy had left, and Nolan was able to see what he had done to his friend. At first he refused to accept that even a human could be so cold, so immune to the purposeless suffering of another. Why had the Lord Maker allowed this to happen? Hadn't Nolan sent a prayer? And begged for protection for Edwud? Was this the Lord Maker's idea of protection? Then there really wasn't much point in praying at all, was there? The Lord Maker seemed not to be interested in protecting. Why was that? Edwud would have had an answer. Nolan tried to think what it might have been, but nothing came to him through the fog of his anger with the Lord Maker.

On the bulletin board, Edwud hung pitifully from the steel shafts pinned through each outstretched hind wing. Against his will, tears formed in Nolan's eyes for the pain and indignity suffered by his friend. Even if he could reach the board, he could never hold on and remove the shafts. Edwud was stuck, helplessly and hopelessly.

Nolan watched Edwud regain consciousness and move his head from side to side, taking in the sight of each shaft. Edwud waved his antennae to show Nolan he was still alive, even though the pain razored through his head and thorax with every twitch. There was no pain from the pinning holes themselves, but the weight of his body pulling downward stretched his underwing muscles beyond belief.

Edwud tried to shift his weight by pulling each wing upward in turn, but only a small shudder resulted, which sent further stabs through his body. He tried flapping each wing in turn, but the shafts were firmly embedded in the cork. Strangely, Edwud felt more sorry for Nolan, whom he could see looking up at him with great pain and helplessness in his eyes. He wanted to call out to Nolan to take the remaining cake chump back to the nimfs, since there was nothing he could do here, but he knew that Nolan wouldn't be able to leave yet, if at all. In a strange sort of way Edwud saw Nolan as more trapped, pinned to something, than he was himself.

The Kitchen door swung open and the Longley female entered. She moved to a drawer near the sink, opened it, and took out a piece of cloth, which she draped over one hand as she crossed the Kitchen and stood directly in front of the heat box, less than fifty leggs from where Edwud hung. She was oblivious to Edwud's existence and hummed a tune to herself. At any moment Edwud expected her to turn around, see him, and rattle his forewings with her infamous screaming voice. The cat had followed her into the Kitchen and Edwud noticed Nolan's antennae pull back out of sight.

The Longley female opened the heat box door and, with her cloth-covered hand, pulled out a sizzling baking dish of half-cooked meat and potatoes. A blast of hot and greasy air cascaded over Edwud, jerking his wings against the shafts. Edwud felt the heat warming his blood. He could hear the oven fan whirring like wind through a pipe as the door was left open while the Longley woman turned the potatoes in their pan.

Edwud saw his wings rattling against the board. With the heat, the pain in his underwing muscles eased greatly and he began to pull and push his hind wings in time with the hot gushing air. He realized that there was more strength available to him; his wings were sliding up and down on the steel shafts, making the puncture holes in the thin membrane larger at each stroke. Edwud flapped harder. The left hind wing, straining against the shaft, suddenly split along the fibrous line out from the hole. Edwud jerked the wing hard toward the shaft's head and wrenched the enlarged hole over the bulbous end. The wing was free.

Edwud's weight slumped downward as he hung from the other wing, which had slipped down to the shaft's head. Beating both hind wings as hard as he could, he lifted his weight, momentarily pulling on the shaft and then ceasing. He dropped suddenly, his weight wobbling the shaft and tearing his wing around the hole.

The Longley female turned toward the heat box, straining to carry the baking dish. Edwud could see that the door would soon be closed, cutting off the blast of hot air. He breathed deeply, thought of Nolan and Sera and Jon B's nimfs, and then flapped both hind wings harder than even he thought he could.

The scream of the Longley female filled the room, masking the sound of the baking dish striking the floor. For a moment Edwud saw the largest spill of his lifetime seep across the floor. He kept flapping as the Longley male rushed through the Kitchen door, summoned by the scream. He kept flapping as the man approached. The heat from the fan mixed with the smell of the spill, and as Edwud looked down he realized he was no longer pinned; he was no longer touching anything; he was floating, hovering in the air.

And Edwud flew. Over the heads of the Longleys, above the spill, past the sink and toward the back door: a perfect moment of floating fayth.

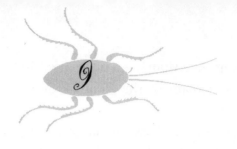

9

The afternoon wind gusted from the south, bending the blades of Kikuyu grass, taunting them to follow. The dried and curled leaves of the lemon tree and the passion-fruit vines leapt and rattled across the paved court-yard, jamming and clustering against the carport posts and the fence. A line of small black ants, leaning into the mouth of the bluster, began their methodical march to the garbage can area amid the rasping sounds of crickets and the lone chuckling of an Indian mynah that swept along with the southerly, riding and fading on each breath.

Nolan sheltered in a ditch originally made by a pot of azaleas, long since removed. Around him crowded several others waiting for the wind to exhaust itself and move on past the fence and away to unknown places. Nolan considered the faces around him: Sera, elegant and calm; Lolli, trying to make everyone laugh with her jokes about the colony; Kerryd, the songstress—no doubt she was weaving the wind into her poetry right this minute; and old Filip, almost totally blind and partially deaf from the chlordane, kept alive now by his friends who placed chumps in his circle, virtually in his path, so that his pride could be maintained.

Directly opposite Nolan was Wulfe—with whom, if it were not for Edwud, Nolan would have nothing to do. Edwud was the only one he knew who could tolerate Wulfe. Nolan considered Wulfe to have a cruel and vicious tongue that he used like a lash against others. Edwud had tried unsuccessfully to convince him that behind Wulfe's cynical words beat the most compassionate heart of any collector in the colony. Nolan often wondered what evidence Edwud had to believe that Wulfe had a heart at all, let alone a compassionate one.

Nolan knew they had not come to visit him; they had come to hear about the Kitchen raid. None of the Stewards would believe that he and Edwud had even entered the Kitchen and they refused to officially inform the Director. The Reverend Viel had spread word that Edwud had made up the whole thing in an elaborate plan to regain respect.

Safe in the hollow, Nolan offered them his remembered view from under the refrigerator. His words hovered between gasps of wind that paused momentarily and then neatly swept them aside—but not before they took shape in the minds of the listeners.

Every time Nolan told the story, he got prickles down the segments of his body and a part of the Kitchen fear slipped silently back inside him, like a moon shadow passing in the night.

Edwud had been seen by almost no one since his escape from the Kitchen. He told Nolan that he wanted to be by himself for some time. Nolan asked why, and Edwud looked at him with a strange expression that Nolan had never seen on anyone's face: a look of preoccupation, of confusion, of determination. Nolan wasn't sure exactly what it was or what it meant. Edwud had gone off somewhere, perhaps even through the fence at the back of the yard and out into the dry concrete expanse that trailed off into oblivion. Nolan couldn't understand how anyone, having undergone what Edwud had suffered in the Kitchen, could possibly want to go off by himself, to be alone, without comfort, without support, without the secure feeling of others near-by. Nolan wondered whether he would ever understand Edwud.

Nolan realized that Wulfe was talking to him.

"What you're trying to tell us," Wulfe said, "is that Edwud pulled his hind wings off these steel shafts that were pinning him to the wall, and while the Longley female screamed at him, he hovered for a while and then flew through the air, straight to the door, and escaped?"

"That's right. That's what happened," Nolan said.

"You didn't happen to spend the night in the drain before you went, did you?" Wulfe scoffed.

"I think it's a beautiful story." Kerryd's lilting voice seemed in harmony even with the wind.

"I wish I could have seen it," old Filip growled.

"You wish you could have seen anything," Wulfe mumbled.

"What's that?" Filip bristled. "Is he saying something about me?"

Sera leaned toward Filip and reassured him that Wulfe was just making one of his jokes.

"I think we all should sing a song to Edwud for his bravery," Lolli said, as she smiled and waved at everyone to come in closer together. "Let's all have a good sing together."

"You're an ant-brain," Wulfe said. "What have we got to sing about? Edwud's a fool—have you seen the holes in his wings?"

"It's just nice when we do," Lolli replied weakly. "You know, all touching antennae and . . . and being like one . . ."

"Is he touching her antennae?" Filip growled.

"No," Sera said. "She wants us to sing together—to Edwud."

"I might not see very well—but I won't have this . . . this . . . touching going on in public. You young nimfs don't seem to be able to control yourselves—keep your feelings to yourselves."

"Feel yourself, huh?" Wulfe said.

"Did he say he's not feeling himself?" Filip inquired. "Why doesn't he speak up?"

"Where is Edwud?" Sera asked.

"He's gone off to be by himself for a while," Nolan answered.

Lolli put her head to one side in amazement. "By himself? Whatever for?"

"To practice hovering in the air, eh, Nolan?" Wulfe laughed.

"To think, is what he said, actually," Nolan answered stiffly. "And I believe he does it better than some."

"Ah, thinking, that'll change things for the better, won't it?" Wulfe said.

"Why, Wulfe, you think that the world can be changed for the better?" Sera asked. Taken by surprise, Wulfe was caught momentarily off balance.

"Of course it needs changing—not that I care, mind you. This world and all who crawl on it deserve exactly what they make for themselves—very little."

"He's depressing, isn't he?" Filip moved farther away from Wulfe.

Kerryd, who had been humming to herself since Nolan's story had finished, spoke up clearly. "Would you like me to sing a song I have just been making? It's not refined yet, of course," she said with a tinge of shyness.

"I think you have a very resonant voice," Nolan said.

Kerryd blushed and pulled her antennae back.

"I know an old war song called 'Milady of the Drains,' " Filip suddenly remembered.

"I don't think that would be quite appropriate," Nolan said.

"Perhaps I'll sing it for you later—when I've practiced it," Kerryd said.

"For the Lord Maker's sake, if you don't sing it soon, Filip here won't be around to hear it," Wulfe said.

"Did he say I won't be around soon?" Filip asked with concern.

"Sing, Kerryd, sing," Nolan pleaded.

Kerryd's voice seemed to slow the haste of the wind and float upward through the overhead branches of a Cootamundra wattle.

"Edwud, the sum of all of our thinking,
hovering hopefully for all of our minds.
Balanced on wings of opposite movement,
one reaching ahead, one pulling behind.

Edwud, the sum of all of our thinking,
pinned by wings so intricate, fine;
wrench free of the nails that painfully hold us
to past misdirections and futures a' blind."

$\mathcal{S}$omething was wrong. Edwud could feel it, like the time when he was a nimf and the first of his brothers failed to return from collecting. Edwud remembered the waiting and the way the light began to fill the sky and the circle of the moon weakening—and still no sign of his brother. All the family waited behind the stack of bricks, facing in the direction from which his brother would appear. And he never came.

Edwud would think about his brother then—and even now, though less often. He would remember before the Longleys, when the garden was wild and overgrown, and the food seemed more plentiful. Edwud wondered whether there really was more food then, or whether life viewed backward filled empty stomachs and leached out old pain. If that was the case, then given enough time, everything painful, unjust or miserable would disappear, and like memory all that would remain would be joy and loving and the peace of a full belly. Perhaps Ootheca was such a place—a memory of the Lord Maker.

Like his torn hind wings, the memory of the Kitchen had not yet been repaired. Edwud shuddered as he recalled the boy's fat little hand appearing like an impossible wall.

And the steel shafts, and the hot blast of air from the heat box fan—and Nolan's terrified face. How could a face show so much horror? Edwud almost laughed out loud. He looked along the concrete curb as if someone might be listening. The road stretched away over a distant rounded hill.

Edwud's underwing muscles were still sore and his front legs both ached where they had struck the Kitchen door as he half flew and fell through the air. It wasn't the pleasant experience he had imagined flying to be.

Along the gutter, the food chumps, trapped in catches of roadside gravel, cans and tufts of grass, were invariably old and dry and tasteless. Occasionally Edwud came across a cigarette pack with a few strands of tobacco caught under the silver paper. He enjoyed two or three bites of the bitter-tasting shred but no more. A mouthful or two more would cause him to vomit rather than experience the warm flush throughout his body.

Almost no one from the yard ventured out into the roadway anymore. The food likely to be found over such great distances would, more often than not, take greater energy in the finding than it supplied in the eating. And there were more enemies here than in the yard: great roaring machines that blasted by in showers of stinging dust that flapped and shook forewings as if they were lighter than air. Edwud had watched from under the fence before he left the yard and noted that only rarely did they run along the gutter, and although it was rougher going, it was definitely the safest track.

The only thing he was sure to be escaping out here

would be other collectors. And that, without knowing it, was why he was traveling the vast rolling concrete desert.

Descending light moved him along faster, as he listened to his own feet pulling at the concrete as if the surface could be spun like road-machine wheels under him. At a large and sharp corner he slipped carefully between the iron grids covering a storm-water channel and climbed slowly down the rough walls toward the bottom. It was dry and dark with a trace of rancid, old water clinging to the air of the chamber like unwanted memory.

Edwud directed his antennae toward the round tunnel of pipe disappearing into the distance on the opposite wall. He could smell nothing suspicious beyond the stale, musty odor. He swung around for a final sweep of the chamber and then settled back, taking body weight from his legs by resting his belly on the concrete.

He thought of Nolan and remembered his hurt and confused expression when Edwud asked him to stay behind and look after Jon B's nimfs. "Can't you think here?" Nolan had said. But Edwud couldn't think with the colony all around him; something had changed in him—as if the Edwud who had entered the Kitchen had been left there, pinned to the cork bulletin board.

Edwud imagined what Sera would be doing precisely at that moment. Returning to her hyde,[1] probably, and dropping a chump at her parents' feet. Edwud couldn't bring himself to like Sera's parents. Before the Longleys, they had been lucky when the garbage cans were moved into

[1] Collector's home.

their circle. For some time they collected more in half a night than the rest of the colony did in a week. They increased their vote and their circle size and quality so rapidly that they were equal with some of the best crests'. And then came the Longleys, who removed the cans and installed an incinerator. Sera's parents had tasted the lingering flavor of power and prestige and their legs had become weaker as their bodies had grown heavier. They fell from grace and influence faster than they had ascended. Their circle was reduced to the minimum, due to the increasingly poor collection, and Sera's mother stopped laying eggs and began to avoid meeting anyone.

Once Edwud took them a chump, more to impress Sera than anything else, and her father had said to him in a cold, thin voice, "We do not require your excess, nor can my influence be won so cheaply." Edwud had blushed, and swung his antennae around in embarrassment so that they struck Sera on her behind, which made Edwud's brain and heart almost stop functioning.

Resting in the drain, Edwud laughed at the memory. The sound echoed across the square chamber and galloped off down the pipe.

The shape of Sera focused again for him and, with his eyes shut to the darkness, he imagined her waiting for him—her antennae lowered, touching the ground, the segments of her body moving against each other in time with her breathing. He imagined himself approaching, raising the short palps[2] under his antennae to give the appearance

[2] Small protrusions from the thorax; organs of touch.

61

of increased size to his chest and plate. And touching her, gently at first, stroking her underbelly and soft forewings, moving closer, as she slowly shivered, opening her wings for balance and . . . Edwud stopped; his heart was pounding. He had the strongest desire to run back to the yard to find her. In the chamber the air no longer seemed to contain enough life for him to draw from.

Outside, the wind and noise machines continued to roll by. From the grid at the top of the chamber the first attacks of sunlight were visible. Edwud realized how cold the chamber was and how stiff and tight his legs and wing muscles were. He lifted one forewing and it took considerable effort. The cold, he thought, was heavy, and when it settled, it brought its weight. The heaviness of cold. The weight of ice. Edwud had seen its effect on water—how hard and stiff and heavy it became with the weight of cold. Heat. Heat could lift the weight of cold. And free the ice. Lift the weight of the cold. Heat could. Like the heat from the Kitchen heat box. The searing heat that lifts the cold—the cold that weighs all things down. The heat could lift, like his wings lifted from the steel shafts.

Edwud stopped in shock. The heat, he thought. It is the heat that entered my body and wings that made me light— that made me fly. Heat, heat that lifts the cold. And after-flight—flight after death—the Orijin story of the Great Fire. The heat from the Great Fire. Was afterflight not the Lord Maker calling collectors to her? Was afterflight not flight after death? Was it the heat? Could it just have been the heat?

62

Please I
to please you,
anything to please.

Please myself
never pleased,
everyone to please.
OLD COUNTING RIDDLE

*E*dwud's legs, losing the stiffness from the long day spent waiting in the storm-water drain, continued their steady rhythm along the concrete gutter. With the intention of returning to the yard in one night, he pushed himself harder than ever before. His mind danced along with his feet, stepping and tripping into fanciful thoughts, whirling and springing back to reason and logic. In the end, to gain some control, he began counting his steps. The regular pattern calmed and smoothed the surface, but Edwud knew that all of his best thinking was done deep below, out of his control, beyond the soothable shallows.

At the back fence Edwud enjoyed a flush of pleasure. He was surprised how good it felt to be back.

His second surprise was to discover that someone was in his hyde, waiting. The scent was confused with his own and with Nolan's, but as he came closer his tiredness began to evaporate. It was Sera's unmistakable fragrance.

An Economy Steward passed by, staring at him. Edwud could almost hear him taking mental note of what implications anything out of the ordinary might have on the economic management of the colony. Edwud forced out a loud "Ho" and an exaggerated wave of his antennae to annoy the Steward with his well-being. The Steward turned his head in the opposite direction as if being called by someone far more important, and scurried away.

"Sera, is that you?" he whispered into his hyde. "Sera?"

"Edwud?"

"What are you doing here?"

"I . . . I was waiting for you . . . to talk with you . . . I didn't think you'd mind. You look very tired."

"I'm not, really."

"I can bring you some food . . . Reverend Viel gave me . . ."

"I'm not that hungry, actually."

Sera looked around Edwud's hyde. Edwud followed her gaze and for the first time saw his hyde as rather unimpressive. He began to invent a funny remark that would allow him and his worth as a collector to rise above the neglected hyde, but something about Sera's unusual state stopped him.

"Are you too tired to talk?" she asked.

"Lord, no—heaps of . . . Lord, no," Edwud replied quickly. Sera rested her legs and breathed in deeply.

"I've been watching . . . and thinking a lot . . . since Jon B's . . . trial. Looking at things in the colony . . ."

Edwud's mind raced ahead, trying to guess what it was she might be about to tell him or ask him. This time he was determined not to mess it up. "Uh-huh," he said, nodding his head.

"Are you sure you're not too tired, Edwud?"

"No, I think I just look tired—I'm a tired-*looking* collector. My mother used to say I learned how to look tired whenever there was any collecting to be done."

"Do you think, Edwud, that the colony has changed?" she asked, gazing directly at him.

"Changed?"

"Do you remember how it used to be when we were nimfs? I do. Do you remember the singwiths[1] we used to have . . . and how everyone would tell stories . . . and how their lives would be devoted to . . . to . . . returning us to harmony and understanding? Do you remember that, Edwud? Do you?" Sera stared straight through Edwud as if he were a memory.

"Has something happened?" Edwud asked gently.

"When I was a nimf," Sera continued as if she hadn't heard him, "I wanted to help meniale families with their collecting—I did that once, did you know that, Edwud? With my friends, we helped . . . we even stayed in their hydes. I used to take chumps from my parents' circle . . . but we stopped doing it. Do you know why, Edwud? Because the more my friends and I collected, the less the meniales did. They began to expect us, night after night, and they became cross if we were late. I wanted to help, Edwud, I really wanted to help—but you can't, you can't help anyone else. You can't even help yourself."

---

[1] Group gatherings to celebrate happy events or milestones.

Edwud wasn't sure whether he could smell an edge of soapsuds on Sera's breath. "I don't know about that, Sera..."

"What's wrong with us, Edwud? My friends, the same ones who helped . . . tried to help the poor meniales, want bigger circles for themselves—more influence, more collections. What has happened to us? The nimfs we used to be . . . where have they gone, Edwud?"

"Perhaps only nimfs can afford to be generous—perhaps the last molt peels away our wishes and dreams to prepare us for what is real . . . what is possible . . ."

"Something's gone . . ."

When she had finished talking, Edwud listened to the sounds of the yard and tested the air with his antennae. There were collectors not far away, and there was an odd smell from something the Longleys had put on the rose-bushes, and some smoke from a long way off.

"I've been doing some thinking myself. Would you like to hear it?" Sera continued to stare through him. Edwud took the silence to mean yes, settled himself more comfortably on the leafy floor, and let pour his thoughts, which filled the hyde with the uneasiness of being too close to an unknown . . . a stranger. "These thoughts have been running around my head. . . . It's about the heat from the heat box in the kitchen. . . . I think that was what made me fly, and then I thought what if the Great Fire, you know, the lifting of our otherselves to Ootheca, what if it wasn't the Lord Maker calling us, but just the heat?"

"Would you touch my face again, Edwud?" Sera asked quietly. "Please."

Edwud moved closer, lowered his left antenna, and stroked the side of her face. "Again, please, Edwud." Edwud repeated his action, extending his antennae along the full length of Sera's body. She began to sway in time with Edwud's strokes. She raised her forewings to brush against Edwud's face and touch the torn holes in his hind wings. Edwud was dizzy with her scent and her rhythmical body and the soft brushing of her wings. He felt her legs slide up and along his soft underbelly. She moved as if half sleeping. Edwud's breathing came fast and deep.

"Gone . . . something's . . . gone," Sera mumbled. But Edwud couldn't hear; the rhythm of his stroking began to match Sera's breathing as they moved in perfect harmony.

*U*nder the Longley house the Director paced up and down, wincing at each step, grateful for the drop in the wind but annoyed with how it had leaked its chill into her joints. And this, she thought to herself, is the most protected hyde of all—warmer in winter and cooler in summer than anywhere in the yard.

Fifty leggs away, behind the concrete steps, her patrimate was fussing with the day's food delivery. His habits, which once she had found amusing, irritated her now. He seemed to take as long fiddling with the arrangement of the chumps as eating them. And he had become broader just where she did not like it—across the gut and above the legs. She shook her head in annoyance.

She looked at her own upper legs—they weren't half as bad. If only he would take her advice, even if it was difficult, and walk at least twice a night. Ha, but he never would. And he never cleaned his antennae properly anymore, except when one of his friends visited. When they were alone, he deliberately let them drag through the dirt, just to annoy her. Not that it mattered, being alone together: he hadn't spread her wings for two ans, at least. And there hadn't been nimfs for . . . for so long, she couldn't even remember. The last lot, since they were voted their circles, had been back to see her once—and then only because they wanted her influence on a vote.

She wondered why she remained in-matri to him—especially when she saw adorable-looking younger collectors like, well . . . like this Edwud K whom she had to see tonight. The thought crossed her mind that Edwud might be impressed with a bit of crest life—not to mention her influence. He was a medioc, but he was the kind who could easily fit in. Still, that wasn't the reason she had sent for him, delicious as it was to moonglaze over—the reason was more serious. Even at this late moment she wondered why she was going to speak to Edwud—and no one else. Why had she not told anyone else?

Edwud smiled at the Director's patrimate as he passed him under the steps. The old collector was absorbed in arranging the neat rows of food delivered by the Steward of the day, and scarcely registered Edwud's presence. But Edwud didn't care. Under his breath he sang a song that he once thought was so overblown with soppy emotion that he had dubbed it "The Froth Song." It concerned a certain smitten collector who slowly starved himself to death because he refused to eat until his young beloved returned. Unbeknownst to him she had gone off to divest herself of her nimfhood's last molt, and on her return he failed to recognize her. Edwud was so happy he began changing the words so that the pair of them would get together just in time to save the smitten one from death.

In her hyde the Director looked quite a bit younger

than in the Remedial Court. Edwud kept his antennae up in respect until she spoke.

"Edwud. Oh, come down here. What a pleasure—the talk of the colony, you are."

"Thank you, Mem."

"Stop that 'Mem'—makes my legs ache. I'm Dell to you."

Edwud forgot about his antennae in surprise at hearing the Director's name. The thought of calling her Dell was about as appealing as standing on his head in the dung zone. His antennae drooped.

"What's all this nonsense about you flying, and having new thoughts or whatever?"

"Oh, well, it was in the Kitchen . . . and I was . . ."

"Would you like a piece of sweet biscuit?"

"Oh, no thank you, Mem."

"You won't mind if I indulge myself, will you, Edwud—I've done a lot of walking today. I think it helps keep the shape of my legs, don't you think?" The Director stretched out her front legs, almost touching Edwud's palps.

"Yes . . . yes . . . they've got a lot of . . . of . . . shape . . ."

The Director pulled her legs back. Edwud tried again. "They've got a very stately . . . sort of . . ."

"Never mind. Tell me about your . . . whatevers . . . thoughts."

"I call them, well, really . . . I think of them just as . . . questions."

"Questions? I don't think we need any more of those, Edwud. It's the others we need—the answers, ha ha ha! Haven't got any of those, have you? Ha ha ha!" The Director nudged Edwud with her foot as she jiggled with her own laughter.

Edwud began with his question about the position and shape of truth: where it could be found and in what form. The truth of afterflight and of the fayth in their return to Ootheca; and the truth of who they were now, in the colony, and why did they have so many enemies and why was there so much suffering, and what if the Lord Maker was watching and waiting to forgive them only when they had returned to her original intention of harmony and balance and generosity—which they seemed to be moving farther away from each night. And what was the reason for such continuous evils as the chlordane and the humans who screamed and killed on sight? And the light, why did they hate the light so much?

Edwud's words frightened the night into stillness and loaded the body of the Director with a weight far greater than the cold—a weight she wished not to have to lift. She moved back slightly from Edwud, holding her antennae together as if in deep thought.

"You have some good questions there, Edwud. It seems that you did not shed these with your last molt as many of us did. There is a time to ask such questions, and there is a time when one becomes . . . seasoned, full-grown, and one learns to accept . . . to develop fayth . . . in . . . in . . ."

"The past?"

"Yes, and in the Lord Maker's design for us. We are the first and last, Edwud—remember that—before everything and after everything."

"I can't help wondering, Mem . . . er . . . Dell, whether

we can find the truth without searching for it? I wonder whether there is anything about us that the Lord Maker would want to take to Ootheca?"

The Director fell silent and stared at Edwud for an embarrassingly long time. Edwud tried not to blush. He wasn't sure whether to stay or leave, to smile or talk. He waited, feeling his head grow hotter, thinking his palps must be glowing.

"Edwud," the Director said, as if she were a huge distance away instead of only three leggs. "Edwud . . . I . . . something has happened . . ."

Edwud felt the change in the Director's tone and saw how her whole proud body seemed to sag toward the ground. He wanted to get out of her hyde instantly—the order of things was being upset in a way that was as frightening as hearing the cat in the garden.

"Perhaps I should go, Director . . . I could call your . . . ?"

"Edwud, hear me . . . there is no one else to tell . . ."

Edwud looked about the Director's hyde as if it were filled with all those who would be honored to hear anything the Director might say, let alone something important: there were the crests, the Stewards, Reverend Viel, even her own patrimate.

"Come closer, Edwud."

Edwud imagined the Director must be able to feel his rising temperature through her antennae, as he reluctantly shuffled closer.

"Our otherselves," the Director whispered.

"What?" Edwud had heard quite clearly. He cocked both antennae upward as if he might ward off danger.

"We're losing our otherselves, Edwud. The colony . . . is . . . losing . . . the . . . the . . ." The Director couldn't finish.

"The Monoocal?" Edwud suggested.

The Director's eyes went wide for a moment, and then closed completely as she slumped into sleep.

Hide! Hide! Hide!
Under the tongue of night,
Before the teeth of light,
Lips that promise, bite.
TRAINING SONG, NIMF STAGE TWELVE

*S*hortly before dawn, Sera climbed through timber beams of the garden shed up to the sagging pine-board ceiling where the Reverend Viel waited, poised on a windowsill. Through the small, sealed window of the shed, much of the yard could be observed. Sera stood alongside the Reverend, looking out—waiting for him to speak.

"Sometimes I stand here in the daytime," he said, "when it is still dark in here, and I watch the movements of the garden. On occasion I imagine that I can fly. I climb to the roof from the outside and move to the edge; I open my forewings, brace each segment of my body, and in my mind I can see myself gliding gracefully through the air to land gently on the side of the sand heap or in the flower bed. But before I leap off, I look down—and the squares of brick paving and the concrete, with all its splits and cracks, rise up to slam into my face. I shut my eyes and step back again—and feel safe."

Sera pictured the Reverend Viel, hidden in the dark of the shed, in the heat of the day, teetering like a dream between real and unreal, between courage and fear. "I have spoken to him," she said.

"Edwud?"

"There are things he has told me."

"About his flying?"

"Yes, and other things."

The Reverend Viel turned from the window, leading Sera along the joists to an enclosure formed by the roof trusses and the ceiling. He offered a bread chump, which she declined. He moved so that his plate brushed up against her side.

"Edwud said that it may be possible that the heat from the Kitchen heat box could have been the cause of his . . . being able to fly."

Reverend Viel stopped to consider this new information. Of course, a strong hot wind, Edwud hanging and flapping his hind wings: of course, it could be true, the force of the wind had kept him in the air—and blown him across the Kitchen. Hadn't he himself been lifted off the ground by gusts of hot wind from the west? Of course, if one was off the ground already at the time, then the wind would lift the wings and . . .

"He asked me not to say anything to anyone until he can think some more about it," Sera said.

The Reverend stroked the back of her head. "I've done Edwud a favor, you know; I've arranged for Jon B's nimfs to be distributed out to some very good families—to take the strain off him." Sera felt embarrassed and pleased at the same time.

"There is something else," she said. "Something about

75

the Longley female—her scream. He said that when Isme and Declan were crushed, it was after the scream that the gas came. First the scream, and then the chlordane: Edwud said he thought the scream brings the chlordane."

The Reverend considered the possibility of the Longley scream. It made a lot of sense—not only in Isme and Declan's case, but before them he understood that a human scream had often been heard during the Kitchen Wars.

"Hasn't Edwud's friend, what's his name . . . ?"

"Nolan."

"Hasn't Nolan been saying that the Longley female screamed when Edwud escaped the Kitchen?"

As the Reverend Viel began stroking her body more vigorously, Sera thought of Edwud, his hind wings spread against the setting sun. It occurred to her that perhaps she should not be here with the Reverend, that his influence and standing might be a poor substitute—but it seemed so much safer with Viel, especially the future. There was little doubt she could become his matrimate, with just a little more effort. And then she could relax for the rest of her life. Edwud was so . . . so risky and odd. It would be so difficult to know just what he was thinking or doing—or, worse still, what he might think or do tomorrow or the next night.

The Reverend was stroking her back. Sera waited a few moments and let her forewings spread just a little; then she gasped politely and shook the Reverend off.

"Please, Reverend," she said in a small voice. "I . . . I . . . couldn't . . ."

14

verday, almost one-third of the yard's circles disappeared from sight. The ground kicked and struggled
at the screaming forceps that lifted out its muddied belly
and carried it away in earth-carrying machines. The day of
loss, and the gaping hole, would long be remembered as the
Great Sink, and it would be taught to nimfs as a reminder
of the defenseless nature of the ground that held their
circles.

Each day following the Great Sink, the vast hollow
would undergo further refinement. Steel mesh lined its
sides, and concrete and pipes and tiles were stuck to its
insides. Finally came the water. More water than anyone in
the colony had ever seen.

Edwud and Nolan lost no part of their circles, but
many of their friends lost portions. Jon B's circle was gone
completely and Reverend Viel had arranged with the Welfare Stewards for the nimfs to collect for unaffected crest
families. Wulfe had lost all of his circle and now collected
together with Edwud in his circle and out on the road.

At least a third of the colony was ruined. At night they
would stand at the edge of the sink with the thought
enclosed in each mind that perhaps their circle would

return. They watched the wind shiver the water's skin where the moon reproduced itself in alternating wrinkles. They would stand patiently, resting antennae against the tiles, waiting, as if the water might be nothing more than the temporary error of a rain puddle. Strange rumors haunted the nights, stories of the ruineds who disappeared or were found floating in exactly the position once occupied by their old circle. The number of sick and weak increased and the tariff supplies were at the lowest level in living memory.

A meeting of the colony was organized. Later it would be called the Loss Conference. Its purpose, in the beginning, was to examine ways to alleviate the effect of the Great Sink. Toward the end it became something else quite different.

The conference was attended by every member of the colony. Packed together, wing to wing.

One of the older Stewards, a crest who had lost a front leg and both forewings during the Kitchen Wars, limped up and down in front of the Director on the brick platform, his head nodding in time with his own words.

"I propose that one small chump be set aside each week from the tariff stores to be distributed among the ruineds—for as long as they need it."

A rumble of approval swept through the attentive listeners. Edwud, sitting at the front, turned to look at the faces behind him: grateful smiles, nodding antennae, pinched faces turned to their friends and family. Another Steward moved toward the war-injured speaker as he continued with increased confidence.

"But the ruineds should not congregate at the tariff stores . . . ah . . . er . . ." The old collector appeared to forget about his limp as he paraded up and down the platform, as if he were about to do battle again. "And they mustn't block the access tracks . . . nor should they be expecting the colony to carry them . . . their loss . . . er . . . for them forever . . ."

To Edwud's surprise, the comments appeared to meet with the approval of the hungry, tired ruineds and the rest of the colony. Many in the gathering were raising and lowering their antennae in appreciation and agreement.

Edwud looked hard into the faces around him, attempting to understand what was running through the minds of those who would be pleased by such a destructive arrangement. A view of eyes: eyes that had the beaten flatness of the black tar roadway, and eyes that moved quickly from side to side as if their own sisters and brothers, in disguise, could eat out their hearts. Eyes that had learned that someone else, someone stronger, wealthier, more clever, knew what was right and fair and would look after them. On the platform, the eyes were different: crest eyes—sharp and clear and confident, the eyes of those accustomed to the bright glow of controlling their own lives, and the lives of others.

Two more Stewards had moved closer to the pompous old speaker. He acknowledged their presence with a flush of pleasure, which seemed to fill the space of his missing leg and almost completely cure his limp.

"Well . . . er . . . we have . . . we have to fight," he continued. "That's right, that's what we have to do." He looked around, needing to nod his colleagues into agreement. "We have to fight and . . . and . . . we have to be brave . . . that's right . . . we have to be brave . . . and that's what we have to do." The old soldier was lost in some past battle. Several of the Stewards closest to him looked at each other in confusion. One of them began to return to his position. "We have to face the . . . er . . . enemy . . . we have, that's right . . . to face the enemy . . . and that's how we . . . that's how we . . ."

From the Stewards, Worik stepped forward quickly, placing supportive antennae on the old collector's back.

"And courage, as my colleague says, is the vital element," Worik said. He looked hard into the faces of the crowd. "The enemy is ourselves!"

"That's right," the old soldier nodded unsurely.

"Ourselves, if we fail to help our own." Worik's voice increased in volume. "We must take care of them as we would our very own nimfs!"

A roar of approval swept through the crowd. Several more Stewards left their positions and joined Worik. Glancing sideways, Nolan could see Edwud struggling—as if to break free like an unborn nimf from his egg—straining to escape the constricting circle that seemed ever ready to seal him in.

"I agree!" Edwud shouted so loudly that the entire conference noise stopped.

All faces turned toward him. Nolan shrank down alongside Edwud in embarrassment.

"Dear Lord, not again, please," Nolan begged.

"I agree that the enemy here is ourselves—that we

must help those ruineds and those hungry and those with little hope of ever obtaining their own circle," Edwud said.

"Good for you, Edwud." The old collector limped toward Edwud. "That's the kind of talk we need."

"But I do not think that we who have circles should donate chumps to the uncircled." Edwud watched the old collector trying to understand. "What we would be doing is taking from them their own future—we would be returning them to nimfhood to remain dependent on our generosity. What of their own nimfs, born into uncircled families—what shall become of them? With no circle from which to collect, they remain without a vote, without a voice, and this voiceless, powerless gift will be passed like a . . . a . . . disease to their own nimfs."

"Edwud, are you saying that we should not help the ruineds?" Worik asked, smiling patiently. An angry muttering rumbled through the crowd.

"There must be some way that they can become circled again, some way that they do not become . . . carriers . . . of such a sickness," Edwud replied.

"But, Edwud," Worik said slowly, so that the crowd might infer that a father was addressing his wayward nimf, "the ruineds, and the . . . others—those with smaller or less satisfactory circles—are able to work harder at collecting to increase their vote. And, Edwud, some of them do improve their circles."

"But most don't. It requires more than hard work—it requires an . . . an . . . amazing piece of luck."

"Ah, but what you call luck, some of us might call—the gift of the Lord Maker."

81

"How can it be a gift, when every time a circle is increased, it decreases another's? And because of the voting power of the wealthy, the decrease seems always to come from those who can least afford it."

The Director moved forward to divide the space between Worik and Edwud. She looked at the gathering, at faces that seemed to move as one from Worik to Edwud, grasping at the words as if they might fill empty stomachs. The Director looked hard at Edwud as if she were seeing something strange—some foreign animal that might smile or bite.

"Is it true, Worik," Edwud asked, "that within your circle there are chumps that are never collected, and spills that are far more than you require?"

"A private circle, Edwud, I'm sure you would agree, is a private business."

Edwud stepped up to the platform, ran to the farthest end, and planted his rear foot firmly in the dust that covered the brick. "Here"— Edwud swung his body out behind the Stewards, trailing his foot, carving a neat curve across the ground in an even arc—"is a circle." The crowd followed his angry movements with fascination. "And here"— Edwud came inside his first boundary and repeated the action—"is another." Faces concentrated on Edwud's determined actions, trying to make sense of them. Inside the last drawn circle, Edwud ran and inscribed again. "And another," he said, and then stopped. The faces waited in anticipation of more movement. Edwud looked at his drawing. "Three circles—where there was one."

The crowd, like one body, held its breath. A heavy figure in the front row pushed forward urgently toward the Stewards.

"There is a story I wish to tell before the vote," the Reverend Viel called. He spread his forewings to increase the effect of his deep and sonorous voice as he stepped up alongside Edwud and Worik. "There is a story that should be remembered at just such a time as this." He looked at the audience carefully and back again to Edwud. "It concerns another colony far from here, a colony that perhaps has experienced something from which we can learn. A yard colony much the same as our own, whose circles were buried under a building to house a road machine."

The audience turned to one another as if many of them might have heard of such a colony.

"The hunger and suffering were terrible: collections were barely enough to feed the nimfs, and eventually the laying of eggs ceased and fighting broke out among themselves—fighting that ended in the death and injury of so many of the brave and loyal." The Reverend paused for every collector present to follow his words. "Eventually there came a division between the circled and uncircled—a mighty battle took place in which more than half of the colony was killed." Not a single sound rose from the audience; even the rattle of dried leaves had stopped. "And the result . . . the terrible . . . awful result . . ." The Reverend's voice rose sharply. "The result was that *no one* would own a circle . . . ever . . . never ever . . . ever again."

A thick, choking gasp rose from the crowd.

"All of the yard belonged to everyone but to no one— and everything collected had to be stored, where later an equal part would be returned to each collector. And no one could collect harder and by his own efforts move ahead—no one. And, of course, as you would expect, collections began to shrink. Why should one work harder when the result was the same? And, I tell you, no one *did* work harder. As soon as a minimum collection was made, each one would stop work. And the collectors of this colony—this once healthy colony—became a yard of broken dreamers, moonglazing of the time when hard work felt good and collections were heavy and nimfs were born into the circles of their family. They dreamed of the time we still have here—here in the yard—and we must not lose it. We must not let it slip away from us by intervening in the design of the Lord Maker—the wisdom of the arranged fates. Surely she has a reason for some to be wealthy and others to be poor?"

Most of the audience was nodding in agreement with the Reverend's convincing tone.

"I would ask you all to pray with me—pray to the Lord Maker that we can accept the plans and happenings she sends us—accept that the Lord Maker in her wisdom, as she fills each egg with love and care, decides who will be born into each family—who will be born into . . ."

"Plenty," Edwud called out rudely, "and who will be born into neverness."

"Neverness?" The Reverend was genuinely surprised.

"It seems to me," Edwud said clearly, "that the Lord Maker may not ever have been hungry and may never have woken in the heat of the day deciding to leave her circle because there isn't enough for everyone . . ."

A shocked outcry burst from the listeners. The Reverend Viel stepped forward, raising his antennae.

"Pray that the Lord Maker will destroy him who would foul the air with such words—pray with me," the Reverend said. "Pray that we can learn to accept bravely what is given to us."

"No!" Edwud called out. Without realizing it, Edwud had spread both forewings and hind wings, creating a huge winged shape behind himself. The nail holes were clear for everyone to see. "It is not necessary to give up the ownership of circles. It is not necessary that we fight among ourselves, nor is it necessary to accept what is done to us, which may or may not have the design of the Lord Maker imprinted on it."

"I want us all to pray," Reverend Viel called out to the gathering.

"A prayer does not gain the strength it needs to reach the Lord Maker from an empty stomach," Edwud said.

At a loss for words, the Reverend Viel rose up and spat as violently as he could into Edwud's face. "You are a traitor to the Lord Maker and to the colony—you are the evil of which the Lord Maker has warned us. It is you who will bring the chlordane, you who entered the Kitchen and caused the Longley female's scream—the scream that will bring the chlordane."

Edwud was shocked that the Reverend could know of his thoughts regarding the scream. He located Sera in the second row and felt the sharp pain of betrayal enter his heart as her eyes refused to meet his.

An angry moblike noise jostled the air. Nolan huddled lower in the front as the Reverend continued:

85

"It is you who have caused the Great Sink. You have brought this punishment upon us from the Lord Maker—you who would defy her will. It is you who would turn us away from our past, which has always held the truth, which has always held us together. Hear me! Hear me! Listen. If Edwud is so certain that his wisdom is greater than the Lord Maker's, then perhaps his own circle should be the first to be shared."

A roar of approval shook Edwud's wings.

"Share his circle . . . share his circle . . . share his circle!" The chant of the mob struck at Edwud like flying stones. He began to speak but the chanting increased to close him out.

"I do not challenge the wisdom of the Lord Maker, but our own," he called out.

"Share his circle . . . share his circle . . . share his circle!"

Several Stewards moved toward the Reverend Viel. The Director stood, raising her antennae high, bringing the voices to a shaky silence.

"I want to hear what Edwud has to say," she said.

Edwud turned to the Director, who smiled enough for him to glimpse an edge of her former strength.

"Go ahead, Edwud," she said.

Edwud turned to face the heated crowd. "I do not have any answers—only questions. I question the right of some to have so much while others have so little. I question the belief that we begin our lives *even*—when one nimf can inherit so much and another so little. I question the idea that we are just, when the poorest, weakest collectors, those least able, have the least productive circles that demand the greatest strength, and when so many die short of their time in hunger. Perhaps if what the Reverend Viel says is true—that everything happening to the colony is the will of the Lord Maker—then that would mean my actions and words are also at the will of the Lord Maker."

Some members of the crowd whispered to those nearest them, trying to gauge what their own reaction should be.

"And if this is so," Edwud continued, "then on this day, at this moment, I relinquish the ownership of my circle in favor of the ruineds."

A huge roar arose from the crowd. Edwud couldn't tell whether it was from shock at his own destruction or the prospect of having a new medioc circle for redistribution.

*B*unches of collectors who previously barely spoke to one another began finding agreement together that there was an appropriate place to deposit their anger and bitterness, which had been hardening inside them like undigested chumps for several ans. If the cause had a name, then it could be defeated. And the name was Edwud K.

Stones were kicked at Edwud's hyde and shouts of abuse rattled the air that Edwud had caused the bad times, even the Great Sink, and that soon would come the chlordane—because of his entering the Kitchen and provoking the humans and the Longley woman's scream.

In the beginning Edwud tried ignoring the attacks, but they were gathering in strength and in number. His friends had brought chumps, and nervously visited, bumping into the long silences that sat like fat accusers, pointing to how no words of any real comfort or wisdom could be offered. Old Filip had demanded to be led to Edwud's hyde and he sounded excited rather than miserable.

"You're going to go, aren't you?" Filip asked. Edwud stared at Filip's blind and useless eyes. "I mean, you'll have to go, won't you? Won't you, Edwud? I heard that they want to bring you to Remedial Court."

"Yes, I'm going to go," Edwud said.

"Ha, I knew it, I just knew it. I knew you wouldn't stay here." Filip waddled around, livelier than usual. "You can share with me, Edwud, you know that, don't you? My circle, I mean. I don't have to say it, really, do I? I mean, you know that, don't you?"

"Yes, I know that."

"Yes, well, not that there's much. Where are you going to go?"

"Damned if I know, Filip, damned if I know."

Filip paced up and down in front of Edwud. "I don't suppose I could . . ." Filip bumped into the raised root of the lemon tree. "Oh . . . no . . . well, I don't suppose I could, ha ha . . . could I?"

Edwud looked at Filip's battered old body.

"I guess I'd be trying to go back again—and that would be a mistake. Do you know, Edwud, you once told me that. You said, 'Never go back, Filip, not because the past has changed, but because *you* have, and you will pass yourself there like a stranger.'"

"I'm full of great advice for others: how to ruin yourself, get yourself into Remedial Court . . ."

"I haven't any food to offer just at the moment," Filip said.

"What? Oh, Lord, I don't seem to get hungry much these days."

"Edwud, I'd like to tell you something. I mean it's not so important, but . . . I . . . could I tell you about something? I mean it is in the past, but I'm not actually trying to go back there."

89

"The Kitchen Wars?" Edwud asked. Filip nodded. "You were there a long time, weren't you?"

"I was, I was. I never really got over the fact that I made it out alive—although some in the colony don't think I did—ha ha ha." Filip laughed. "Think I'm more dead than alive, some of them do."

"I've never seen a dead collector bump into a tree," Edwud said.

Filip laughed again. "I helped someone die, during the Kitchen Wars—I hardly knew him, really. I mean it wasn't like he was a close friend or anything, but I sort of picked him up, right off the ground, ha ha. I was a lot stronger then and he seemed to feel a lot better. I wasn't embarrassed or anything—and he was very polite; he said, "Thank you," and we just stayed like that, not saying anything for—I don't know how long. Then he just died. I kept holding on to him, and I think now that I believed that if I could prevent any part of him from touching the ground, then somehow it would be all right. What would be all right I didn't know then, and I don't know now. I held him up off the ground for as long as I could, and . . . and . . . then he just seemed . . . to be sort of . . . lighter. Probably my muscles locked in place or something and . . . and . . . I've never told anyone about it all these years. . . ."

Edwud placed an antenna across Filip's wings. "Why don't you come with me when I go?" he said.

16

*T*he Director's patrimate burst into Edwud's hyde, breathless and shaking.

"You have to come," he said.

Edwud turned to face him—the smell of drain suds on his breath. "What?"

"You have to come, Edwud. The Director . . . she . . . keeps calling out . . . and she doesn't make sense . . . she won't . . . she hasn't eaten for . . . she won't listen . . . she can't get up and . . . she always walks every day and she can't get up . . ."

"I'm not Edwud. I'm Lennod . . ."

"She keeps calling out things I can't understand and she says your name . . ."

"She doesn't say my name . . ."

"She does: she says, 'Edwud, you know, don't you, Edwud?' "

"Well, that's just the point, see. I'm not the one who knows everything. Edwud is the one who knows—Edwud knows anything and everything—you ask him . . ."

"Please, Edwud, come and talk to her . . . you can make sense of . . . and get her to eat something. You can get her to eat something, I know you can . . ."

"I could probably get her to drink something—now that's my strong area . . ."

"Please, will you come?"

"Why not, lead on. I've never known everything—even for a little while."

The Director's patrimate had already disappeared into the darkness. Edwud lurched off after him. The cold air provided a refreshing edge to the warm flush of his sotted state.

At the bottom of the Director's hyde, the Director's patrimate stepped aside and pushed Edwud forward toward the outstretched and collapsed body of the Director.

"It's Edwud, dear," he said breathlessly.

The Director raised her antennae.

"Edwud? Is that you, Edwud? You know, don't you, Edwud, you know. You know why it's all happening, don't you, why we have lost the protection of the Lord Maker? We're cut off, aren't we, Edwud?"

Edwud shifted his weight backward, the effect of the suds wearing thinner.

"Err . . . ah . . . Mem, why don't you, er . . . have something to eat . . . er . . . ahh, Mem . . . ah, something to drink. . . ?"

"I have a soft cake chump here," the Director's patrimate said.

"The Lord Maker isn't taking us back, is she, Edwud? She has given up on us, hasn't she, Edwud? We're not returning to Ootheca, are we, Edwud . . . ever . . . are we, Edwud? Can't go without . . . without . . . I've lost it . . . for us . . . I've lost it . . . can't go now . . . I've lost it . . ."

Edwud turned toward the Director's patrimate. "What is it she's talking about?" he whispered.

"Don't call me 'she,' Edwud. . . . I can still hear."

"Sorry, Mem, I was just saying we might be able to find it," Edwud suggested hopefully.

"Find it? Find it? Find what? Ha ha ha, you don't understand—you don't understand . . ."

"Actually, Mem, you're quite right—I don't understand. You see . . . I never understand. I'm not the one who understands—I'm the one who never understands anything . . ."

The Director stretched upward and stared at Edwud.

"You don't understand . . . ," she said.

"I will look for it. I promise I will look for it"—Edwud turned to the Director's patrimate and spoke from the corner of his mouth—"whatever it is. . . ."

"I'll leave the two of you to discuss it," the Director's patrimate said as he backed quietly away.

"You don't understand," she said again.

"I will look for it and I will find it . . . all right? Is that all right?"

"Will you, Edwud, will you?" The Director laughed again, a strange laugh that sounded as though it could only be shared with herself.

"I will find it. Edwud and I . . . I mean . . . *I* will find it."

"But you can't find it," the Director said.

"Yes I can," Edwud said with conviction. "Damn, yes I can. It's the Monoocal, isn't it? That's what's missing, isn't it? The Monoocal . . ."

The Director stared at Edwud. "The Monoocal . . . ," she said.

"I know you can't tell me . . . but I know . . . that's it, isn't it?" Edwud began to leave. He stopped and looked back at the Director. "Why me? Why did you tell me? You could have told . . ." Edwud noticed the strange look on the Director's face.

"Don't you know?" the Director answered, looking with great compassion at Edwud. "Don't you know what I have just done to you?"

But Edwud, half-sotted as Lennod, didn't know. He didn't know that the Director had passed to him a weight, a pain, a journey that would change his life forever—with only the slightest possibility of saving the colony or himself.

Even though the Director never said exactly what it was that was lost, Edwud felt he had been chosen to find for the colony—its otherself. And that could only mean the Monoocal.

For the first time in his life, Edwud dreamed of the Monoocal. He knew it was the Monoocal even though he had never seen it. He knew the stories from his nimfhood—his father and mother would tell of the Orijin Chronicles together, each one excitedly cutting in on the other. And the story of the Monoocal was the most mysterious and reason-defying of them all.

"The Monoocal," his father said, "is round, round as the moon—and only slightly larger across than the length of my own body."

"You can see through it," his mother cut in, "and everything on the other side is larger . . ."

"But from the other side, everything is smaller," said his father. "It depends on which side you're standing."

"Obviously," said his mother.

"Have you seen it?" Edwud remembered having asked.

"Of course not," his mother said. "It's kept at the bottom of the Director's hyde—only Directors ever see it . . ."

"And before the Director dies . . . ," his father cut in.

"She shows it only to the one who will be the next Director."

"How do you know what it looks like, then?" Edwud

recalled his questions often annoyed both parents.

"Because we know, just like you know now—and like you will tell your own nimfs."

"But that isn't the best thing about the Monoocal," Edwud's father said in a loud whisper.

"It's what you can see in it," said his mother.

"Why won't you let me tell the nimf, Adel?"

"Because you're so slow . . . and you're going to frighten him."

"Frighten him?"

"I'm not frightened," Edwud had said.

"See, he's not frightened."

"Just because he says, doesn't make it so."

Edwud remembered his mother repeating that phrase a thousand times throughout his nimfhood: "just because he says, doesn't make it so."

"What do you see in the Monoocal?" Edwud had asked.

Edwud remembered his parents looking at each other as if waiting for the other to speak, and then his father said, "Sometimes . . . when you look into the Monoocal . . . you see . . ."

"Your otherself," his mother finished.

"Your what?" Edwud had asked.

"Your otherself," both parents whispered, "your otherself who will fly to Ootheca."

Inside run tubes and pipes that flood with fluids,
connecting and disconnecting
all parts of the body and brain,
so that each piece may work in harmony with every other.

NIMF BODY LESSONS

*A*n angry mob had gathered outside Edwud's hyde. Murmurs and rumblings passed from one to the other, like nimfs playing touch—of how Edwud had somehow managed to poison the Director, that she was dying. Some said she was already dead because she hadn't appeared for the last ten nights. The Law Stewards were nowhere to be seen; the Reverend Viel stood watching through the window high up in the shed. Sera reasoned and pleaded with him to intervene, but the Reverend swayed back and forth, tempting his dizziness and fear into being and then leaning back into safety. More than Edwud himself, the Reverend wanted the *idea* of Edwud to be destroyed, but as with his fear of height, he would never be able to acknowledge it—especially to himself, because he knew that it was possible to hate only those who were superior.

Edwud was not in his hyde. He had left with Nolan before dark to wait in the drains for Filip. The smell of fermenting water from the sump underneath encouraged Nolan to poke out his head into the night air between the iron slats, which formed a gridlike cover over the drain. Nolan hated the drains and always avoided them.

"Filip is never going to find his way here." He turned to Edwud, shaking his head and reaching for fresh air. "He'll keep bumping into things and the nimfs will probably lead him off somewhere and leave him."

"We'll wait a little longer," Edwud said.

In the distance they could hear the noise of the mob growing stronger. Nolan seemed more agitated than usual and Edwud knew it involved more than the anxiety he felt about breaking away from safety. He wondered whether he should tell Nolan the *real* reason he was leaving—to find and bring back the Monoocal. He could barely accept it himself; the Director hadn't made it clear—she hadn't said "go and bring it back," and yet the notion of doing exactly that had insisted its way into him, dispelling doubt as surely as the dark replaced the light. Edwud decided there was no benefit in weighing Nolan down with the burden of such an unreasonable thought.

"We might have one or two more . . . ah . . . sort of . . . like . . . traveling companions," Nolan said.

"You told someone else?" Edwud asked.

"It didn't seem right to . . . to . . . lie when they asked me."

"They?"

"Just a few."

"How many?"

"Ah . . . let's see . . . ah . . . Kerryd . . ."

"Does she understand where we are going?"

"*I* don't understand where we are going!"

Edwud thought to himself that that was true enough. Nolan continued, "And . . . ah . . . Wulfe."

"You don't even like Wulfe!"

"And . . . ah . . . Nik."

"Nik! Sweet Lord, Nik!"

"Apparently he's lost the rights to almost his whole circle for illegal collecting."

"And Lolli . . ."

"Have they all given up their circles?"

"What was left of them."

A cursing, thumping sound broke through the darkness. Edwud and Nolan jerked their heads down out of sight. Wulfe appeared, holding firmly to one of Filip's antennae.

"You don't have to tear it out of my head, you know," Filip growled. "I can find my own way around."

"Am I supposed to listen to you cracking your thick skull against every rock, tree and brick in the yard?"

"I can smell the drains," Filip said.

"I thought it was you," Wulfe answered.

"Edwud will be down below the cover—you can let me go now."

"Good, plunge into the sump. Then at least you'll stop complaining."

"You're an obnoxious snake . . ."

"Filip, Wulfe," Edwud called, "down here." Still gripping Filip's antenna, Wulfe descended into the drain along-side Edwud and Nolan.

"Edwud, I can't see how he's going to make it." Wulfe indicated Filip, who was attempting to get his bearings by smell.

"Did he say he can't take it? Edwud, is that what he said?" Filip sidled up to Edwud. "I think he's right—I don't think he'll be able to take it. He's soft and he never stops complaining—he'd better be staying behind."

"Did you pass anyone else on your way here?" Edwud asked.

"We passed Kerryd's hyde, but she wasn't there," Wulfe said.

"I didn't want everyone to know . . ."

"Well, Nolan . . ."

"Yes, I know—it doesn't matter now. We should go as soon as possible and try to cover a good distance before light," Edwud said.

"I'm not holding anyone up," Filip said.

"Of course not," Wulfe replied. "You can hardly hold yourself up."

And the others came—Kerryd, Lolli, Nik and, last of all, Sera. Nolan turned his back to her as she slipped through the grid and clung to the wall alongside them.

"I haven't come to go with you," she said to Edwud. Nolan ignored her as Edwud tried to look at her eyes.

"Why did you tell the Reverend Viel?" Edwud asked.

Sera looked around at the others, who pretended they weren't listening. "He's really a very good . . . I mean he believes in what he's doing—the good of the colony. It really is important to him. I think he sees you as . . . as something destructive . . ."

"Come with us," Edwud said. Nolan swung around in surprise at Edwud's invitation, resentment of Sera clinging to his face like stale crumbs of food.

"I can't."

"Have you fallen-in-fantasy with him?" Edwud forced himself to ask.

"I think so," Sera answered.

"If you're not sure—then you probably haven't."

"I have, then," Sera quickly replied. Edwud realized his words had once again taken him to a place he did not want to go, and as usual he listened to his own words push him dangerously onward.

"I think you're afraid," he said.

"I am not." Sera flared in anger at him. "Afraid of what?"

"Afraid to take the risk of losing the safety that Viel could offer you for . . . for something . . ."

"You mean with you?"

"Yes, with me."

"But you aren't offering anything, Edwud."

"Like the Reverend, you mean?"

"No. Well, yes . . ."

"What is it he's offering?"

"It's not as . . . as . . . cold as that. . . . You don't understand."

"Tell me, then—let me understand."

"The Reverend is . . . is . . . solid—he doesn't think

something today and then announce tomorrow that he thinks something different—he's consistent, and he's . . ."

"Powerful."

"Yes, he is—and you say it as though there's something wrong with that."

"With power? I don't think there's anything wrong with power, only that it seems to be like washing suds—savor it once and everything else becomes tasteless."

"But you fight with Reverend Viel specifically over power—you want to have even greater power. You want to change everything, our whole Sistum, to your way of thinking. Isn't that wanting power? Isn't it Reverend Viel's power that you resent and envy?"

Edwud looked hard at Sera; his belief in the rightness of his own thoughts was being shaken by the throat. He knew something was wrong with the colony in the yard— he didn't know that he was right because he didn't really have any answers that might fix things. But the Reverend Viel wanted no thinking, just acceptance—no responsibility and no change—and that, Edwud thought, is why his power is different from mine.

"I am sad, Sera, that you cannot see the difference," he said.

"And I am sad that you cannot see the need to remain strong and stable and consistent when everything is so . . . so . . . hard." Sera was crying. Edwud reached out to touch her. She drew back.

"Don't," she said.

"If you are happy with the Reverend Viel, what are you crying for?"

"For you, Edwud. I'm crying for you."

"That's ridiculous—why cry for me? I'm doing what I want to do—I'm doing what I believe in—just like the Reverend Viel."

"Yes, but you don't really understand . . ."

"Understand what?"

"You don't understand how . . . how . . . collectors are . . . it's you who won't accept the truth—and it's you who will be destroyed." Sera stared hard at Edwud as if imprinting his shape in her mind. She brushed at her tears, smiled at Edwud, stopped for a moment, and touched Edwud gently with her antennae. She stepped backward and disappeared up through the drain cover.

Lolli looked toward Edwud, her antennae and palps extended as if she might wrap him up and insulate him from the pain she felt must be dripping from the very air. Edwud stared after Sera like a leaf trying to catch a wind that has already passed. Edwud could not stop the pain that pierced his body more sharply than the cruel steel pins in the Kitchen.

The group listened in silence to the night. Music sneaking out between the cracks of the house, road machines spitting as they passed, creaks of the buildings giving back the heat of the day. The realization, the meaning of leaving, surrounding them in sounds already calling them back to safety, to comfort, to home. The smells of the yard seemed even to press the drain stench into submission: the rhododendron, wisteria, jasmine and laburnum—and the old lemon tree, and the azaleas in their pots and the bougainvillea—all telling the would-be leavers that leaving any long-committed past may be the greatest pain of all.

The minds of the would-be travelers grappled with images of their own pasts—as secured to the place, to the yard, as the conduits that connected their hearts to every particle of their bodies.

19

I've learned something of the way to walk drains. To walk too high along the inner walls of the pipes exhausts the legs after they have traveled only a short distance. To walk too low risks being caught in a sudden flood of effluent and being swept away. To walk the middleway, which seems the most sensible, can cause so little to happen that the purpose of the journey may become lost in the safety of the process. Better that all three levels are carefully chosen to extract that moment when each will give the most strength to each walker.

EDWUD'S TALKS TO THE TRAVELERS

The flushing tide of the drains seemed to have a rhythm, a beat, a purpose of its own. Murmuring and sobbing behind the walkers, pleading with them to wait—and then rushing to catch them, clamoring, chattering and flooding the space of the hollow such that at times they would need to cling to the roof of the pipes until the swill, laughing and splashing at their fear like a group of disobedient nimfs, departed ahead of them.

Walking became a product of will spread across time, with day dressed as night and heat following cold in any order. Minds became fixed on the sounds of the moving feet in front of them, and eyes turned upward to the occasional splintered shaft of light from an opening that promised clean air and the possibility of fresh food and open space.

They walked on. Farther than any of them had ever traveled. Talk became rare and expensive in the quest to draw on energy that had never been so demanded. Edwud listened for Filip's steps to falter or drag, but his beat was as regular as any of theirs, and like the others', his weight levered forward on every note that Kerryd sang—her lyrical voice filling the pipes with echoes that begged to remain trapped forever.

Between the rushes of fluid, Wulfe, at the rear, began listening for the rhythm of their feet—as if the sound, as he counted the steps, might remain a testament to their journey.

But something in the echo was wrong. It was in another rhythm—shorter and sharper. Wulfe stopped. It became stronger. He climbed toward the roof and waited. The walkers in front began to fade farther ahead. Wulfe listened to his own breathing and the approaching sound of footsteps. Clinging to the round upper surface was tiring, and Wulfe felt annoyed with himself for not stopping the whole group. What was he expecting? The footsteps were directly below him. He moved his antennae silently in the dark. It was a collector—there was no doubt. Wulfe moved down the side of the wall behind the steps and began to follow their sound, slowly gaining ground on the unknown follower so that a shape began to emerge in front of him. Purposefully he increased the noise made by his own feet. The collector ahead stopped for a moment and then began moving faster after the others. Wulfe ran to catch up. He called out. The collector in front seemed to disappear. Wulfe stopped. He moved cautiously forward, step by step. He looked up to see a small body desperately gripping the roof of the pipe.

"Get down here!" he called. The small collector scrambled down obediently. "Jinni B! What in the heap . . . are you doing?"

She looked squarely at Wulfe and shook her wings. "I don't have to tell you," she said as she turned and walked off after the others. Wulfe stood watching with his mouth open.

"Wait!" he called out. He quickly caught up with her and fell into beat alongside her. "Edwud's going to be furious."

"He doesn't own the drains." Jinni's voice gave away her tiredness and left an edge of doubt.

"Have you been following every night?"

"None of your business, is it?"

"Well, we'll see what Edwud has to say."

" 'We'll see what Edwud has to say,' " she mocked. Wulfe felt decidedly uncomfortable with this young brat—but impressed with how she must have struggled to keep up.

When he recognized her, Edwud sighed, shaking his head from side to side—realizing the futility of ordering her to return.

"Have you eaten?" he asked.

"No, I live on air," Jinni replied. Edwud and Wulfe looked at each other helplessly.

"You could do with more manners," Wulfe said.

"You could do with more brains," she snapped back. Wulfe stared for a moment, hearing Filip, behind him,

107

unsuccessfully trying to smother a laugh by covering his mouth.

"I don't see what you've got to laugh at, old fool," he called to Filip. "It's because of you she was able to catch up with us at all."

"What?" Filip's antennae shot up into the air. "That's not true, is it, Edwud? I haven't slowed you down, have I, Edwud?"

"Of course you haven't—shut up, Wulfe."

"He shouldn't be laughing at . . . at anyone . . . ," Wulfe said.

Nik pushed past Filip and Wulfe and faced Jinni. "I think she needs a good thump,"[1] he said. Involuntarily Jinni stepped backward toward Edwud.

"That's what happened to you, was it?" she spat at Nik. "Too many thumps around the head?" Her voice, lacking conviction, trailed off. Lolli came from behind, placing an antenna comfortingly on Jinni's back.

"She's only a nimf—and she's very tired . . . ," Lolli said.

"I'm tired too," Nik said, "but we don't have to be so rude."

"She doesn't mean it, do you, dear?" Lolli said soothingly. Jinni moved out from under her touch.

"Yes, I do. They don't own the drains—I can come down here anytime I like. They can't make me go back or anything—they can't make me do anything I don't want to do. And I'm not tired—I could keep walking as long as any of you. I'm not going back—and I'm not tired—and I'm not

[1] Out-of-date method of nimf control by striking the back of the head.

108

frightened of any of you—and . . . and . . ." All of them stared as tiny, reluctant tears gathered in the corners of her eyes, swelled, and rolled down her face, as if they were completely unimpressed with courage. "I don't care what you say. I'll go back when I want to—and I'll go forward when I want to—and just anyone try and give me a thump . . . and . . . and . . . I . . . I'm not . . . I don't . . . I'll go back when it suits me . . ."

Edwud touched one of the tears with his left antenna. It held fast and slithered down like a frightened baby nimf to splash against his head.

"But we're not going back, Jinni," he said.

Every great and small event
began the same: with not the least
part of its potential understood.
THE ORIJIN CHRONICLES

*A*t first the frightened earth hummed to itself, but this would seem not comfort enough. Now, as the pipe branch chosen by Edwud slowly rose toward the surface, the tidal swills came rushing to meet them head on and the quaking increased.

Through his feet Edwud could feel the vibrations. Not continuous, but in short, warning bursts. Behind him Filip's breathing had become louder and more labored. The temperature increased as they moved slowly upward toward the surface.

Wulfe caught up with Edwud and whispered to him that a small break might be a good idea. Especially as he didn't want to end up carrying Filip on his back. Edwud smiled at Wulfe's disguised concern for Filip and waved everyone to stop at the next intersecting pipe, where the joint provided a protective lip for them to rest in safety. All of them flopped down gratefully.

"I don't like that rumbling—do you feel it, Edwud?" Nik asked.

"It seems to be coming from up there—where we're headed," Nolan said, as he shook his head back and forth worriedly.

"They're doing something to it up there," Filip added ruefully. "I don't see why they can't leave the ground alone."

"That's the way they are," Kerryd said. "It's what they do, I think—do you think that, Edwud? I mean—they seem to want to change things into other things all the time." Kerryd's voice and mind drifted off. Edwud knew that a song would appear some days later, whose words and melody would follow the dreamy passage of her present thoughts.

"I don't know—it could be large road machines," Edwud said. "I'm going to have a look. Wait here—I won't be long." Edwud strode off up the pipe as the others waited and watched.

"I'm not sure we ought to be heading toward that—whatever it is. I'm thinking it may not be a good idea," Nik said while pointing his antennae down the pipeway suspiciously. "We could be heading for trouble."

"Well, that won't be a new direction for you, will it?" Wulfe said.

"How would you like to float down with the next wash?" Nik stood to face Wulfe.

"Oh, now come on, you two." Lolli made little noises of comfort. "Ooh . . . oh . . . we all have to, oh . . . stick together . . ."

"Stick what together?" Jinni asked.

"Ooh . . . oh . . . I suppose . . . yes . . . that's right . . . stick

111

ourselves together—no, I mean we all should be, ah . . . together . . . I think . . . like we all should be pulling on the one side . . ."

"Lolli's right—we're all a bit tired," Nolan sighed.

"And hungry," Nik added, "and I'm not so sure Edwud really knows what he's doing. He won't talk about his plans."

The group fell into a brooding silence. The rhythm of the shaking earth began jarring against their thoughts. The remembered comfort of the yard seemed in a process of being swept down the channel from which they had come.

"Perhaps we shouldn't have taken the upturn back there," Lolli said. "Perhaps we should have continued farther on down . . ."

"I was thinking that myself—at the time," Nik said.

"Why didn't you speak up, then?" Filip called to him.

"I'm not the leader, am I?"

"You certainly are not," Filip replied.

"And what does that mean, you old . . . you old . . . cripple?"

"I'm hungry," Jinni said.

"Good," said Wulfe.

"It's not very nice to feel happy about someone's hunger, Wulfe," Kerryd said, shaking her head in disapproval.

"I'm not very nice," Wulfe answered.

"We don't need to be told." Jinni twitched her antennae at him.

"Perhaps we should have a vote about what we should

do—and when Edwud gets back . . . ," Lolli said.

"I'm not voting," Filip's stubborn voice echoed.

"Useful members only . . . ," Nik said.

"I don't even know why I'm here . . . ," Lolli began.

"I don't know why you're here either," Wulfe responded.

"You can be very cruel." Lolli began to cry.

"And I'm not even trying," Wulfe added.

"I don't like you," Jinni said.

"Who, me?" Nik asked, leaping to his feet.

"Any of you . . . you're all . . . you're all . . . small."

"Small?" Nolan said, surprised.

Wulfe stood up. "You're the smallest here," he said. The whole group looked at one another as if it were suddenly necessary to see who was really small and who was not. The males stood up, stretching their legs to give added height, spreading their wings to give the impression of bulk. The females moved closer together.

Jinni called out to the males, "You all look silly!" The males looked at one another and lowered their legs and wings. "I meant small up here." Jinni tapped the side of her head. Kerryd and Lolli burst into giggles.

"Up where, did she say?" Filip tried to whisper to Nolan.

"Oh, Lord," Wulfe groaned.

"Well, I couldn't see. I'm not the smallest . . . am I? Lord, I hope not. Nolan, I'm not the smallest, am I?"

"Look out, don't step on old Filip, Nolan," Wulfe shouted in mock alarm.

"What?"

"He's so hard to see," Wulfe said. Even Jinni smothered her laughter under her wing.

"Very funny, Wulfe. You'll get old one day—and I hope I'm around to see it," Filip said.

A lull in the shaking encouraged silence. Everyone settled flatter into the earthenware pipe. The waiting for Edwud continued. Occasionally one of them would peer down the pipe in the direction Edwud had taken. When the shuddering in the ground began to build again, Nik began pacing.

"Where is Edwud, anyway? How come he's not back?"

"It might have been better if we'd all gone together," Lolli said. "I can't see why Edwud had to go off by himself." Lolli's head moved in time with Nik's pacing.

"He's probably just checking whether it's safe for us up ahead," Nolan said.

"Safe for us?" Nik gave a laugh. "Safe for us? You must be joking—why would he do that?"

"Because that's how he thinks," Jinni said.

"Or doesn't think," Nik said.

"I doubt that this is the best way for us to . . . would you like me to sing for you?" Kerryd's voice hesitated in the air. "I could sing about home . . . the yard, I mean."

"Well, it's not home anymore, is it?" Nik said abruptly. Lolli fixed her stare on the space vacated by Kerryd's voice.

"Does . . . does anyone think about . . . about the yard? I mean . . . ," she faltered. Filip's deeper voice brought Lolli around to face him.

"I do," he said.

"Oh, do you?" she said, relief easing the tension in her tone.

"I remember it all—the trees and the flowers and the

shed and the lemon tree . . ."

"And the old brick pile—and the rock garden and the sand heap," Nolan joined in.

"And the Great Sink!" Wulfe's voice was hard and shocking. "And the ruineds and their starving nimfs— and the look in the eyes of those who came back from the road with nothing—yes, I remember." The words of the others, lost like shadows attacked by light, left them empty and confused.

The approaching and fading rumble through the ground and the pipe and the thick air began to shake loose the tenuous threads linking courage to behavior, and they began trembling with the earth as they lay in the dark.

"One of these swills could have chlordane in it, you know," Nik said, as he watched the effluent tide rise and fall. "Did you think of that, any of you?"

The group stared at the bottom of the pipe. Filip coughed and said, "Well, there hasn't been any yet."

"You'll only know about it once," said Wulfe.

"Well, it will never be a bad memory, will it?" Filip shot back. Jinni moved closer to Filip.

"It wouldn't be strong enough with all the other swill, would it?" she asked.

"Ha," Nik said, "have you ever seen anyone after chlordane? They can't balance, first—can't tell which way the world slopes—and they bump into things and fall onto their backs—and their eyesight starts to go—and they see things that aren't there—until eventually they don't see anything at all and the pain eats out their stomachs . . ."

"Shut up," Wulfe said, glancing toward Filip. Lolli and

Nolan and Kerryd focused on the swill.

"We'd be trapped here if it came," Lolli said.

"We couldn't even outrun it," Nolan added.

"Nor could we stop breathing long enough to get out of here." Kerryd's voice was a pitch higher than normal.

"I'm not going to die trapped down here," Nik announced.

"No!" Filip called out.

"I want to breathe the open air again."

"And feel the moon . . ."

"And the wind . . ."

"It could even be coming toward us now—the chlordane—we wouldn't even know until it was too late."

The seven of them paced up and down, bumping and jostling each other, watching the swill and slowly moving up the pipe in the direction Edwud had taken. And then Nik stumbled against Wulfe, lost his footing, and rolled over and into the swirling filth below. Lolli screamed; Wulfe immediately lowered his antennae to Nik, who grabbed at them with his legs, but the swill was a large one and the pressure easily pulled Nik's legs away, floating him off down the pipe.

Wulfe ran hard along the middleway, not stopping at each pipe junction that momentarily slowed the rush. He could see Nik's head bob up through the froth of the swirling liquid and disappear again—a wing reached upward and flapped wildly. Nik seemed to be rolling over and over helplessly. Wulfe, as he ran, considered whether he should stop, but his legs pounded on down the pipe; he was amazed at how clearly his mind was working. He didn't even like Nik—what was he doing trying to save his life? The thought persisted that they'd all be better off if Nik disappeared with the swill. Still, his legs ran on as if guided by more powerful thoughts to which he had no access.

Ahead, Wulfe knew, there was a large trough they had passed earlier and a branching of the pipe where the swill would slow down. He tried to increase his speed to beat Nik's rolling body to the trough. He could see nothing of Nik at all. The froth had increased with the swill's speed and he knew Nik would be dragged under with the pressure. Nik would not know where the surface was as he was turned over and over in a mad watery world that had stopped making sense.

Nik hit the bottom of the deep trough with the heaviest sludge of the swill. The water was calmer but deeper. Instinctively he gripped the bottom of the trough as something solid and stable to hold on to. His head was spinning in a dizzying, aching whirl. Both forewings had been stretched to breaking point and the pain, he knew, was waiting for its moment. He needed air, but fear had locked his legs to the bottom of the trough—letting go might be a worse fate, he reasoned. He knew he would die, and wondered if dying would be painful. He wondered if his other-self would rise in afterflight to Ootheca—to the Lord Maker—where everything would make sense and even he would be loved. He began to relax his muscles. To Ootheca, where circles are filled with rich spills and chumps. Nik's mind drifted as his muscles weakened. The Lord Maker would welcome him—as if he were the same as everyone else, as if he were loved like Edwud or Kerryd or Nolan. He

117

would be like them at last. Nik floated upward—the need for air seemed less important. His wings opened and spread outward, beating gently against the water, lifting him up, and up, raising him toward the surface.

Wulfe stopped at the trough, realizing that this was the only possible place where Nik could be rescued. He peered into the darkness, hoping to sense Nik's presence, knowing that if Nik was to survive, to live, he had to come to the surface. Nik would have to let go of everything.

Behind him Wulfe heard short, sharp breaths and then watched Jinni appear. "Where is he?" she asked, gulping for air.

"I can't see him," Wulfe said. "If he doesn't come up now . . ."

"There he is!" Jinni shouted. In the middle of the trough, Nik's back rose like a black moon through the suds.

"I can't reach him!" Wulfe shouted.

"He won't be able to breathe," Jinni announced to herself.

"I can't reach him!" Wulfe's voice was high-pitched.

"You can paddle out to him," she said.

"What! I can't do that."

"Yes, you can—I've seen a nimf do it. You just keep running your legs really fast and you spread out your forewings so they sit on top of the water and you sort of kick and run real fast all at the same time—and you go across the top of the water."

"I can't do that! I'll swallow the swill and then I'll go down to the bottom like . . . like he did—and I won't come up," Wulfe said.

"He came up."

"He's probably dead!"

"You could paddle out and hang onto his antennae with your teeth and drag him back here, and we could lift him out," Jinni said.

"Why don't you do it, then?"

"I'm only a nimf. I wouldn't be strong enough."

"Your mouth would be," Wulfe snapped.

"Are you going to do it?"

"No!"

"Just do what I said—kick your legs a lot and spread out . . ."

"My forewings—I know. Look, I don't think he's alive— he's not moving."

"What if it were you out there?" Jinni asked.

"I wouldn't be so dumb as to fall into it in the first place. And I wouldn't expect anyone to be dumb enough to come in after me."

"Well, I'll have to do it, then—get out of the way."

"Oh, dung, dung, dung . . ." Wulfe spread his forewings and leapt off the edge of the trough, his feet thrashing the air, his antennae sticking straight upward in terror. He hit the frothy swill with panicking legs and wings flapping.

"Keep your wings still!" Jinni shouted. "Kick with the legs! The legs, not the wings!"

Wulfe flapped, kicked, and thrashed every movable part of his body. The froth seemed to part in front of him—but he wasn't sinking. He aimed in the direction of Nik and kept churning. He could hear the brat of a nimf's voice shouting something at him, but he didn't care what it was

119

she was saying—she had already got him into this . . . this
. . . dung of a mess. He couldn't see far through the foam,
which floated in around him after he passed. Jinni was still
calling out something to him. His legs were aching.

And there was Nik. Facedown in front of him. Wulfe
lunged forward, thrusting his legs underneath the limp
body. He kicked out hard. Nik's sodden body rolled over.
Wulfe couldn't see whether he was alive or dead. He pulled
Nik's antennae closer to him with his forewing and bit hard
into them. He began kicking out to return to the edge and
began to realize how exhausted he was, as the weight of
Nik's body pulled him back and forced his head into the
stinking swill every time he moved forward.

Nik had not moved. Wulfe thought with disgust that his
efforts had been a waste—Nik was dead and now he was
going to join him. Wulfe knew he had very few kicks left in
him. He would have called for help if he hadn't had his jaws
clamped tightly on a dead collector's antennae. What a stupid way to go out, he thought. The anger kept him kicking.
What in the Lord Maker's name was he doing in this dumb,
dumb situation—kicking himself toward death in a sewer
with a dead collector's antennae in his mouth, while a nasty
little brat of a nimf yelled insults at him? Heaps of dung!

"Here!" Jinni's high-pitched voice penetrated Wulfe's
reverie. Through the foam he could barely see her shape
leaning toward him. There was no feeling left in his legs
and his forewings had stopped flapping altogether. Even if
he could make it to the side of the trough, he knew he
would never have the strength to pull himself and Nik up
onto the edge. Wulfe's brain told him clearly what to do—

let go of Nik—and Wulfe observed his body, his teeth this time, ignoring the command.

A large flush of swill poured into the trough, swirling him farther from the edge. Wulfe considered that he was in the process of drowning already, and if so, maybe it wasn't so bad—maybe it would be peaceful. Peaceful sounded good to him.

His left antenna seemed to be caught on something. Wulfe tried to flick it off but it wouldn't move. It annoyed him to think of his most sensitive antenna stuck onto something while he was trying to drown peacefully. He yanked harder and felt the pain through to the top of his head. Anger made him kick harder toward the caught antenna. The foam parted and revealed the small but wildly flapping wings of the brat, as she clawed at the edge of the trough with Wulfe's best antenna between her teeth. Wulfe realized she must have leapt in. He was shocked and pushed hard toward her to allow her to scramble up the edge. He watched her claw at the concrete edge, and with the easing of tension on his antenna, she struggled up the face.

Wulfe thought he might make it if she could take some of the weight from him. The weight he felt he had been carrying forever and ever. The weight, the dead weight of collectors—and his own unbearable heavy failure to be anything, anything but small.

His feet hit the edge of the wall. He glanced back at Nik, still motionless on his back, the foam moving over the lower half of his body. Wulfe threw himself at the wall and felt Jinni's strength hauling on his antenna. He clawed at the concrete and felt Nik's weight through his teeth and down his neck. His front legs and then his back legs grappled with the pocked surface, lifting him up. He struggled up the flat edge. And then they were both hauling on Nik's sagging body. Wulfe realized that his teeth would bite through Nik's antennae at any moment. Nik's head caught on the sharp edge of the concrete and both he and Jinni leaned backward, increasing the strain. Wulfe's teeth sank further into Nik's antennae. Slowly the body rose, pivoting around his head, which remained caught on the edge. Nik's body wavered for a moment and then flipped over, back first, onto the concrete beside them.

For several moments neither of them moved. Then Jinni looked hard at Nik.

"We should roll him onto his stomach and face him down the pipe. If there's any water in him, it might run out," she said. Wulfe looked at her as he struggled for breath.

"What?"

"He may not be dead," Jinni said. Wulfe helped her lever Nik onto his stomach. A trickle of liquid flowed out. "See, look!" Jinni pointed at the tiny flow. "He's breathing, look!" A clump of suds wavered back and forth in front of Nik's mouth.

"Heaps of dung!" Wulfe said.

The two of them watched as Nik's breathing began to get stronger. Wulfe speculated on how it might have been better if they had left him in the swill.

"I can see how you might feel like that," Jinni said.

"What do you mean?" Wulfe squinted at her.

"He's not going to be happy with you."

"Why?"

"Look." Jinni pointed at Nik's neatly severed antennae and the other halves, which were still stuck to the side of Wulfe's face.

Wulfe brushed them off quickly with a shudder and looked squarely at Jinni with horror. "Oh, my Lord," he said.

"He certainly looks different, doesn't he?" Jinni said.

"Oh, my Lord," Wulfe said again.

"Sort of . . . pruned."

Wulfe and Jinni looked at each other. She reached out to wipe a clot of foam clinging to Wulfe's face. At first, without thinking, Wulfe pulled his head away, but she persisted. He struggled to control his face not to smile, but it was becoming more like the disobedient nimf it was staring at. Jinni brushed his face clean, finally becoming embarrassed by Wulfe's peculiar gaze.

Since deciding to leave the colony, Edwud had begun a secret daily program he called "preparation." The program consisted of three parts. The first part was what he called the "ant dance," where he lifted an object, carried it for fifty leggs, and then carried it back. Edwud learned the technique from watching the small black ants near the can area of the yard. They could lift enormous weights for their size, and Edwud spent hours watching and talking to them. Rarely did any of the ants stop work to even chat with him—so Edwud, to the amusement of many collectors, would trot alongside, inquiring and making mental notes. Edwud reasoned that the ants had a lifting, holding and locking technique that made the whole task easier. He noted that the more they lifted, the more they were able to lift, and that after a while the process took on the rhythmical appearance of an artful dance.

On his first try Jon B's nimfs saw him struggling with a rock and they thought he had gone mad. Never having seen a collector lift anything that wasn't food, they fell about in the dust imitating Edwud's grunting, straining stagger. Edwud stomped off many times, vowing to do his lifting in private, with the nimfs always sneaking about trying to follow him for the best entertainment in the colony.

The second part of his program Edwud called "thinking." Here he did calculations such as counting the number of steps from one object to another and noticing exactly where the wind touched his face, so that when he closed his eyes and laid his antennae to rest, he could trace the direction of the path and end up exactly on the object. "Thinking" also included remaining alone and very still, so that only his long slow breaths remained in touch with the outside world. In this way Edwud allowed his mind to dwell on the "why" of things. Such as, why did the Lord Maker leave collectors with wings if they were not able to fly? And what was the purpose of sending the suffering of the Great Sink to the colony when it seemed only to hurt the weakest collectors in the yard? And why did he feel the way he did about Sera when she had betrayed him to the Reverend Viel, and why did she cry for him? And why did Nolan and Wulfe and Kerryd and the others, why did they come with him? And where was he going? Where were they all going? And how would he find the Monoocal when he didn't even know what it looked like? What if he did find it—how would it help the colony?

Sometimes he created answers to the "whys" and chose from among them when he needed to act; yet rarely did he end "thinking" with any real sense of sureness.

The third and perhaps most difficult part of Edwud's daily program was both painful and frightening. Every fiber of his being resisted, yet he persisted. He called it "light." Each morning when all of the colony's collectors were tucked away and hidden and safe, he would force himself to stand in the open as long as he could bear it, facing into the vicious streaks of the sun. Each day he would try to face the light a little longer. Sometimes he thought he was gaining and sometimes he fell back toward the safety of the dark, his eyes watering and his head throbbing. He wasn't clear about why he wanted to torture himself like this; he knew he would never be able to explain it to anyone else. But he reasoned that so many things changed from night to night that they must have occurred in the light of day, and perhaps if he could overcome his collector's fear, then it might be possible to see much farther—to see much more—and to see it all more clearly.

Walking back down the pipe toward the others, Edwud was pleased he had again completed his secret program. He had a few surprises for them concerning what he had learned up ahead on the surface—the rumbling noise, particularly. And using the ant dance, he had carried with him a huge chump of something that looked like a vegetable of some kind.

He began thinking of Sera. He knew he had fallen-in-fantasy with her. She hovered in gorgeous perfection in his mind: the least movement, the tiniest gesture, a sublime act; every word, a graceful and elegant truth; each touch, a throbbing promise. Brushed aside were any momentary thoughts of the real Sera: the Sera who had joined with the Reverend Viel, the Sera who had betrayed his confidence, the Sera who was afraid to risk her heart. Edwud thought that there must be two of himself, to love two Seras: one that operated with the real, the visible, the certain; and one that floated like one of Kerryd's songs and cared only for what might be. Edwud laughed to himself; perhaps one of them, one of the Edwuds, was this Lennod that Nolan was always telling him about?

"Edwud!" The shout rang out through the pipe. Edwud dropped the large chump with relief. It was Nolan running to meet him. "Where have you been? Everyone is . . . is . . . terrified. . . . Nik fell into the swill and Wulfe and Jinni ran down the drain after him . . . and . . . and Kerryd is keening to herself . . ." Nolan stopped in front of Edwud. "How did you carry that chump by yourself?" Without waiting for an answer, Nolan continued, "Everyone wants to go back . . . to the yard . . . they don't . . ."

In the distance Edwud saw Kerryd and Lolli and Filip running toward him.

"Edwud!" they shouted.

"We were so frightened," Lolli said. "About the chlordane . . . Nik said it could be in any one of the swills . . . and . . ."

"Everyone started smelling it . . ." Nolan said.

"We didn't know what had happened to you," Kerryd said.

"I wasn't frightened," Filip said.

"Yes you were," Lolli snapped at him.

Edwud's legs and head throbbed with pain and anger. "Dung damn!" he yelled. The others fell quiet and lowered their antennae like small nimfs. "Dung damn you," Edwud said again. "I'm not your father, I'm not your mother. I'm not the one responsible here—I'm not . . ." Edwud was too angry to make sense. The others stood around the chump, heads down, as Edwud strode off down the pipe. "Dung damn you," he called back at them.

Fifty leggs in front of him, Jinni, Wulfe and Nik appeared as if in one lump. Jinni and Wulfe seemed to have Nik's front legs perched on their backs as they half led, half

127

dragged him forward. Edwud stopped and felt his anger slide away, to be replaced by relief.

"He's all right," Jinni called.

"Thank the Lord," Edwud mumbled to himself. He took Jinni's place under Nik and led them back to the chump. "Do you lot want to go back as well?" he asked Wulfe directly.

"They jumped in the swill." Nik's breaking, unsteady voice was high with emotion. "They jumped in. Him." Nik pointed at Wulfe. "Him . . . he jumped in . . . and her . . . she did too . . . and they pulled me out. I was gone . . . and they pulled me out." Nik turned in a dreamy state to Wulfe and Jinni. "And I love them," he said. Wulfe dropped Nik's legs to the floor of the pipe in disgust. The others looked at Nik in shock. "I love them," Nik said again.

"I knew I should have left you there," Wulfe muttered.

"I still love you," Nik said hazily.

"I bit off both of your antennae—you stupid collector," Wulfe snapped.

"You what? You did what?" Nik asked.

"He was pulling you out with his teeth," Jinni said. "It was an accident."

"My antennae?" Nik seemed confused.

"Did someone eat his antennae?" Filip asked.

"My antennae?" Nik wobbled his head. "Aaagh!" he screamed. "You ate my antennae!"

"That's more like it," Wulfe said, as he turned to take a piece of Edwud's chump.

ll of them quietly followed Edwud up the wheels, along the axles and between the drainage holes in the floor of the railway car. Grateful to be out of the stench and danger of the drains, although they all knew that they would have to go back into them again.

Edwud knew that the railway car was going to move; he had watched them when he came to the surface as they made the terrible rumbling noise. He decided not to tell the others—partly because he wanted to see the shock on their faces when the whole room moved. He chuckled to himself every time he thought about it.

The car had carried wheat and alfalfa in the past—the smells were unmistakable. Only tasteless, dried pieces of the alfalfa stalks were left, but jammed into the cracks between the floorboards were dozens of untouched wheat grains, enough food for two ans, Edwud calculated—not that he'd want to stay here as long as that.

When the car lurched forward with a groan and a shudder, Edwud spun around to watch the faces. Horror! Lolli's scream was drowned in the groaning of the car; Nolan grabbed at Wulfe, whose antennae sprang up so fast they appeared to shoot off from his head. Kerryd seemed to enjoy the sensation, and Nik prayed. Edwud noticed Filip grinning widely—obviously he knew about trains.

23

Clip track
clump pack
road slog
trod.

Clop trick
plug stick
slug long
plod.

TRADITIONAL MARCHING CHANT

he train squealed and jiggered throughout the
night, careening around steel curves, as the small
group of collectors gripped the splintered floorboards, drifting in and out of sleep through dreams of racing landscapes
and whirling shadows.

Edwud dreamed of the Monoocal. It rolled like the train
wheels, just a little in front of him. As he ran to catch up, it
changed direction, rounding on unseen rails invisible to
him; always in front of him, always on invisible tracks.

Edwud considered what hope he had of finding the
Monoocal, of returning to the colony, and he wondered if he
had condemned himself and his friends to a pointless
death. Perhaps death was always pointless, he pondered,
which would mean that life, also, was pointless. Then why
was he clinging to this thundering human machine as if he

were going somewhere—as if there were somewhere to go? Sleep. Sleep, he decided, was when the Lord Maker's thoughts entered the unguarded mind, settling far back like shy nimfs waiting for the time when they could step forth and show their cleverness.

The train stopped. All of the collectors woke. Edwud signaled them to move quickly toward the exit.

Grateful to escape the noise of the rail yards, the group moved quickly in single file behind Edwud as if he had some kind of map visible only to him. The group's reliance on him both pleased and annoyed Edwud. He loved the feeling of importance it gave him: collectors responding and following his directions, swapping their own views for his. He wondered by what mechanism, what motivation they chose his thoughts as more followable than their own. Perhaps he should tell them about his quest for the Monoocal. But something stopped him. Perhaps they were not ready yet to hear it.

Edwud had no map and no idea of which direction to follow. He struck out at first along the easiest pathway, a paved track, until a sudden surge of human feet came pounding out of the sky at them. Cleared pathways, they had learned as nimfs, were always the most dangerous. To be seen was the most foolish risk; to cease expecting death was to invite it in; to draw no attention was the greatest wisdom.

Climbing through the grass at the side of the track, the group made much slower progress, struggling up and over and around more often than onward.

131

The air was different here, Edwud decided—lighter, innocent of many of the smells of the yard. This would be the country he had heard about, where there were fewer humans on the ground but less food as well. Edwud sighed: the Lord Maker did that a lot, he thought—matched a generous situation with a mean one. Like Sera—beautiful, thoughtful and sensitive on one side, but fearful, unable to lose sight of the boundaries of the yard; like the cool protection of the night turning to the harsh, revealing day. Perhaps Ootheca was double-sided also, like the moon, with a dark side that could not be seen until afterflight.

Light was falling quickly as Edwud led the tired group under the door of an iron-sheeted building. The smells were heavy and clung in oily lumps close to the concrete floor. The air was damp and stale; old and rotting grains littered the floor amid droppings of animals from long ago. There had been animals here—pigs and chickens and a horse or donkey. All of them could detect the faint old odors now mixed confusingly together. Edwud decided it was an abandoned farm and the others agreed.

"At least it will be quiet," Wulfe said.

Filip and Jinni and Nik slumped together onto the floor, too exhausted to talk. Lolli tried to smile at everyone in turn but each of them either ignored her or avoided her eyes. Kerryd was making tiny musical noises by puffing and sucking air over her teeth in different ways. Nolan sidled up to Edwud.

"What do you think?" he asked Edwud.

"I don't know," Edwud said. "It feels safe—we can look for food after we've rested."

Satisfied, Nolan lowered his body to the floor and enjoyed the strain leaving his legs. The eight of them, like sodden leaves in a pool, began gently sinking into sleep as the sun tapped and ticked on the corrugated iron walls of the shed.

It had been dark for some time when Edwud began to wake and feel that something was not quite right. The feeling came down his antennae in shivers like low notes sung slightly out of tune. He strained to see farther into the darkness. He could sense the others beginning to wake. What was it? He listened and moved his antennae slowly in a wide arc.

"What is it?" Nolan asked.

"Can you smell something?" Nik wanted to know.

"I can," Filip said. Everyone turned toward him. "I don't know what, but I can smell something." Without realizing it, the group moved closer together.

"Don't push at me!" Wulfe turned angrily on Nik.

"I wasn't pushing—it was Nolan. He keeps shoving backward into me."

"I've hardly moved," Nolan complained.

"Where's Jinni?" Edwud asked. "And Kerryd?" The group fell silent. "Jinni! Kerryd!" Edwud called out loudly. There was no answer.

"Would they have gone outside?" Lolli asked.

"Kerryd! Jinni!" Edwud called again.

The cloud screening the moon shifted; then the pale light drilled through the nail holes in the roof and Edwud saw what was disturbing the air around them. About thirty leggs in front of him and surrounding the group was a large gathering of huge brown collectors. Edwud guessed there could be twenty at least. Their bodies were thicker and their heads were considerably smaller than the yard collectors', and amazingly, Edwud noted, they had no wings at all. And even in the midst of his fear he was desperate to know how, without wings, they would ever rise in afterflight.

"Ho," Edwud called.

The brown collectors looked at one another as if searching for a clue. Some appeared puzzled, some suspicious, and some threatening and angry. They twitched their antennae around constantly.

Edwud tried again. "Ho, have you seen two of our friends? They seem to be missing."

"Edwud, we're all right." Kerryd's voice floated over the heads of the circle of collectors.

"They won't let us through," Jinni called out. "They keep blocking our way."

"Aah, we came on the train . . . aah . . . we're . . . aah . . . looking for . . . aah . . . something . . ." Edwud's voice trailed off.

"I don't think they can talk," Wulfe said, loud enough for everyone to hear. Nolan rolled his eyes and smiled at the brown collectors to apologize for Wulfe's rudeness. As each of them had spoken, the antennae of every brown collector waved and wiggled and followed the speaker, like nimfs watching their first spill pour from the sky.

"Do you . . . aah . . . talk?" Edwud asked, smiling as he spoke. The brown collectors twitched their antennae at Edwud's mouth. Filip moved up to Edwud.

"I've got an idea," he said. "Tell me what they do." Filip

lowered his antennae and then rapidly wiggled them up and down. The brown collectors reared up the front of their bodies, revealing the underside of their protective plates, and bared their small white teeth in a threatening manner.

"They're about to tear your head off," Wulfe whispered to Filip.

"That's how they talk!" Filip declared with satisfaction.

"What did you say to them?" Nolan called out anxiously.

"How would I know?" Filip growled back at him.

"Well, they didn't like it," Nolan complained.

"I'm frightened." Lolli began to cry.

"Now that'll be a big help," Wulfe said to her.

"They would have attacked us by now if they were going to," Edwud noted soothingly.

"Don't let him start waving any more messages to them," Wulfe said as he glared at Filip.

"Lord, you lot are a bunch of . . . of . . . flutterers," Filip said.

"A bunch of what?" Wulfe asked.

"Shut up!" Edwud said. "And keep your antennae still. Kerryd, can you hear me?"

"Yes," Jinni replied.

"That girl needs a good thump," Wulfe mumbled.

Edwud continued, "Kerryd, can you sing something . . . anything . . . so long as it is loud and clear?"

"I don't think this is a good time for singing," Lolli said, to admonish Edwud for his lightheartedness.

"I think we should make a run for it," Nik whispered to Edwud.

"And what about Kerryd and Jinni?" Wulfe snapped at

him. "I should have left you floating in the drains . . . you . . . you . . . flutterer!"

Kerryd's voice started low as if it had burrowed through the ground beneath the brown collectors and burst out into the air above their heads. It was a song that only Filip had heard before, a long time ago, before the Kitchen Wars. It told of a favorite collector of the Lord Maker's, called Minna, who was given the power to have again any moment that she wanted—any time that she found pleasant or happy enough she could call back.

The brown collectors swung around to face Kerryd. They listened with their antennae pointed at Kerryd, absorbing the vibrations of her voice. The song told how Minna became obsessed with trying to feel again the happiness of past moments—her first love, the admiration for her brilliant collecting, her lost friends. Each time Minna returned to the moment she wanted, it was exactly the same; however, *she* was not the same. Minna came back into the moment knowing where it was headed, what it meant; and there was no joy in the return. She began spending more of her time desperate to recall the exact feelings she had once enjoyed and less of her time collecting food for herself. Gradually she became thinner and thinner, until one day she was as thin as her own forewings and was lifted on the northern breeze into the air.

On quiet nights when the gentle north winds blow, Minna can be heard whispering to those foolish enough to listen—how to recall their favorite moments, how to summon them up and make them appear within their minds. Kerryd's voice became softer.

"Once again," she sang. *"Once again."* Her voice fading like the notes of a bell in the distance. *"Once again."*

The brown collectors parted in front of Kerryd and Jinni as they walked toward Edwud. Not one of the country collectors moved as Edwud led his friends out of the animal shelter and away into the night.

Once outside the shed, Edwud broke into a run and the others followed without argument. The thought of the thick brown collectors coming after them kept them skeltering through the night without even a backward glance. Filip was the first one to stop, limp and breathless. He told them to continue and he would catch up, but no one considered leaving him behind. They flopped to the ground, silently grateful to have old Filip take responsibility for the rest that they all desperately wanted.

"Why do you think they couldn't talk, Edwud?" Wulfe finally asked when his breathing returned to near normal.

Edwud had no convincing idea. He had been thinking about it as he ran. Perhaps they didn't need to talk—perhaps they were able to communicate everything they needed to by moving and signaling with their antennae. Perhaps talk was banned—perhaps someone had discovered that words were how lies were made—without words, perhaps they thought they could remain closer to the truth of things.

"I don't know," Edwud said.

"I think their mouths were too small," Nik suggested.

"So that the big words wouldn't fit through?" Wulfe replied with sarcasm.

"I think they were too stupid to talk," Jinni said.

"Do you know you are very bitter for a young nimf?" Lolli said as she shook her head at Jinni. "Didn't you get taught properly by your . . ." Lolli stopped, remembering Jon B, Jinni's father, losing his head at the Remedial Court. Everyone realized what Lolli was thinking, and they were shocked at how it now seemed to have happened so long ago.

Jinni turned angrily on Lolli, but saw the innocence in her face and stopped herself from saying something calculatingly vicious. She glanced quickly at Wulfe to see if he was enjoying her discomfort, but saw only pain. She was surprised—was Wulfe suffering pain for her? Wulfe turned away.

"Why did they let Kerryd and Jinni pass, Edwud?" Nolan asked. "What did Kerryd's singing do? I don't understand, how did you know . . . to get Kerryd to sing?"

Jinni couldn't help herself. "Why do you all think Edwud has the answer to everything?" she said.

For a while the group remained silent, considering Jinni's accusation; then Nolan said, "Somebody has to know . . . I mean . . . somebody has to be the . . . the . . . decider . . . otherwise . . ."

"Otherwise you'd have to work it out yourself," Jinni said. All eyes were staring at her intently. "And then you'd also have to be responsible if you got it wrong," she continued, secretly enjoying the attention. She began walking off. "You know, sometimes I think I'm not really the youngest collector on this journey." The others stared after her in amazement.

24

*A*s the group walked on through the countryside, Edwud became concerned with Filip's deteriorating strength. More and more often one of the group would pretend to be exhausted so that Filip could take a rest without losing face. In the beginning all of them, except Edwud and Wulfe, thought that Filip had too much pride, and it was always tempting to try to get him to admit any weakness at all. Surprisingly, most of the time, when they virtually had the old collector at their mercy, something stopped them from dipping his face in his failure. Perhaps they remembered their own embarrassing defeats as young nimfs or perhaps they were learning the difference between vanity and dignity.

Food was spread over large distances, they discovered, but there was always a grain or two or a chump, a berry or a seed on most days. After meeting with the thick brown collectors, they were careful to avoid other collectors and their circles.

Jinni had grown quite a bit since they had left the drains. She walked close to Edwud most of the time and was often arguing or disagreeing with him. To everyone but

Edwud, it was clear that she had fallen-in-fantasy with him. Kerryd wanted to sing about it, but the others decided it would be too embarrassing and there was no telling what Jinni might do if she discovered her feelings were about as secret as Filip's failing legs. So many of the important things, Kerryd was beginning to understand, were the unacknowledged ones—the ones not spoken about. What, then, was the purpose of words? she wondered. To cover our embarrassment? To protect our dignity? If this was so— then it was the "unacknowledged," the "underneath" things that she wanted to sing about. These would be the things that would join collectors, she thought, the things that would reveal the fact that only words make us differ- ent, only our words harden the spaces between us—and underneath the words there is just one collector with many different names.

Since Jinni's accusation that the reason he asked Edwud for answers was that he did not want to take the responsibility for being wrong, Nolan had resisted asking questions of anyone. At first he was angry with her. How dare such a young and untried nimf make such . . . such pompous announcements as if they were wisdom? Nolan was convinced that wisdom came with time, but as he walked on in silence he realized that Edwud was no older than he was himself and that Filip, then, should be the wis- est among them.

Nolan didn't like thinking: it turned everything about life into a decision; it made straightforward things bend, and nice choices less attractive. Look where thinking had got Edwud—dispossessed, holes in his wings, and he had

140

lost Sera. Which makes me a bit of a flutterer for following Edwud in the first place, doesn't it? he thought.

Regardless of how annoying it was to him, he had to face the idea that Jinni had something that he didn't have, some particular kind of courage, some particular need to understand the truth of things—Edwud had it too. Perhaps the real reason Nolan stuck close to Edwud was that deep down, underneath all his words, he envied this in Edwud; and perhaps there was always some consolation in being close to the misery it caused his friend, which somehow, if only for a short time, made Nolan feel superior. When Nolan thought like this, it frightened him and after a while he would drive the thoughts away with a scatter of words to the others. Without needing to think about it, Nolan knew the power of words to drive away thought.

Traveling in the rain was the worst experience of all, the group decided. Being caught in a low-lying area meant that the runoff water rushed in from all directions, weakening the earth into mush and forcing them to climb rapidly to higher ground. The rain was always cold and the ground sucked at each step, unwilling to let go. Each of them would plod on, head down, eyes fixed on the next best foot space, silently hoping for any kind of shelter.

It was during a sudden downpour early one night that Edwud hurriedly led them into the largest, most elaborate building any of them had ever entered. Kerryd was enthralled the moment she passed through the doorway. Dozens of human voices were singing together in deep tones that held most notes for the longest possible time.

141

Edwud found it disturbing and turned to leave, but the others refused to go back out into the rain.

Kerryd tried to hum along with the singing, but her voice seemed to have too much hope in it to blend with the dismal tone of the singers. Keeping to the shadows against the baseboard, she led the group deeper into the building. No one dared say a word as they passed by the humans engrossed in their songbooks. Kerryd climbed up three sets of wooden steps, which were polished so smoothly that she slipped several times before reaching the top. Reluctantly the others followed, cursing under their breath and annoyed that Edwud had let her take the lead. Farther along, they struck a carpeted area that was more difficult to negotiate than the newly cut lawn back at the yard. Where the carpet ran out there was a small gap between the wall and the floorboards. Kerryd slipped under the baseboard and behind the wall, and the others followed.

Below them they could smell stagnant water. It was too dark to see anything, but they could envisage the stale pools of old water under the building that created such a musty, unpleasant odor. Edwud found a timber beam and began climbing upward toward the roof, and the others followed. At the top they spread out across the beam.

The singing was considerably muffled by the ceiling plaster and Edwud thought it sounded better. He swept his antennae slowly across the area around him. There had been some birds in here some time ago, he could make out, and a small number of ants and, as he expected, quite a number of collectors. There were several areas of visibility around the light fittings that had been cut into the ceiling.

As Edwud adjusted to the dark, he saw several collectors clustered around the edge of a light-fitting hole. At that distance he couldn't be sure whether they had noticed him and his friends, but then, amazingly, one of them seemed to be waving toward them with a signal that back at the yard would have been a "come here" message.

"Do you see that, Edwud?" Nolan asked.

"They're white!" Nik blurted out.

"I think we should get back down out of here," Nolan said.

"How come they're white?" Nik said.

"How many of them do you think, Edwud?"

"A lot," Nolan said emphatically.

"They're all white," Nik repeated.

"Get Kerryd to sing again," Lolli suggested.

"Why don't they come over here? Signal them to come over here, Edwud," Wulfe said.

"Point me to where they are. I'll damned well go over there," Filip growled.

Edwud turned to Jinni. "What do you think?" he asked.

"If they were going to attack us, they would have—as we were coming up the beam," she said. Edwud nodded.

"Who thinks we should wave them over?" he asked. Kerryd, Wulfe, Filip and Jinni raised one antenna.

"Why don't we get just one of us to go over there?" Nik suggested. "Filip, here, said he would go—we could see what happens."

Edwud glared his annoyance at Nik and waved at the distant collectors to approach them. One of them broke away from the group and strode directly up to Edwud, antennae down in a welcoming gesture. Edwud dropped his antennae in greeting.

"Ho," Edwud called.

"Ho," the white collector responded, slightly surprised. "You talk, then?" he said.

"We're from the . . . aah . . . the yard . . . a long way off," Edwud said.

"Well, goodness, you must be tired . . . and hungry. Why don't you come over to the light hole? We have some chumps there we can share with you," the white collector said as he turned abruptly and headed back the way he had come. "I'm called Brother Four." Edwud glanced at the others to consider their reactions, which seemed mixed and confused. He turned and followed the white collector toward the light hole.

"What sort of a name is Brother Four?" Wulfe mumbled to Jinni.

The white collectors bustled around in a friendly manner, offering pieces of very dry biscuit and asking questions about the yard colony and the country collectors and the journey through the drains and the ride on the railway car. Edwud and his friends were most impressed with the generosity and kindness of the white collectors. Edwud wondered if the yard colony would be so generous to a strange group of outsiders.

"You certainly are a very . . . aah . . . dark-looking lot," said an older white collector, called Sister Nine. The other white collectors appeared slightly embarrassed by her observation.

"Don't take any notice of her," Brother Four said.

144

"She doesn't mean it the way it sounds."

"It sounds all right to me," Filip said. "I like being dark."

"So do I," Jinni agreed.

"The humans will be going soon," Brother Four said. "They never stay long."

"Why do they sing like that?" Kerryd asked.

"Like what?" Sister Nine asked.

"So . . . hopeless . . . sounding?"

The white collectors looked at each other as if someone had made a bad smell.

"What she means," Jinni said, "is why does it all sound the same . . . you know . . . as if something depressing keeps happening?"

The white collectors changed responses; they began to smile as if their new, dark visitors were limited in their knowledge of important things. An older white collector pushed himself forward. "You have to understand . . . what it's all about . . . what they're saying," he said with a self-satisfied grin. "I'm Brother One. Perhaps we could teach you."

"I don't think we'll be staying that long," Edwud replied.

"There's plenty of food. Why don't you stay for a while? We'd be happy to teach you about the singing," Brother One said enthusiastically.

"We already have a singer," Filip replied roughly. "And she doesn't sound as mournful as that lot down there."

"Don't take any notice of him. He's been in too many fights," Nik apologized. The white collectors smiled patiently as if Filip were a naughty, stage two nimf.

"We don't have fights here in the Sanctuary," Brother One said.

At the sound of the word *Sanctuary*, the white collectors, in unison, closed their eyes, bowed their heads, and mumbled rapidly, "Blessed be the Sanctuary."

The yard collectors were amazed. Filip reared up as if he were about to be attacked. "What! What's happening?" Filip swung around, trying to face all of the white collectors at once. The white collectors ignored him.

"We don't have any fighting here," Brother One repeated.

"Nor any stealing," Sister Nine called out.

"Nor any illegal joining," someone added.

"Nor any lying," said another.

The white collectors were smiling and nodding at each other with a controlled decorum, which allowed a generous display of modesty. They spoke loudly and continually looked up at the roof as if someone were listening.

"It all sounds like a lie to me," Filip mumbled to Jinni.

"Why don't you stay with us for a little while?" Brother One said. "Perhaps we can teach you something of our ways here in the Sanctuary."

"Blessed be the Sanctuary," mumbled the white collectors.

The yard collectors settled together in the west corner of the roof, as far as possible from the Sanctuary collectors without giving obvious offense. Filip and Jinni didn't like anything about their new hosts, but Edwud was very curious about how they could have organized such a peaceful, generous colony and how they could maintain such a thing. He fell asleep dreaming of the pure white collectors chanting "Blessed be the Sanctuary" to the sound of the humans' dreadful singing.

Over the next few nights, Edwud learned many of the Sanctuary's beliefs and attitudes. He was most impressed with Brother One's explanation that long ago it was known that the Lord Maker received her knowledge through sound alone. Even the humans knew this, Brother One explained, as they communicated through singing and talking and praying. What was important to the Lord Maker, then, was what she *heard* from collectors.

Early one night Edwud was walking across the rafters with Jinni and Wulfe when they came across two white collectors locked in battle. Edwud wasn't sure what he should do. One of the white collectors was considerably larger than the other and was in the process of biting through the other's wing. The strange thing about the battle was that neither of the combatants made a single sound. If it hadn't been for the bleeding wing joint, Edwud would have dismissed it as harmless.

"Stop it!" Jinni screamed out. Her voice echoed against the roofing tiles and stopped the two white collectors dead.

The larger one climbed off his opponent's back and glared at Jinni. Edwud stepped forward between the two, raising his antennae. Wulfe followed Edwud's lead.

"What do you think you're doing?" Edwud growled at him. The white collector looked to the roof. Edwud and Wulfe looked at each other.

"We were just playing," the smaller one said.

"Playing!" Edwud echoed. "You weren't playing, you were fighting!"

Both white collectors rolled onto their backs as if Edwud had struck them across the face. "Blessed be the Sanctuary and the words of the Lord Maker," they chanted over and over. Wulfe, Edwud and Jinni shook their heads in disbelief.

"Get up," Edwud ordered them. The two ignored him.

"At least they've stopped fighting," Jinni said. At the sound of the word *fighting* the two supine collectors moaned their blesseds louder. Edwud shook his head and led Jinni and Wulfe away.

Back at the west corner, Nolan was making the point to Nik that except for the first night's food, the white collectors hadn't actually given them a single chump, even though they kept making generous offers.

"Have you realized that, Edwud?" Nolan asked. "In fact one of them came sneaking back and stole a chump from us when he thought we were sleeping."

"I like them," Nik said. "They have beautiful manners. One of them said she hoped we could stay."

"I'm not staying with them," Jinni said.

"Neither am I," Filip agreed. "There's something strange about the lot of them—all that 'blessed be the Sanctuary' stuff gives me a sharp pain in the thorax."

Gradually the group began avoiding the white collectors as much as possible, keeping to the west side of the building most of the time. So they were surprised one night when a number of the Sanctuary colony, led by Brother

One, dropped by to invite Edwud over to their area to share a spill and some talk. Wulfe asked whether he might accompany Edwud, but the hosts made it clear that only Edwud was to be their guest. Wulfe was suspicious and annoyed, but Edwud asked him to cooperate and went off with Brother One, pleased that they would want to share with him and hoping to bring something back.

On the east side, around the edge of a large light-hole cutting, dozens of white collectors peered down into the building below where humans had begun trickling in. The white collectors made room for Edwud, who joined them, thankful that the singing had not yet commenced. Beneath him, Edwud could see the rows where the humans would sit. In front of them, on a raised step, stood a human that Edwud considered must be their leader. Dressed in long, fancy robes, the leader was about to speak to the gathering. Edwud had a momentary twinge of jealousy for the respect and appearance this leader had compared to his own.

"In a moment he will talk to them," Brother One said. "And they will talk back." The other collectors nodded in agreement. "And then they will all sing."

"There is something special down there," Sister Nine said excitedly. The others looked at her with annoyance. One of them dragged her away from the edge of the cutting.

"What she means is there is something wonderful down there," Brother Four said.

"To drink," Sister Nine called out. Edwud concentrated on finding something wonderful to drink in the scene below. He slipped one of his antennae through the cutting and systematically scanned the room below.

"We don't usually tell anyone else about it," Brother One said, smiling so hard at Edwud that Edwud felt obliged to return it with a smile that said "I understand." "It's very special to them," Brother One continued.

"And to us," Brother Four interrupted.

"One of us, from the Sanctuary, managed to drink some of it a long time ago," Brother One said. An attractive, large collector moved closer to Edwud. Her name was Sister Three. She said nothing but looked at Edwud with some interest. Slowly she leaned very close to him and whispered so softly that Edwud wasn't exactly sure what she had said.

"And he . . . ," she said.

Edwud looked at her and then down below again, searching for the wonderful drink. The white collectors had gathered very close around him but he had failed to notice this as he searched methodically with antennae and eyes. And then he saw it. A silver container with a beautiful red liquid, which as he concentrated with his antennae had a very attractive odor. The red liquid was directly below him, such that if he fell through the crack from where he was at this moment, he would fall into its center. Edwud tried to move backward at that moment and discovered how close the white collectors had moved around him. In fact he couldn't move back at all, nor sideways; they were just too close.

"Could you move back a little, please?" he asked. The collectors around him made no reply. They appeared to move in slightly closer.

"Did you see the red drink?" Brother One asked.

"Yes, thank you. Now could some of you move back, please, so that I can get clear of this hole?" Edwud said, with more control than he felt.

"Would you like to try it?" Brother One asked as he smiled.

"No, thank you," Edwud said as chillingly as he could muster.

"We'd like you to try it," Brother One said.

Edwud realized that he was trapped by the circle of collectors. The only way past them was down through the ceiling hole. There wasn't enough space for him to turn and grasp the ceiling from the other side, which meant that if they pushed, he would fall into the hole, down through the air, and plunge into the silver container of red drink below. In front of so many humans, he would be bound to be seen by at least one of them, which would mean that before he could take a mouthful, one of them would pound him flat with his foot. The attractive Sister Three moved closer, nudging him with her palps.

"This is violence!" Edwud shouted. "I thought Sanctuary collectors did not believe in violence?" The advancing collectors stopped, jerking their heads toward the roof as if the Lord Maker had just landed there.

"Blessed be the Sanctuary," they chanted in unison.

Edwud shouted at the roof. "Listen to this, Lord Maker. The Sanctuary collectors are about to push an innocent collector to his death—a very violent death . . ." The white collectors, in one horror-filled movement, opened their wings, rose up high on their legs, and then rolled onto their backs with their legs waving pleadingly in the air. Edwud

151

was stunned. He began to pick his way between the prostrate bodies, resisting the urge to tread on the previously smiling faces, particularly the attractive Sister Three, who had, for a moment, got Edwud falsely excited.

These collectors were demented, Edwud decided. They seemed to think that their actions were free of their words—that so long as they said good things, right things, then everything would be fine and they could do as they liked. The idea of a Lord Maker who could hear but not see was ludicrous and infantile. Why did they want to push him into the red drink anyway? Edwud pondered. Why sacrifice a life for nothing? Perhaps they had been watching the singing humans too long; perhaps some of their mindless ways were rubbing off?

Edwud was still angry when he got back to the group in the west corner.

"We're leaving," he said. "Right now."

"Good," said Jinni. Wulfe nodded.

"Wait a moment," Nik said. "I'm not ready to leave yet. I quite like it here."

Edwud turned on him. "They're not sane; they just tried to kill—push me through the ceiling light hole into a bowl of red liquid."

"What!" Filip said. "Where are they? Where are they, Edwud? Let's give them a fight to remember. Let's toss a few down the hole. What was it a bowl of?"

"What did they do?" Jinni asked, beginning to shake.

"They surrounded me—around the hole—they're mad. I pretended to talk to their Lord Maker and they fell over onto their backs. I don't know how they think; they may come after us anyway."

"This doesn't make sense," Nik said anxiously. "I was getting along so well with them."

"With Sister Three, you were getting along well," Jinni said.

"Look, Nik, she was the closest one to me and whispered something to me before she started pushing me toward the hole," Edwud said consolingly. Nik was more than surprised; he was hurt and it was obvious to the others.

"Come on, Nik, she probably did like you—she didn't try to push you down the hole," Lolli said, and then realized what a dumb point she had made; it was hardly better that Sister Three preferred to kill someone else. Surprisingly Nik seemed to find the thought comforting. He smiled his resigned-to-failure smile at Lolli.

"If we leave now, we might get out of the building before they start that awful singing," Edwud said. "And when we get outside, we'll get Kerryd to sing one of her beautiful songs for us." Kerryd blushed in appreciation and everyone knew she was already planning her song from that exact moment.

Outside the building, in the fresh night air, the group immediately began feeling lighter and more cheery, except for Nik, who kept glancing back at the building as if he'd forgotten something. Kerryd began to hum and Filip and Jinni stamped their feet as they walked to beat time for Kerryd.

Wulfe was annoyed that Jinni and Filip spent a lot of time together and enjoyed each other's company. Unable to accept the idea that he might be jealous, and how he felt about Jinni, Wulfe tramped along behind them, occasionally tossing a barbed comment at their frivolous behavior, which Filip couldn't hear and Jinni ignored. Wulfe could also see how Jinni had fallen-in-fantasy with Edwud; it was painfully obvious. He knew that Edwud was unaware and he wondered how it was that Edwud could be so clever about some things and so dumb about others. He wondered whether he, himself, had clever areas and dumb areas, but at the moment he didn't want to explore the possibility in case the number of dumb areas overwhelmed the clever.

At the front Lolli walked with Edwud. She asked him how he was able to decide which direction to take. Edwud didn't have a satisfactory answer. He had noticed that there was some kind of urge within him at different times to choose one path over another. At first Edwud thought that these choices of direction were random and related to nothing more than a guess or an apparent advantage; but as the journey progressed, he began to see that, perhaps influenced by some internal memory of his combined with the direction of constant winds, the overall path they had taken so far had the shape of a huge arc.

Was the Monoocal itself "calling" him—like a mother gathering her nimfs? When he failed to respond—or tarried along the way—was he being disciplined to return to the purpose of his journey? Suddenly Edwud had a painful surge of homesickness for the safety of the yard.

"Wait!" Nik called out from the rear of the line. The

group stopped. In the distance behind them appeared a lone white collector hurrying to catch up.

"What is it?" Filip demanded. "What's happening?"

"It's Sister Three!" Nik called out joyfully. The group gathered around Nik and waited for Sister Three to catch up with them.

"She doesn't look so white out here," Wulfe snapped.

"I thought she tried to kill Edwud," Filip said.

Sister Three stopped in front of Nik. "I didn't try to kill Edwud," she said. "I tried to warn him . . . I tried to whisper to him what they were going . . ."

"Why didn't you do something—say something to stop them . . . ?" Jinni asked angrily.

Sister Three didn't have an answer to Jinni's charge, and she looked down at the ground. Nik wheeled around to face the group. "She was probably too afraid to speak up . . . I know what that's like. . . . Haven't you all been too afraid sometime?" he said.

"But she was helping them," Jinni snapped back.

"I had to get near to try and warn him," Sister Three said, trying to make contact with Jinni.

"Why have you caught up with us?" Edwud asked.

"I want to come with you," she said.

"Oh, no, you're not," Jinni immediately responded.

"You're not the leader," Nik shouted at her.

"She can't come with us," Lolli said evenly. The whole group turned to face Lolli. "How could she fit in?" Lolli continued. "She's so . . . so . . . different . . ."

"What's that got to do with it?" Nik said.

"She doesn't think . . . things . . . the same . . . as us. . . .

She might roll over and say that silly 'blessed be the Sanctuary' . . . and . . . and . . . she's not dark like us." Lolli began losing confidence in her thoughts as they appeared in words.

"Is she going to fall on her back?" Filip asked.

"Why do you want to come with us?" Edwud asked. Sister Three kept looking at the ground and did not answer.

"I know why," Kerryd said. "Because she wants to be with Nik, and I think it's wonderful and you're all being silly." Kerryd extended her antennae in a welcoming gesture to Sister Three and led her past the others along the track. They stood in awe as Kerryd strode past and began a song about fear and loving.

To do nothing
is the saddest
failure of all.
THE ORIJIN CHRONICLES

he yard had changed since the departure of Edwud and the others. The Director was believed to be seriously ill, as she never ventured out of her hyde. Rumors of someone having poisoned her seeped through the colony like a relentless oily spill, contaminating the meniale ranks and encouraging acts of disorder and confusion. Worik had gained the support of most of the Law Stewards and half of the crests and was desperately attempting to stem the outbreaks of illegal collecting, violence and unlawful gatherings. A new law was introduced that anyone found guilty of making statements about the unfairness of circle size and distribution would have his or her own circle resumed for redistribution.

Several young collectors who had spoken out had now become dispossessed, moving from circle to circle each night asking the larger owners whether they needed help in collecting in exchange for a small part of any chumps or spills they might find. They became known as "drudges" and were looked upon with a mixture of pity and contempt, as they spent most of their nights toiling in other collectors' circles. Most in the colony were afraid to speak about anything at all to anyone in case it was reported. Old friendships evaporated like summer rain, and in their place came the dry lifelessness of doubt, suspicion and betrayal.

After the death of her parents, found floating in the Great Sink early one night with their antennae twisted together and their faces at rest, Sera became the Reverend Viel's matrimate and joined her circle with his. She had not shed a tear as she watched the ants carry away her parents' bodies. She wondered at the time if it was because she was no longer able to care or because she believed they were likely to be better off now—waiting for afterflight.

The Reverend was a good patrimate, attentive, reliable, confident, but something about him puzzled Sera. He talked powerfully about love and forgiveness, and yet at the same time spoke of how those not invited to Ootheca by the Lord Maker would be left behind to grieve forever for their weaknesses and mistakes. And Sera was frightened by her own thoughts—thoughts that she quickly chased from her mind—that here, now, in the colony of the yard, could *they* themselves be the uninvited, the ones left behind? Had the Lord Maker already summoned all those of worth? It seemed to Sera that every collector she knew would not qualify by the Reverend's standards, that they were all flawed in some particular way.

Sometimes Sera let herself think about Edwud and his friends, what it would have been like to have gone with him. Were they hungry all the time? Did they fight and argue and disagree? Were they lost out there in places no one had ever known? What new enemies had they encountered? Were they still alive? And what had they gone for anyway; what did it achieve? She would wish him back, then, and Nolan and the others—regardless of how she blocked it in her mind. The times with Edwud would drift into her mind at odd moments, and for short seconds they became warmer and more satisfying than the Reverend's safe hyde and his store of food.

I went searching
for I don't know what,
and found two friends
who had two friends
whose two friends
searched
for I don't know
what.

ANCIENT UNSOLVED RIDDLE

"It's glass," Edwud said. "The whole roof—see how we can see the moon through it." The others tilted their heads back and saw that it was true. The entire roof was made of glass. The walls seemed to be made of some very hard green plastic; in fact it seemed to be green everywhere—hundreds and hundreds of plants of all types and sizes, row upon row of them, making it the strangest building that any of them had ever seen, let alone entered. There was only one door, which had not been closed properly, Edwud discovered when they came across the building, and there had been just enough room for them to squeeze through. However, while they slept inside during the day, the door had been shut tight.

Sister Three had been reluctant to enter at first, even though she had been with them on the track for at least a hundred nights. Nik seldom left her side, night after night explaining about the yard colony and how they had come to leave and how Edwud was looking for something. Sister Three never seemed to understand or trust anyone fully, and Nik had to push her through the partly opened door of the glass house as she closed her eyes. When inside, she seemed to be terrified. Edwud had the absurd idea that perhaps she believed the Lord Maker could now see her behavior quite clearly through the glass roof.

Apart from the plants there were no other living things in the glass house. Edwud checked every corner and crack—although under several plants he found the bodies of a variety of moths and several caterpillars, who had been dead for a long time. There were pots and pots of exotic flowers, which none of them had ever seen before, and tubs of various-sized plants of tomatoes, strawberries, peppers, kiwifruit and lettuce. There were shallow trays with small seedlings and a workbench with packets and packets of seeds of every shape and color imaginable. Edwud was pleased—there was so much food at hand that none of them would need to walk more than fifty leggs for a total meal.

Running along the benches were solid pipes with plastic nozzles every one hundred leggs or so, and Edwud could sense that they carried water. On the evening of their second night the nozzles exploded with a fine spray, which formed a foggy mist in the air and settled on the plants like the gentlest rain.

"Is that rain?" Filip said with surprise.

"It's coming from the pipes on the benches," Edwud told him.

"Wo ho!" Filip said.

"This is wonderful, isn't it, Edwud?" Lolli danced around Edwud.

"Give us a song, young Kerryd," Filip said.

Kerryd sang a dancing song of nonsense words that they knew from nimfhood, as all of them, except Sister Three and Nik, skipped and hopped together under the falling mist, splashing one another as often as possible. With so much food and beautiful soft rain, they all felt they could live in the wonderful glass house forever. As Edwud danced, the thinking part of him, like a nagging parent, remembered that the brightest part of every gift was its wrapping.

Not long after the sun rose on the day following the water-pipe shower, the group began to notice the dramatic rise in temperature. It became impossible to sleep during the day as the sun appeared to ignore the roof on the way into the glass house, but failed to find its way out again. Trapped inside, the sun's heat kept pouring in, drawing the moisture from the plants and flinging it in foggy layers onto the inside of the glass roof, making it even more difficult for the heat to escape. Droplets of moisture formed along the bodies and wings of all the collectors, no matter how shady a spot they found for themselves under a plant or beneath the bench. Movement became unattractive as it generated more body heat, and so the soggy collectors lay in the shade puffing and gasping, imagining cool northerly breezes from the past.

Shortly after nightfall, however, with the sun gone, the temperature fell rapidly and the sodden collectors forgot the misery of the day and went about enjoying the pleasures of their new home. Edwud encouraged them to carry a supply of seeds from the bench down to the coolest place they could find in preparation for the following day.

In a short while, most of them became extremely tired and irritable from lack of sleep during the day. They began to argue and deliberately annoy one another more than usual.

Edwud discovered he could roll seeds off the bench using his self-taught lift-and-lock technique. As the seeds crashed to the ground, Jinni was complaining that Nolan, Wulfe and Lolli should not be benefiting from Edwud's labor.

"He's the only one who can do it," Nolan said to her.

"Why don't you learn, then?" she snapped back.

"Why don't you learn some manners?" Nik snarled at her.

"Manners would have helped a lot when you were drowning in the drains," Jinni spat back at him.

"Edwud doesn't mind," Lolli said.

" 'Edwud doesn't mind,' " Jinni mimicked sarcastically.

"Ignore her," Wulfe said, as he continued to drag a seed to his shady spot under a small palm. Jinni realized that Wulfe had already delivered two seeds to her own temporary hyde nearby. She looked at Wulfe closely for only the second time, the first time having been the exhausting moments after rescuing Nik, when she had wiped the foam from Wulfe's face. This time she recognized in Wulfe's expression something she had no words for but felt was simultaneously annoying, confusing and slightly thrilling. She turned quickly and climbed up toward Edwud.

By the middle of the following day, the collectors were amazed at how they could have forgotten during the night just how hot, humid and steamy the daylight hours could be. All of them swore privately that they would insist to Edwud that they must leave this glass heat box as soon as possible.

As the dark squeezed out the light and the temperature again fell rapidly, the collectors' memory of the day's heat seemed to evaporate with the moisture that had clung to their bodies. To give up such a bountiful and safe home just because of a little discomfort would be madness, they agreed. Edwud and Kerryd weren't so sure. Kerryd had become so tired that she had stopped making up songs, and her singing was restricted to a soft blowing noise she made over her teeth during the heat of the day. Edwud found that his thinking had deteriorated considerably, making it difficult to arrive at decisions and creating a new kind of reluctance to concern himself with the well-being of the group. For no reason at all that Edwud could understand, into his mind rolled some notion about the Monoocal—almost as if it were calling him: he knew he had to go.

That night Edwud dragged himself around the entire boundary of the glass house and discovered a truth he had been afraid to think about: there was no way out of this new world they had found. Under the earthen floor was a layer of concrete, which met flush with the solid plastic walls. Unless the door was left ajar again, there was no way out.

During the long days Edwud thought about the glass house a lot. His thinking was slower and thicker in the heat, but he pondered the question of why such a glass house should be built at all. It seemed that the purpose was to make the area of plants produce more than they wanted to by sweating them in the sun trap. He would have liked to be able to tell the humans that there could be another side to this unnatural glass-house world they had created to force such a generous situation for themselves—perhaps a dark side.

The collectors spoke less and less to each other, and when they did, it was with suspicion and bad temper. Trust between them sagged out in the heat. All of them gained weight, as different plants dropped seeds or ripe fruit virtually at their feet. Edwud had not told them there was no way out, but surprisingly not one of them suggested leaving. The increasingly easy food collection and safety of the glass house had made them resist the more risky option of trying to find a better place.

Nik had joined with Sister Three but there seemed little joy in the union, as they went about collecting together and sharing the one hyde. Edwud had tried to arrange a singwith for them but enthusiasm was so low that the group went through the motions of being joyful without any of the real joy. Edwud wished for a good quaff of the soap-sud foam from the drains back at the yard, so that he could lose himself just for a while. He wondered if that was why he did it—became sotted—to escape himself, as if he could run from himself the way he had run from his father as a tiny, frightened nimf.

None of them was prepared for the door to swing open early one morning and swing shut behind a large, male human. Sister Three was the only one exposed, and foolishly she ran hysterically across the width of the bench in full view of the human. Edwud watched as the man swiped his hand at Sister Three, missing her by no more than ten leggs. She clung to the underside of the bench for a moment and then began running rapidly toward her hyde. The human lost sight of her. He bent down and moved several of the pots near the bench, but Sister Three was long gone. The man peered closely at the leaves of several plants nearby, turning them over and inspecting their underside. He examined the floor where it was visible and looked hard into some flower buds. Standing straight up, he walked to a set of cupboards situated under the bench, opened the door, and took out a plastic container and a metal pump. Edwud aimed his antennae at the container. When the male removed the container's cap, Edwud detected a strange, foul odor. To his relief it wasn't chlordane, but he knew that, coming from a human, it was unlikely to be anything to enhance life for the collectors in the glass house.

Having filled the pump, the male human walked to the farthest end of the glass house and began spraying the leaves of each plant methodically. Automatically Edwud held his breath and crouched down farther in his temporary hyde; he could see none of the others but he knew they would have registered what was happening. The foul-smelling spray filled the already heated air and made Edwud gasp. He tried breathing through some dead grass stalks but wasn't sure whether this filtered out some of the spray or not. No wonder there was nothing alive in the glass house besides plants, he thought.

Eventually the man stopped spraying. Edwud noticed he had a cloth held over his mouth and was coughing. Good! Edwud thought. I hope he falls over. The man slammed the door shut behind him as he left. Edwud poked his head out.

"Stay underneath something or in your hyde until the fumes have settled," he called to the others as loud as he could. "It's not chlordane."

The spray seemed to take half the day to settle. By the time night began crowding into the glass house, the air was clear again. Edwud asked the others to gather near his hyde. He looked at them closely as they arrived.

"Where's Nolan?" he asked.

"I didn't see him in his hyde as I went past," Wulfe said. "I thought he had gone ahead."

"Has anyone seen Nolan since the spraying began?" Edwud asked. The collectors shook their heads and looked at each other.

"I feel sick," Lolli complained.

"So do I," Nik said.

"I don't think we should eat anything until the water from the pipes washes the spray off," Edwud said.

"Good thinking, Edwud," Filip agreed.

"You're all too fat anyway," Jinni said.

"So are you," said Wulfe, and immediately regretted it as Jinni swung around to face him with surprise. "For a young nimf, you are," Wulfe amended.

"I'm not a young nimf anymore, if you look closely enough," she said.

"Oh, he looks closely enough, all right," Nik said accusingly. Wulfe was at a loss for words in his embarrassment and turned away.

"I'm going to look for Nolan," Wulfe said, as he quickly walked off. Edwud caught up with him and together they began a systematic search of the most likely areas. When they had moved out of hearing range of the others, Edwud turned to Wulfe.

"You like Jinni, don't you?" he said.

Wulfe looked at his friend, wondering how much truth he would be able to offer Edwud. "Yes," he finally said.

"But you think she's fallen-in-fantasy with me?"

Wulfe looked straight ahead, rather than at Edwud. "Yes," he said again.

"Why do you never say what you mean?" Edwud asked. Wulfe stopped walking and considered Edwud's question.

"I don't know," he said. "Edwud, I don't know."

"Seems like Sister Three has to mean what she says, and you have to say what you mean." Edwud laughed.

"It's not something to laugh about," Wulfe snapped.

"I'm sorry." Edwud controlled himself.

"How do you learn how to say what you mean?" Wulfe asked seriously.

"I don't know, Wulfe. I really don't know," Edwud reflected. "What do you think would happen if you did say what you really feel . . . to Jinni?"

Wulfe thought for a moment. "She might laugh at me," he said.

"What would happen then?"

"Then I'd get angry and say something nasty . . . or . . . something."

"Why?" Edwud stopped walking and faced Wulfe.

"Why?" repeated Wulfe, as if the answer was obvious. "Because . . . because . . . if someone is going to laugh at you, the best way to stop them is to . . ."

"Attack them . . . laugh at them first?" Edwud suggested.

"Yes, that's right, Edwud." Wulfe was now more certain. "But what would happen if you just let them laugh at you?"

"They wouldn't respect you, Edwud, you know that."

"And if they didn't respect you?"

"What? If they didn't respect you? Well . . . you might as well give up . . . I mean give up everything . . . give up breathing."

"Why?" asked Edwud.

"Why? Edwud, that's a silly question," Wulfe said with a snort.

"What would happen if they didn't respect you?" Edwud asked again.

"I . . . I . . . suppose . . . I wouldn't . . . really like myself."

"Do you like yourself now, Wulfe?" Edwud asked.

Wulfe stopped dead in his tracks and looked at Edwud. It was true he didn't like himself as he was now. So what was he likely to lose if someone did laugh at him, or if someone didn't respect him: nothing. As he looked at Edwud, Wulfe knew that something within him had been swept aside as suddenly and permanently as rotting leaves in a southerly gale.

Before Wulfe could speak, beyond Edwud he saw Nolan lying near the workbench cupboards. Edwud stopped in alarm. His friend was out in the open, clearly visible. Something was wrong.

"Nolan," Edwud called. Nolan made no movement or sound. Edwud ran to his friend. Even before he reached him, he could hear Nolan's short and sharp breathing. "What is it?" Edwud asked.

Nolan looked at Edwud and said, "Bad luck, Edwud, just bad luck."

"What happened?"

"I must have been directly under the spray—it must have dripped on me."

Edwud could smell that Nolan was completely covered with the stinking spray. "I don't think I can move properly," Nolan said. "The world is spinning."

"You're covered with it," Wulfe said, turning his head away with distaste.

"We'll have to get it off you." Edwud voiced his thoughts. "Wulfe, go and tell the others to come here, quickly." Without a word Wulfe turned and ran.

Assembled at a slight distance, the group gazed with sympathy on Nolan.

"We could carry him to a water-pipe nozzle," Jinni said, "and wait for the water to come."

"That may not happen for days," Edwud replied. Nolan coughed, making a dreadful clacking sound from deep within that unsettled the onlookers. "I've tried rubbing it off with a leaf, but it's dry and hard," Edwud told them.

"I once saw someone covered with a spill," Filip remembered, "and they covered him in dirt and a lot of the spill soaked into the dirt and they brushed it off."

"What happened to him?" Nik asked.

"He died a day later." The others groaned. "Well, I was only remembering," Filip said.

"I have an idea," Edwud said. The others listened carefully. Nolan coughed again. "We could try and wash it off him ourselves." The listeners appeared confused. "With our own mouths—our own spit." Edwud tried to sound confident. They looked at Nolan and back at Edwud, taking in the vile odor rising from Nolan.

"You mean, lick it off?" Jinni asked with amazement.

"Then we would get poisoned," Nik said.

"We could keep spitting it out," Edwud suggested.

"But we'd still get a lot of it into our bodies," Nik answered quickly.

Nolan coughed again and all of them tried to look somewhere that didn't have Nolan in view.

"It wouldn't help if we all got sick," Wulfe said.

"You're right," said Edwud. "If only half of us do it, then the other half can remain safe."

"I think Edwud should pick who washes Nolan down," Filip proposed.

"I think it should be by volunteers," Nik said.

"That should save you," Wulfe replied viciously, without thinking. "I'm sorry," he said quickly. The others looked at him in shock: Wulfe apologizing! They were amazed.

Wulfe walked past them and over to Nolan. He smiled at him, pulled his head back, and spat hard on Nolan's plate. He leaned across Nolan and began licking and scrubbing at the sticky mess. For a moment the group stood motionless, and then Kerryd walked to Nolan's other side and repeated Wulfe's actions. Edwud smiled at Nolan's embarrassment. Even in his deadly predicament, Nolan would probably have preferred to die quietly rather than have this done to him. Edwud moved forward and started on a forewing, forcing back the nausea that threatened to make him vomit on every lick. Jinni approached Nolan head on, telling him to close his eyes and to try not to cough in her face. Edwud watched her as she worked, realizing how much she had grown up.

"Where exactly is he?" Filip complained as he bumped into Wulfe. They all braced themselves for Wulfe's biting reply, but it didn't come. Wulfe led Filip to Nolan's side and continued his work. Behind him Edwud saw the other three watching. It seemed as if they were being pressed flat by some invisible weight; they shifted from leg to leg and let their antennae droop.

"I think it is wonderful to help someone in such need," Sister Three said, without moving any closer to Nolan. Nik looked at her with some confusion. Lolli looked away.

"Some of us should try to stay healthy," Lolli said.

"Exactly," Nik replied. "Imagine if we all ended up like Nolan."

"I shall certainly help anyone who gets ill," said Sister Three, glancing up at the roof.

As if lifting a great weight, Lolli moved slowly toward Nolan, took a deep breath, and joined the others. Only Nik and his matrimate, Sister Three, stood apart watching.

Over the following days all of them became ill. Painful

vomiting and coughing spasms racked their bodies. Walking became difficult, as the world could spin around their heads at any time without warning. Strange aches and pains emerged every night and the group would gather around Edwud's hyde and discuss the newest and most debilitating of them. Nolan had improved a little but was still the most seriously ill of them all; he seldom found the energy even to talk. Not surprisingly, Nik and Sister Three were the least affected.

The poisonous spray had settled on everything edible in the place. None of them had eaten since the fumes had settled and the excess fat they had been carrying was fast disappearing. Edwud hoped for the water-pipe nozzles to come on and wash some of the food clean, but night after night the glass house remained dry. The heat was clearly increasing every day: Edwud could tell by the way even the plants would droop by the afternoon. He no longer slept in the day and began to think that the world they were in—the glass house—had become the most double-sided of all of the Lord Maker's gifts: on the one side, a place brimming full of rich and exotic foods, and on the other, each mouthful guaranteed to make them sicker and sicker.

Standing in front of the door one evening, Edwud had an idea: when they entered the glass house in the first place, it was because the door had not been shut properly—what if the next time the door opened, it did not shut properly again? Perhaps they could all wait by the door and hope that by chance it might happen again. Edwud paced faster back and forth in front of the door. What if something prevented the door from closing? he thought.

Something that got in the way. What could get in the way? he wondered.

Above his head a seedpod burst, showering featherlike spores into the air. Edwud watched as they slipped through space in a zigzag fashion, stopping their flight suddenly and heading in the opposite direction, but always floating downward. He could put something in the way! He could wait until the door was opened and put something in the way of it closing. Perhaps whoever entered wouldn't notice—perhaps if they were all waiting, they would have enough time to get out in exactly the same way they came in.

Edwud made them all gather around Nolan as if it might preserve the little energy he had left. Looking at them, he suddenly realized how much they had changed since entering the glass house. Tiny changes day by day that went unnoticed until a shock recognition forced acknowledgment.

"We are going to get out of this . . . this . . . trap," Edwud told them. Hardly an antenna lifted in interest. "Wake up!" Edwud shouted.

"I'm awake!" Filip reassured Edwud.

Edwud revealed his plan: they would all wait by the door, and when it was opened, Edwud would carry a stone and drop it in a position that would stop the door from closing tightly, hopefully without being seen by whoever entered. Then they would all squeeze out as quickly as possible, once again, hopefully without being seen. None of them believed Edwud's plan had much to do with reality. They stared back at him with half-thought-out objections beginning to form at the back of their minds.

"How would we know when the door would be opening?" Wulfe asked.

"We could be waiting there forever," Nik said.

"You couldn't carry a stone large enough, could you, Edwud?" Kerryd wondered.

"Yes, I can," Edwud said confidently. "I've practiced for a long time. And I think I know how to get the door open." Edwud explained how he had been watching a seedpod bursting, when it occurred to him that the whole purpose of the glass house was to make plants grow faster and produce more seeds for planting. So that if between them they could bite off enough heads of flowers and pieces of ripening fruit and seedpods, then he was sure that when the human saw what had happened he would be drawn into the house. The others were not so sure.

"What if the stone didn't stop the door and it shut tight, and the man began to spray again?" Wulfe said.

"We'd never survive another spraying, Edwud," Lolli said. Edwud knew she was right and also that Wulfe's point was a good one.

"I think it's a good plan," Wulfe said. Jinni looked at him and he looked directly back at her. "I'd prefer to get killed trying to get out than to slowly bake and choke to death here," he said as he smiled at Jinni.

"Me too," said Filip. "I'm with you, Edwud."

"I agree," said Jinni. The others mumbled together for a while and then agreed that the alternative wasn't all that attractive.

At first dark Nolan was helped to the door, while Filip, designated as his guardian, complained bitterly that he was capable of doing the tougher work of biting through stems. They worked all night, even Sister Three who kept talking to the roof every time a flower bud or seedpod fell. By morning the floor was littered with dozens of decapitated heads and hearts of plants. The weary collectors lined up behind Nolan and Filip against the wall as near to the door as possible. Edwud chose a large stone close to the wall, lifted and locked it in place, and staggered to his position right in the doorway.

"Do you think you should stand so much in the open?" Jinni asked him. Edwud released the stone and felt how exhausted he had become.

"I will only have a half blink to block the door," he gasped. "I have to be as close as possible." Wulfe and Filip wanted to help but Edwud knew they would only get in the way. They settled down to wait.

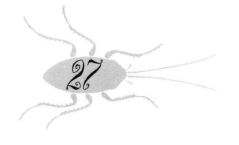

*W*hen the door of the glass house swung open, the entire group of collectors was asleep. The human male entering swung the door open so hard that it slammed against the wall of the building. Edwud's wings automatically opened in fright. The human's boot passed within three leggs of his head. Edwud guessed that the man was so concerned about his plants that he was staring straight ahead at the clipped stems rather than at his feet. For a moment he wasn't sure whether to call to the others or lift the stone. He decided on the stone. He spun around, mentally practicing his lift-and-lock technique.

There was no stone! Edwud spun around again. The others were watching him with confused expressions. Stupidly Edwud kept looking where the stone should have been. And then he saw it. Pressed completely into the ground. The outline of the man's boot surrounding it like a frame. Edwud bent down, gripping it as best he could, and tried to lift it.

Wulfe, Jinni and Kerryd ran to help him. They stood around the edge of the stone, gripping it like Edwud, and tried to lift. The stone did not move. The door to the glass house swung shut with a crunch, blowing a wave of air over the four of them and rattling their antennae.

Near the wall Lolli started to cry. Filip kept asking what had happened, and Sister Three, forgetting where she was, chanted, "Blessed be the Sanctuary." Wulfe considered correcting Sister Three's prayer to "Blessed be the Cemetery," but he resisted the temptation. He saw how tired Edwud looked and how sick Nolan was. Nolan seemed oblivious to what had happened; he lay in the same spot to which he had been helped and watched the activity as if he were looking through the glass roof at them.

"Well, that's it," Nik said, shaking his head. The others looked at Edwud and back at the embedded stone.

"Could you carry another stone, Edwud?" Kerryd asked. Edwud considered that the nearest stones of a size large enough were a distance of five hundred leggs away at least. It would take half a night even if his tiredness did not turn his legs to mud. He shook his antennae at Kerryd.

"Well, that's it, then," Nik said again. Wulfe had plunged a leg down into the earth beside the stone and was scratching away methodically as they talked.

"What are you doing?" Jinni asked him.

"I was wondering if we could dig it out," Wulfe replied. The others looked at Edwud for an opinion. "It's not packed so tightly," Wulfe said. Edwud bent down alongside Wulfe and felt the earth around the stone. Wulfe lifted out a thick piece of mud. "See," he said triumphantly.

Behind them the male human had retrieved most of the ruined flower heads and seedpods and was preparing the pump. He banged the container down hard on the bench and started talking to himself.

"He's going to spray us again," Sister Three wailed.

"Get over here and help us dig!" Edwud shouted at her. The group looked at Edwud in surprise; he had never shouted like that before. Sister Three hurried to the stone and bent down with the others. "You too, Nik," Edwud said coldly.

Those with the longest legs worked at the stone, passing the mud back to the others, who dumped it out of sight along the wall. Fortunately the man had begun spraying at the far end. He had tied a white cloth around his mouth and was spraying much more thoroughly than the previous time. Edwud knew that if they didn't get out as the man left, then they never would. Progress on the ground around the stone was slow and Edwud wondered whether—even if they managed to clear it—he would be able to lift it out of its hole. There wasn't enough room for anyone to help him, even if they knew how to lift.

As the man came closer to where they worked, Edwud and Wulfe carried Nolan and guided the others to a temporary hyde among the pots. The air filled with the choking fumes worse than before. Jinni and Nolan broke out with coughing spasms. Edwud watched the man closely, and as soon as he turned back to the bench, he led the group back to the stone.

Edwud knew that the man would not stay long, and each time he withdrew mud from around the stone he glanced up to estimate the man's arrival time at the door. The smell of the poison was overpowering and the need to vomit was clutching at all of their throats. They worked even as they coughed and saw the world spinning around their heads.

Edwud saw the man slam the pump away into the cupboard under the bench, turn, and head directly for the door. He yelled at the others to run for the wall. As the boots of the man approached, Edwud leapt into the hole surrounding the stone. He was too tired even to pray to the Lord Maker not to end his life under a human foot. The door burst open and Edwud, who had closed his eyes, realized he had not been trodden on.

He leapt out of the hole, gripped the rock in his ant lock, and lifted. The stone did not move. He tried again. Nothing. Edwud was furious; without realizing it, he stamped at the ground in anger, grabbing at the stone and opening his wings, which flapped wildly. The stone made a sucking noise of complaint and then rose steadily out of the hole. Too angry to think clearly, Edwud paused for a moment and then recovered. He ran hard toward the door, which was swinging closed again, flung the rock down against the doorjamb, and held it in place.

The vibration of the door striking the stone passed through every fiber of Edwud's body, rattling his plate and making his head hurt instantly. But they had trapped enough space for them to escape.

In the outside air the collectors marveled at how they had forgotten the smell of a fresh breeze, how it rattled and teased the leaves and grass as it passed with promises of somewhere better to go, somewhere better to be. With the weight of the glass roof gone and nothing between them and the sky, they felt lighter and more confident with every step down the concrete path away from the poisonous world of captive plants.

Nolan rested one front leg on Edwud's back and the other on Wulfe. Half the time he was dragged by the two of them, as his legs gave way or refused to move properly. Kerryd followed anxiously behind, occasionally trying to sing a tune of encouragement to him. From time to time they all stopped when Nolan slumped into a coughing spasm that lasted too long. Edwud wasn't sure whether he had injured himself when lifting the rock, but every one hundred leggs or so a stabbing pain shot down his whole body.

When they stopped, Jinni would take the opportunity to leave the track and vomit quietly away from everyone. No one mentioned the behavior, as they knew how embarrassing it would be to her. When it started to rain, Edwud insisted they stay under it, turning themselves over and over, washing the powdery, glass house poisons from their bodies.

Late in the evening they rested under a stack of old timber. Nolan couldn't seem to get warm, even though they took turns, two on either side, to rub his body from head to wing tip. Edwud sat talking to his friend, even though at times Nolan sounded more like he was dancing through his nimfhood dreams and talking to his parents, long since gone.

"Edwud and I are going to explore," Nolan said happily, in between coughing fits. "Places no one else has ever been." Nolan was grinning. He shivered and Edwud massaged his plate. Nolan slipped into a momentary sleep and out again. "Edwud can think better than anyone . . . he's been out on the road already," Nolan continued.

"Sshhh," Edwud comforted his friend.

"You don't talk with me anymore, Edwud," Nolan said, sounding clearer and more like his old self as he looked closely at Edwud. "You talk with Jinni or Wulfe or . . . even Filip. I wonder what it's like to be you, Edwud, I wonder. Did you ever wonder what it's like being me? It's not much being me, Edwud, not much at all. Not much at all."

"Could you eat some grass seeds, Nolan?" Edwud asked. Nolan didn't answer but slid into half sleep again.

"Things will get better, Edwud," Nolan said, as if he had never dozed off. "You just have to be patient. Things change. They get better. Nothing, not even bad things, stays the same—everything changes." Without knowing how he knew, Edwud realized his friend was dying and there was nothing he could do.

"You're my closest friend, Nolan. You've always been my closest friend," Edwud said.

"I am, Edwud, aren't I? I always have been, haven't I? You and me, Edwud, before all the others . . . just you and me. We went into the Kitchen together. Do you remember when we were both so small we followed the black ants into their hole, Edwud, do you remember?"

"And they jumped all over us," Edwud said, finishing the memory. He moved closer to his friend and began gently rocking him like his mother had rocked him when he was too small to remember. Nolan slowly drifted off to sleep again.

The night was still and warm. A lone magpie and several sparrows argued at each other from different trees. In the distance the constant groan of road machines muffled the smaller sounds nearby. Steam rose from the wet ground and mixed with the smells of decomposing leaves and the fresher promise of new seedling shoots.

"You'll find it, Edwud, you will." Nolan smiled at his lifelong friend. "And my otherself . . ." Edwud picked up his friend so that no part of him was touching the ground. "My otherself . . . will fly to Ootheca . . . ," Nolan said, staring directly at Edwud. Edwud realized that somehow Nolan had come to know the purpose of their journey—perhaps it was clearer at this moment to Nolan than it had ever been to Edwud.

Edwud struggled to hold up his devoted friend. And then perhaps Edwud's legs locked into place, for Nolan was as light as the feathery seeds that burst from the pods in the glass house and floated with perfect fayth to the ground.

Edwud refused to talk to anyone after Nolan's death. He felt he had let Nolan down in some way. Perhaps Nolan should never have come on the journey, he began to think. Perhaps there was something seriously wrong with Edwud as a leader. Perhaps he wasn't a proper leader at all. A leader led people, led them *somewhere*. He was leading them nowhere. He missed Nolan more than he thought possible. Nolan had always been nearby, just a little way off, no matter where Edwud went or what mess he made of things. As long as he could remember, Nolan had been exerting just enough weight to balance Edwud's life. Edwud had never considered what his life would be like without Nolan around. He told the others to do whatever they liked, for he was not going to lead them anymore.

What Edwud failed to notice was that they were all suffering the loss of Nolan. He became angry that after Nolan died, everything moved along as before, as if nothing had changed at all. When Nik complained about the rough pathway they were on, Edwud turned on him in a fury.

"You choose!" he shouted at Nik. "Go on, choose a path! Make a decision and I'll complain." He glared at Nik with such hostility that even Sister Three could read Edwud's resentment that Nik was alive and Nolan wasn't—as if Nik were some poor substitute for Nolan.

Nik wasn't hurt by Edwud's attack. It was only more confirmation of what he had always known about himself: that he *was* a poor substitute for Nolan, and in fact a poor substitute for anyone. The only good thing about himself, Nik believed, was that he held no illusions about his worth. His one good friend, an old and traveled collector called Salmo, who disappeared not long after Nik left nimfhood, had told him once that his problem was that he refused to see himself clearly. Nik had scoffed when Salmo told him that just as nimfs have within them their different stages, which are revealed as they shed at each molt, the full-grown have within them many collectors and at different times they can call forth whichever one they see fit to call.

"You make the wrong choice," Salmo had said, all those ans ago, "like a blind collector afraid of overstepping the boundary of his circle, who fails to reach the sweetest chumps." Nik had never forgotten those words, and often since then had pondered what old Salmo had meant. Why would he make the wrong choice? If he had the chance of choosing to call up, to be, a better collector, why on earth would he not choose it? "Because," Salmo had said to him, "you have judged that the one you choose, the weaker one, is the one you deserve to be, the one that others have told you to be."

Lately Salmo's words had come echoing through his mind as he walked. He remembered his father never speaking to him unless he made a mistake, and then never shutting up. Since his joining with Sister Three, many

185

things had changed. He knew that Sister Three was not as stupid, frightened or hypocritical as she appeared to the others. He could see kindness and strength that just never seemed to get a chance to appear. Sometimes, when he was alone with her, without the opinions of the others pressing on them, two different collectors did seem to emerge. Perhaps, Nik thought, he should have listened more closely to old Salmo that long, long time ago.

At different times, as they walked and a decision on direction had to be taken, the group would come to a halt and they would look at Edwud, who stared blankly and defiantly back at them. A discussion would ensue and the most confident-sounding voice would win his or her choice of direction.

Even through his anger Edwud became interested in the process of these decisions. First there would be confusion, and then someone would voice an opinion. Immediately, before any time for thinking had passed, another would object. The objector would rarely have a recommendation to make, but would object to the next opinion expressed also. Gradually they would all form into three bunches that Edwud labeled "proposers, objectors, and neutrals," and each collector was drawn to his or her most comfortable bunch. Jinni and Filip were always proposers; Nik and Sister Three always objectors; Lolli remained neutral. Wulfe occasionally lapsed into the mistaken comfort of the objectors, but mostly gave considered and intelligent support to the best ideas. Kerryd moved among all three groups at different times.

To Edwud's surprise, the directions finally settled upon

were always the ones he felt in agreement with, which made him wonder whether there was an invisible map planted at the back of all of their minds.

During the day Edwud sat apart from the others and discouraged friendly approaches with an icy silence. In the middle of a hot day when the others were sleeping, Kerryd ignored Edwud's barriers and rested beside him. For a long time she said nothing and then softly she began singing a song she had made up since Nolan's death:

> *"Circles*
> *within circles,*
> *one inside the other.*
> *One life, one life,*
> *all of us making*
> *one life.*
>
> *Circles*
> *within circles,*
> *ripples over water.*
> *One life, one life,*
> *all of us losing*
> *one life."*

And Edwud cried quietly for a long time, for his friend, for himself and for them all.

*S*lowly, night by night, Edwud moved back within the group. Occasionally someone would mention Nolan and they would each have something to say about him. A world without his friend was taking shape for Edwud, but he knew its form would never be the same as before.

The need to tell the others of his secret burden—the search for the Monoocal, passed to him by the Director—weighed heavier and heavier each night. Finally Edwud assembled them solemnly and announced his bewildering, and probably impossible, quest.

He was surprised at how calmly they took the news—as if it made more sense to them than it did to him. They agreed that it must be found and returned to the yard. They had all heard of it as nimfs: how it was completely round and somehow was a key of sorts, that you could see through it and in it, that it made things larger and smaller—and in it you could see your otherself. With the Monoocal gone, Edwud told them he believed that collectors had lost their otherselves—that their perspective of things had become distorted, that there would be no return to Ootheca.

When they asked him whether he had a trail to follow in his search, Edwud didn't know how to answer.

"A general direction, yes," Edwud said. "Not an exact track." The others seemed concerned at his vagueness, but they were too pleased to see Edwud at the front again to make much complaint.

As they walked each night, the need for talk about things that could be seen grew less. They had come to know one another well enough to predict reactions and opinions, but not well enough yet to recognize what it was that connected them to one another.

The direction they chose became heavier with road machines and human houses each night. They had become quick to react to the scent of cats, humans and dangerous spills, and had learned to freeze in place if there were no temporary hydes immediately available. The variety of chumps increased and part of the weight they had lost in the glass house came back.

Edwud noticed how much of a toll had been taken on all of them, especially Jinni, who was the only one who still regularly coughed and occasionally needed to vomit. She failed to gain much weight and seldom ate with the rest of them.

Wulfe was constantly looking for something especially fresh or unusual to tempt her into eating. He was returning to the group one night with a sweet-smelling, milky-looking chump for Jinni, when he overheard her and Filip talking together a little way from the others. Wulfe put down the chump and moved closer to the pair of them without making a sound.

"What was she like, your matrimate?" Jinni asked.

"Bidilio?" Filip gave a little chuckle. "She was . . . ah, what would be the word . . . ahh . . . physical . . . yes, that's it, she was physical."

"How was she physical?" Jinni demanded. Wulfe knew he shouldn't be listening, but he was fascinated at how Jinni insisted on getting the facts about everything, and he was more afraid of making a noise and being discovered if he tried to leave. In front of him, old Filip was smiling to himself as he opened the door to memories sealed as fresh as a wrapped chump.

"Strong as a cow ant, never got tired, couldn't get enough . . . enough nimfs," Filip said. "She warned me about going to the Kitchen Wars before we knew about the chlordane. 'I may not be waiting here alone until you get back,' she used to say. But she was always there when I returned." Filip shook his head as if he could shake the memories loose and out onto the ground to dance in front of him.

"Wulfe likes me," Jinni said, coughing loudly.

"We used to fight all the time, about anything at all," continued Filip. "She would never believe I collected long enough or hard enough, that we never accumulated enough votes to get a better circle . . ."

"When you were poisoned . . . afterward, I mean, did your eyes . . . did they get . . . did it happen . . . quickly? I mean, did you just wake up one night and you couldn't see?" Jinni asked.

"What?" Filip said, surprised to find that Bidilio had turned into Jinni. "Of course Wulfe likes you; so do I."

"No, I mean, Wulfe likes me . . . physically . . . Like

Bidilio," Jinni said.

"Oh, does he?" Filip said, surprised. "Poor old Wulfe, fancy that."

"You know, Filip, I can't see very well anymore," Jinni said.

From his hiding place Wulfe pretended to be walking as if he had just arrived, and then burst forward with his special chump.

"You won't be able to resist this," he said to Jinni as he dropped it in front of her, staring at her the whole time. Filip leaned closer to hear better. "Even he can smell how good it is," Wulfe said, indicating Filip with his antennae.

When Edwud led the group through the back
entrance of a large building, it was to escape
both rain and a surge of human feet that burst out of
nowhere late at night. He had no idea what sort of building
it was. They huddled together behind a huge white screen,
shaking the water from their wings. Edwud climbed up the
plastic-looking fabric and discovered it had eye-sized holes
cut into it at regular intervals. Through the holes he could
see a vast room with row upon row of seats. There were
sweet-smelling chump odors drifting from all directions in
the room. He climbed down again and informed the others.

They separated and spread out across the carpeted
floor of the vast room, heading to the rear where they
would meet up and consider their collection. Wulfe refused
to allow Jinni to go by herself and accompanied her,
oblivious to the sound of her annoyed insults. Edwud took
the center, keeping Filip in sight in the dim light as he
searched. It was hardly a search, Edwud quickly realized, as
sugary chump after chump sat beneath the rows of seats.
Occasionally an even sweeter spill had soaked into the carpet. It was the richest source Edwud had ever experienced.

When the floor began to vibrate slightly, Edwud
scanned his antennae in a circle about him. Something was

moving toward him, something large. With no further warning seats began crashing down above and around his head; human feet came at him from both directions. Edwud leapt for the metal legs of the nearest chair and climbed quickly to the underside of the seat. Human legs dangled from the chairs all around him and human voices made their noises at each other. Edwud offered a prayer to the Lord Maker that the others had found safety before the herd of feet got to them. He couldn't see Filip where he had been before, and he dared not risk moving out of his hiding place. Edwud waited, with the heady mix of sour human odor and sugary chumps almost overpowering him.

The lights in the room seemed to sink rapidly, Edwud noticed, until there was just a very dull silvery glow bouncing off the faces of the humans. Despite his fears, Edwud was curious about what so many humans could be doing sitting together silently in a dark room.

He came down from under the seat, taking a direction that was as far from human feet as possible, and headed across the carpet toward where Filip was last visible. He found Filip about fifty leggs away, clinging to a young female human's shoe. When Edwud told him what it was he was holding on to so earnestly, Filip leapt off with a yell that Edwud thought the humans must surely hear. Together they ran until they reached an open space that had no chairs. Jinni and Wulfe joined them and they hurried toward the rear of the room.

The others were waiting for them, and Edwud saw how they were all as relieved as he was to see that no one had been crushed or injured. Edwud led them up the back wall and onto a plaster lip that formed part of the ceiling cornice.

"What are they doing?" Kerryd asked. She was fascinated with the sound that was coming from large boxes high up in the corners of the room. "It's like music," she said. The others considered it sounded more like suffering animals. Edwud watched the white square of material with the small holes that they had climbed upon earlier. It was now glowing brightly with gigantic humans dancing across it. The others followed his gaze and were equally amazed.

"They're all staring at it, Edwud," Lolli said.

The square kept changing to different things as they watched, from gigantic mountains poking into the sky to a thunderous river and back to the giant humans leaping across the bright, white square. Could this be their worship, some kind of devotion for the giant humans and mountains and rivers of the white square? There certainly was a reverential atmosphere, as hardly a human moved or spoke while they sat gravely attentive to the changing scenes flitting in front of them.

Edwud had climbed on the material and he knew it was flat. How could these things exist on it? Was the white square a window into another world of life, a larger one that humans hoped to rise to? Was it the same for them as Ootheca was for collectors? Was this the window through which they all had to pass? Edwud's head was spinning as if he had reached the limits of his thinking at that moment. He wished for something real, something sure, something solid on which to base his beliefs, so that he could act.

" 'Better to believe in anything that allows you to act,

rather than drift on an ocean of possibles,' " Sera had quoted to him once. Edwud longed for her functional thinking as he bobbed and swirled in a sea of doubt and confusion.

He watched more closely and noticed that the white square beamed light back to a point directly below them, and as the white square world changed, so did the light. Edwud had to get nearer to the point of light below. He told the others to stay exactly where they were as he climbed over the lip of the cornice down toward the light source. Could this be the important key to understanding every important question he had ever asked himself?

There was something to be learned here of great importance—Edwud believed he could feel it. He climbed across the top of a small room that housed the light point, and moved down the wall toward his objective. In front of him he could see where the light entered the small room through a glass square set into the wall. He crawled carefully closer.

The heat from the light was increasing as he moved. The brightness was unbearable, but Edwud forced himself to look at the world of the white square. He paused at the glass, concerned about the heat and the intensity of light, fearful that it could kill or blind him. He wanted to scurry back to the others and leave the knowledge hidden, but something in him refused. He moved out over the glass, feeling the heat come from inside the small room. He turned his eyes away from the unbearable brightness toward the white square and called out in shock at what he saw. Across the full size of the square was a perfect outline of himself.

Sunlight shakes the shadows' mark
and stretches until snap,
though nothing without shadows seen
but dark and dark and dark.
SONGS OF LIGHT-EXPERIENCE

A roar from the seated humans rose up so suddenly that Edwud lost his grip on the glass and slid halfway down the wall. Even as he fell, he kept watching the white square where he had briefly appeared. The humans settled back to watch quietly again and he was no longer on the square. Edwud was very excited; over and over to himself he kept saying, "My otherself, my otherself, I've seen my otherself . . ." Not surprising, Edwud thought, that the humans sat so patiently looking through the giant window.

Still shaking with fear and excitement, he climbed back up to the cornice, where the others gathered around him, joyful to have him back.

"What happened?" Wulfe asked on behalf of all of them.

"Did you see it? Did you see, there on the white square?" Edwud pointed his antennae to the front of the room.

"I didn't see anything. Edwud, what's going on?" Filip demanded.

"I saw," Jinni said.

"Did you?" Edwud asked. "Did you? I didn't imagine it, then."

"Was that you, Edwud?" Jinni asked in a confused tone.

"I don't know," Edwud replied.

"Was that who?" Filip asked angrily.

"Edwud appeared on the white square . . . as large as . . . as large as . . . as a hundred collectors," Jinni answered.

"Did you, Edwud?" Filip asked. "How did you do that?"

"I don't know," Edwud said absently. Almost to himself he whispered, "But I will find out, I will find out."

Edwud couldn't sleep. He watched the others spread out along the cornice, noticing how much smaller the distances between them had become since they began their journey. Jinni's wings touched Filip on one side and Wulfe on the other, Kerryd and Lolli had crossed antennae, and Nik and Sister Three had locked their legs together in sleep.

The room had emptied, and was dark and silent except for some tiny yellow lights high up around the walls. Edwud gazed at the white window, which seemed to be closed. He thought of Nolan, and smiled to himself at how disturbed he would have been by the whole episode. He could imagine Nolan's expression, his agitated pacing up and down and the cautious tone he would take with Edwud. He could very well be standing alongside me now, Edwud thought. No wonder my back is aching, carrying Nolan around every-

197

where I go. He laughed to himself. How he would have enjoyed telling Nolan about the window and what he intended doing next.

Having checked that they were all lost in sleep, Edwud began climbing back to where the blinding white light had come from. It was more difficult in the semidarkness, but eventually Edwud located the glass set into the wall. This time there was no heat radiating from the glass and no light. Edwud crawled out carefully onto the glass; he checked the large square window at the other end of the room to see if it opened—it remained dark. He turned to look through the glass, to the source of the blinding light. It was dim inside and he waited until his eyes focused clearly on what lay beyond.

Slowly it took shape; Edwud felt his legs go weak, his breathing increase rapidly, and his body lighten as if it would float across the room. There in front of him, round, clear, glassy and beautiful, was the Monoocal.

hings had gone from bad to worse at the yard. A large number of very strange collectors arrived one evening and proceeded to make themselves at home in the colony. The Director, who never ventured out of her hyde at all anymore, was not even consulted as Worik and the Reverend Viel established themselves as joint administrators of a committee to deal with the newcomers.

Known as Gerscapheos, the new collectors had habits that variously horrified, terrified and disgusted the yard collectors. They dug spiral burrows into the ground and dragged dry leaves and various earth litter into their burrows to feed themselves and their nimfs. They were never particular about the privacy of dung zone placement, and once several of them were observed consuming blood from a dead lizard that had been mauled by the cat. At night, whenever the moon was largest, the strangers would form circles, wing tip to wing tip, and stamp their feet as they chanted an incomprehensible song to some incomprehensible Lord Maker.

The yard collectors began to hate the Gerscapheos more each day as rumor inflated rumor and every strange habit became a possible threat.

"Gerscapheos eat their nimfs when food is short," someone said he was told.

"They collect in the day," another said.

"And they don't care about private circles."

"There'll be nothing left for us soon."

"They're so stupid they can't even talk properly like us."

The Reverend Viel and Worik established that the foreigners came from the coast after they had traveled for a hundred nights in vast metal boxes on a boat that came across the top of the ocean. They had no intention of going back.

Although the yard colony outnumbered the intruders, the Gerscapheos had such a very different attitude to life, death and violence that the colony felt extremely nervous about a physical confrontation. The strangers believed that to be killed was much more attractive than dying quietly in one's hyde. They sang, danced, and spoke so much about beautiful and violent deaths from their enemies that the yard collectors came to believe that most of them couldn't wait to be crushed, poisoned, or eaten. It was one thing to die violently while fighting one's enemies and being held in glorious regard afterward, but quite another to hold that regard *before* actually dying. This was not an enemy they wished to meet in battle.

A plan was devised by the administrative committee to encourage the new collectors to embark on a Kitchen raid. Each night various tempting chumps were placed closer and closer to the Kitchen door so that the intruders would be drawn toward the dangerous house of humans. The plan worked beautifully and the yard collectors held their breath as they learned that a large number of Gerscapheos had entered the Kitchen.

After six nights inside the house, half the foreign collectors straggled out, sick, injured and defeated. They told the others of the horrors they met, from invisible poisons to human boots. The committee couldn't agree quickly enough to attack the strangers in their weakened state, which allowed them time to retreat into the garden shed.

The Reverend Viel was furious as the Gerscapheos took control of the shed, including his own hyde, refusing entry to any yard collectors. Entry holes were blocked and sealed by both sides except for the strip under the door, which was guarded by both sides. At times, when the shed light was on at night, the underdoor gap sliced a demarcation line that divided the two groups as neatly as a blade. It became known as "The Strip," and very young nimfs who had never seen Gerscapheos had nightmares of The Strip and what lay beyond it.

34

The Monoocal could not be moved. Edwud had managed to get inside the small room that housed the large and complex equipment that made the blinding light, but there was no way that the round and glassy Monoocal could be set free. He climbed over and over the machine until he was dizzy, wondering the whole time how the Monoocal could have been taken here and sealed so permanently into such a complex machine.

Edwud remembered the Director's strange laugh when he told her he would find the Monoocal. "Find it? Find it?" she had said. "But you don't understand, you can't find it." Thankfully he had been only half-sotted at the time, but he did remember the Director's strange laugh following him out of her hyde, and it had accompanied him secretly on his journey. She was half-right, Edwud thought. I have found it, but I can't bring it back.

For several nights Edwud remained with the others on the cornice. Each night the humans would pour in, clattering the seats and talking to each other until the lights retreated and the great white window lit up, and then they would stare rapturously at it until it closed.

When the humans left, the group of collectors would descend and marvel at the sweet chumps and spills left behind. Jinni's cough began to clear up, and Filip lost some of the aches and pains in his legs. They quickly fell into a pattern of rapid collection and retreat to the cornice. Before eating, Edwud would always climb to the glass square and gaze in at the Monoocal. He had taken them all with him the night after his first discovery, but they had not been as impressed as he thought they should be, and so he went thereafter by himself. At least he could be near it, Edwud thought, as he studied the Monoocal each night.

Although they were comfortable and were enjoying the regular and easy collections, the group had experienced enough to know that peaceful times did not last.

Filip was the one to herald the end of their time in the vast picture room. In the middle of the day he suddenly woke up. Something had disturbed him. He had been dreaming of one of the last battles of the Kitchen Wars, when less than a quarter of them were left alive. All over the Kitchen, the humans had placed tiny plastic boxes with cavelike entrances that had at their center a rich, saucy-smelling chump. Many of his hungry friends entered the caves and gorged themselves without discussing whether the chumps might be poisoned. Filip remembered thinking at the time that perhaps many of them didn't care anymore. They couldn't get out of the Kitchen the way they had come in, as the humans had nailed a rubber strip to the bottom of the door. Before daybreak his friends had died an agonizing death. Filip had watched the poison virtually eat away the inside of their bodies. In his dream Filip imagined the final days, when the chlordane began falling like rain. Although in reality he had escaped through a ventilation grid high up on the wall, in his nightmare the chlordane hosed down on him wherever he went; and when he reached the ventilation grid, he found it sealed, and the choking chlordane sprayed into his face and eyes and mouth.

Filip woke up gagging. For a moment he was still in his dream, the smell of chlordane deep inside him, and then slowly he adjusted to his surroundings: the sleeping collectors, the large room. His antennae kicked up with a jerk, automatically aiming at the doorway where the humans always entered. There below him were men in white, and from the containers strapped to their backs came the unmistakable and deadly odor of chlordane.

"Get up!" Filip shouted, running along the cornice, bumping and tripping over the sleeping bodies. "Get up! Get up!"

Edwud led them down the far wall and under the seats for protection. As they ran, they watched the white-coated humans spread out across the room at the rear. The scent of chlordane was unmistakable. If they had waited even a few more seconds, they would have been trapped where they slept. Edwud glanced at the great white square as he passed and led them out under the door through which they had entered.

The daylight struck at them as they reached the street. It was so much hotter than before. The noise of traffic after the silence of the picture room was jarring. Edwud hurried along the concrete gutter, trying to look ahead—he knew they would not have long before they were seen by some passing human. A storm-water channel appeared at a junction in the gutter, and Edwud gratefully plunged down into its darkness.

When he turned to check that the others had followed, Edwud once again noticed how most of them had changed. Wulfe was virtually carrying Jinni, who could barely keep pace; Nik followed behind Sister Three, with his wings spread in a protective gesture to give her courage; Kerryd and Lolli took turns leading and sometimes pushing Filip, telling him all the while that he was actually helping them, and how grateful they were. How much they had changed, Edwud thought.

"I'm sorry I ran so fast," Edwud said between breaths. No one felt it necessary to answer. Edwud wanted to say something more. "I was frightened, actually," he said. The others looked at him with surprise. Edwud, afraid? Of course they knew he was often afraid, but *saying* he was afraid, that was really something else.

"So was I," Wulfe said. This was greeted with even more astonishment.

"I'm always afraid," Lolli said softly.

"What did she say?" Filip demanded to know.

"She said she's always afraid," Jinni said.

"What of? What's she afraid of?" Filip asked.

"I'm afraid of . . . of . . . everything," Lolli said, determined to be truthful.

"How can you be afraid of everything?" Filip wanted to know. Lolli was embarrassed, and she looked around for support, regretting her outburst of honesty. Filip sensed her predicament.

"Well, it must be . . . ah . . . really . . . ah . . . difficult to . . . ah . . . to . . . ah, do things," Filip suggested. "Mind you, it's very sensible to be afraid of some things."

"Oh, it is difficult," Lolli agreed. "You wouldn't even know what it's like; you never get frightened," she said.

"I never get frightened!" Filip said in mock amazement.

"Well, not like me, you don't," Lolli said. Filip shook his head; his antennae swung around sensing how everyone was listening closely.

"I'm frightened every time I wake up. I'm frightened that some part of me isn't going to work properly; that I won't be able to keep up with the rest of you; that I'll be left alone; that the new ache in my legs is all the chlordane I've taken finally doing its job. I'm frightened when I go to sleep that the nightmares will come, more real than any battle; that I won't wake up at all, and if I do, that the last of my sight and hearing will be gone," Filip said.

Edwud watched how all of them moved closer to Filip. At the beginning of the journey he knew that such a confession would have driven them away as if the fear itself might be contagious.

"I didn't know," Lolli said comfortingly. "Oh, it's so . . . so . . . wonderful to hear. . . . I don't mean it's wonderful that you . . ." Lolli tried to explain and apologize at the same time.

"What I do is," Filip continued, "I make this picture in my mind—ha ha, see more clearly there than I can all of you lot," he joked. "I see a picture of myself being outrageously brave—I . . . I . . . have saved the lot of you, many times . . . in my mind—and then I find I like it so much that I can't quite give it up just to feel safe."

"That's wonderful. Oh, I'm going to do that next time I'm afraid," Lolli said with enthusiasm. The others looked at her with some doubt.

"What I do," Nik cut in, "is to ignore it—whatever I'm afraid of, I just ignore it, pretend it isn't there."

"Oh, that's a good idea," Lolli said.

"No, it isn't," Filip said with disgust. "That's really stupid. That's how it gets you. It sneaks up without any difficulty because you won't look at it, and then it gets inside you, worse than chlordane." Filip rattled his antennae impatiently.

"Filip's right," Wulfe said.

"Did he say I was right?" Filip asked.

"There's only one thing ever to be afraid of," Wulfe said, turning to contact each one of them. "And you have to find it out for yourself."

"Couldn't you tell us, Wulfe?" Lolli pleaded.

"You wouldn't believe me," Wulfe answered, "until you were ready."

"I'm ready," Lolli said.

"I didn't fear anything when I started out," Jinni said wistfully. "Now I seem to discover a new fear every night."

"Only a fool or a nimf can remain fearing nothing," Wulfe said, gently leaning toward Jinni. "And you are neither one."

Edwud had said nothing; he was so impressed with the way the group had talked that for once he had nothing much to add, although part of him was disappointed that they didn't turn to him for his opinion. Edwud was most impressed with Wulfe, who appeared to be more calm and certain than ever before. It felt to Edwud now as if he could pass some of the invisible weight he was carrying to Wulfe.

"Could Kerryd give us a song? I love to hear her sing," Sister Three asked timidly. Kerryd jumped up, delighted with Sister Three.

"I think we should walk as Kerryd sings," Edwud said. "Would you like to lead, Wulfe?" For a change Edwud followed at the end of the line as they made their way along the drains in the way they had learned. Kerryd's voice spiraled down the pipes:

> *"Color of loving,*
> *color of fear.*
> *Heat of loving,*
> *cold of fear.*
> *Colors, colors,*
> *night and day,*
> *cold and hot*
> *that never stay."*

After a while Edwud began feeling better about leaving the Monoocal behind. He wasn't sure why. Two possibilities constantly returned: that there might be more than one Monoocal, or that what he thought was the Monoocal was, in fact, something quite different. The drains this time did not seem as depressing as before, and it was quite relaxing being at the rear of the line where he could allow himself much more time to think. He had conversations in his mind with Nolan and enjoyed taking Nolan's part so much that he would laugh out loud from time to time, and the others would turn around in front of him and give him worried looks. He remembered Kerryd's song:

"Circles
within circles,
one inside the other.
One life, one life,
all of us making
one life."

Nolan was certainly with him, he thought. And the others walking in front of him, small ripples as yet, but growing all the time. Edwud thought he would like to make up a song and surprise them all by singing it to them. For the rest of the night he tried different tunes and thoughtful words, but not once would it come out right. It seemed so easy for Kerryd, as if she just opened her mouth and the melody poured forth. Such a gift from the Lord Maker had to be spread thinly among collectors, he thought, else there would be too many makers of music and not enough appreciators.

For some time, as he walked in the dark, Edwud had known that floating by them was the identical soapsud foam that, back at the yard, he would have quaffed to become sotted. He tried to ignore its heady odor as it swirled past by concentrating on his song, but it only succeeded in making the frothy spume more attractive, and the song even worse.

The others didn't seem to notice the potential of the swill passing by them, and Edwud realized that probably Nolan and Filip were the only ones who could have easily recognized it. Without intending to, he fell farther behind the others. To verify that the swill contained the ingredients he imagined, Edwud dipped one leg into the foam as he passed, and tasted. It was the right stuff, all right, Edwud conceded to himself. Nolan would be saying to keep away from it in his "dire warnings" voice. Edwud scooped another mouthful of the foam as he walked. It had a slightly different taste from that in the yard, but only someone as practiced as himself, Edwud thought, would be able to detect it.

Every one hundred leggs, Edwud would take a mouthful of the foam. It could, at any time, run out completely, he reasoned, and he had not indulged himself for a very long time. Several times he lost sight of the others in front of him, forcing them to wait for him to catch up. Eventually Filip drifted back to walk with him.

"Strange to have you all the way back here, Edwud," Filip said amiably. "This is more like my position." Edwud did not answer. "Did I ever tell you about my own nimfs?" Filip could hear Edwud counting to one hundred, stopping for a moment, and then starting to count again. "Are you counting something, Edwud?" he asked. When Edwud failed to respond again, Filip tried a different approach. "I don't suppose you could actually give me a bit of assistance, Edwud. The old legs are a bit exhausted. If you could let me lean on you for a while, I won't fall too far behind."

"Lennod," Edwud answered.

"Oh, Lord, I thought so," Filip muttered. "Edwud, you have to stop drinking that foam. I knew what it was almost as soon as we entered the drain. Nolan warned me . . ."

"Nolan's dead," Edwud said.

"Yes, I know," Filip replied. "That foam, Edwud, can do terrible things . . . I've seen it before."

"Lennod," Edwud snapped. "You've seen everything before, haven't you—so full of advice—so full of warnings—how come you're the one who is nearly blind and deaf, huh? How come you're the one who has to be helped all the time?"

"I know that's not you talking, Edwud."

"Lennod! Edwud is the one at the front—I'm the one at the back!"

Filip called out to the others, as he tried to come between Edwud and the foam below. Edwud laughed and easily slipped past the old collector. "Don't do this, Edwud, please," Filip pleaded. Edwud remained at the level of the soapy foam, not even bothering to count to one hundred any longer.

As the others arrived, they listened to Filip's explanation. Edwud had consumed all he could for the time being and sat staring at them with an odd and unsettling expression. Wulfe and Jinni lowered themselves down alongside Edwud. "You should be up at the front," Wulfe said. Edwud smiled a strange smile.

"Edwud, what's wrong?" Jinni asked with concern.

"Lennod! Lennod! Lennod!" Edwud shouted. Jinni jumped backward with shock at Edwud's fury.

"It's the foam," Filip told her. "It brings this . . . this

211

Lennod out."

"You're Edwud," Wulfe said. "And you've taken too much of this . . . spume . . . and it . . ."

"We need you at the front of us, Edwud, to lead. You're the one who . . . ," Kerryd said quietly.

"No, I'm not. Edwud is the one who knows. Edwud is the one who is always sure, always right. I'm Lennod, and I don't know . . . go away!"

"We will not go away," Wulfe said, as he leaned toward Edwud and began pushing him up the side of the pipe away from the foam. Edwud turned on Wulfe, opening his hind wings aggressively and flipping Wulfe on his side. Edwud grabbed Wulfe's forewing and tore a piece out with his teeth. Wulfe and the others were horrified.

"Edwud!" Jinni screamed.

"What's happening?" Filip demanded. Edwud attempted to tear another hole in Wulfe's wing, but Wulfe was too quick for him—he leapt out of range, lowering his head and plate at Edwud for protection. Edwud advanced again, but Jinni stepped forward and blocked his way. Edwud hesitated, staring at Jinni, and then with a flick of his front legs pushed her aside. Jinni rolled onto her back and slid halfway down the side of the pipe before finding her feet.

"All right, Lennod," Wulfe said. "We won't force you to do anything." Edwud appeared to relax a little. "We'll just wait here for a while. Are you all right, Jinni?" Wulfe asked with concern.

"Of course I am," she called. Jinni was more embarrassed than injured and felt very foolish. Sister Three was praying to the top of the pipe for protection against the mad collector. Nik alternated between keeping an image acceptable to his matrimate and the others, and putting a long distance between himself and Edwud. In fear, Lolli pressed up against Filip, who wasn't sure what exactly was happening but reasoned that it might be better if he didn't keep asking, and it was very pleasant having Lolli's body pressed against him anyway.

Kerryd watched closely as if she were in some sort of slow and grinding pain, as she tried to understand how such a thing could occur. The foam itself does not carry this Lennod, she thought: like the door of the Kitchen opening to let the cat out into the yard, it can only release what is already there. Kerryd hated the idea that Lennod could exist within Edwud. She had put her hopes, even her life, under Edwud's guidance. Perhaps that was unfair, particularly since Edwud had never asked for it. But that was how it was.

Filip had been brought up to date with what had happened. He was the least agitated and he moved closer to face Edwud. "I know you," he said. Edwud turned angrily, ready to attack. "I know you, Lennod," Filip said again. "I knew you when you were a tiny nimf, before you could even collect."

Edwud was confused. "You old fool, you can barely see me, let alone know who I am," Edwud scoffed.

"I don't need to see you. I remember you very well," Filip said. "I knew your father and your mother."

"Your brain is rotten with chlordane; you can't remember what you collected last night," Edwud sneered.

"You did a terrible thing, Lennod," Filip said quietly.

The others were baffled and Wulfe drew near to Filip to ask him in a whisper what he was doing. Filip reassured him with a confident smile and a wave of his antennae. "A terrible thing," Filip continued.

Edwud opened his wings and rocked from side to side as if he was finding it difficult to balance. His plate was raised and his antennae pointed directly at Filip. "You know nothing, old collector, but silly stories of . . . of . . . Kitchen Wars . . ."

"You found your father collecting illegally, Lennod, didn't you? When you were too young to understand what it would mean. You talked about it and he lost part of his circle."

Edwud was turning around as if he couldn't quite recognize his surroundings or the collectors watching and listening so closely to him. His wings dragged as he turned, keeping him balanced. All those ans ago. His father.

"He never spoke to you again, did he, Lennod?" Filip said, as he stood up and stretched his old wings in front of Edwud.

Edwud saw his father rising up in front of him in anger and hurt and disappointment. He saw his father slowly give up, retreat into himself in silence, becoming physically smaller and more lonely with every night. Never to speak to him again; not a smile, not a wave, not a moment when his father's eyes would even see him. And then there was Lennod to take the blame, Lennod to be cut off from his father—not Edwud, but Lennod. Couldn't his father see that Lennod did the bad thing, not Edwud? Edwud was the good one who loved him.

35

*W*hen Edwud had slept off the effects of the foam, he had no memory of Lennod nor of what he had said and done since becoming sotted. He knew it must have been something embarrassing from the way that the others kept avoiding the subject and smiling at each other in acknowledgment of the shared secret. He made no objection when they all agreed to climb out of the drains as soon as possible, and he followed along behind for a while until they all insisted he take the lead again. He realized that he felt more comfortable at the front than at the rear and determined to think about why that was so when he had a quiet moment later.

The streets had turned hotter and more windy as they emerged late at night. The road machines and humans were in small numbers only. Edwud led them out of the gutter and up onto the footpath, past steps and cans over-flowing with rubbish. Filip and Jinni would not be able to walk for long in such humid conditions, Edwud thought, as he began sampling possible doorways for access and safety. From under one came a strong, musty, moldy odor. Edwud reasoned that such a place would be unlikely to house many humans, as mold grew best in the dark and humans liked neither dark nor mold.

Inside, from the floor to the ceiling, were dark, wooden shelves packed solid with books of every shape, color and size imaginable. Sister Three informed them of how humans stored things inside the books, which, when opened, caused them to talk or sing. She said proudly that Sanctuary collectors had known about books for ages and ages. They were so valuable, she told the others, that the humans were never permitted to take them away; they were always collected and stored to be used again. Furthermore, Sister Three said, they did not get used up; the same songs and talk came out of the same books every time they were opened.

The group looked upon the vast collection of books with great respect. Kerryd wanted to know how the songs were put into the books, and Jinni wanted to know what an opened one looked like. Sister Three said the paper in the books had tiny marks as dark as the yard collectors' wings, but unfortunately she had no idea how the songs were put into them. Kerryd imagined putting her songs into a book so that every time someone opened it, he had to sing. It made her very happy to think about it.

The musty smell was a comforting one—it seemed to hold no dangers like the air from the glass house and the Kitchen, or the fumes from the road machines. In one corner there was cool air blowing out from a metal box, and Edwud signaled them to follow him. Settling under the lower edge of the air box, the collectors enjoyed cooling their legs and feeling the heat begin to leave. Above them a large table with ornately carved legs stood against the wall. On its surface they could all see that there were several books stacked and that one of them lay opened. Wulfe and Nik scanned the area for chumps or spills.

Kerryd insisted on climbing up to the tabletop with Edwud. Jinni wanted to go with them, but Wulfe was adamant that she was not well enough. The others were content to wait for a report. Edwud had trouble keeping up with Kerryd in her excitement to get to the open book.

The only light came from reflections off the walls from road machines passing in the street outside. Edwud felt the residue of the foam from the drains still in his body. He knew the feeling well: a dryness that seemed to make it difficult to move or think clearly. It was at times like this he promised himself that never again would he go near the terrible spume, no matter how depressed he became. It was also when he most wanted to sink into a pool of the suds and never emerge again. The possibilities of the open book were interesting enough to keep him climbing. Edwud laughed to himself; there was always something he could find or invent, some little thing, that made going on hold possibilities, even when he felt so terrible.

Kerryd reached the open book first and paused, waiting for Edwud. They swept the area around them with their antennae. No sign of danger. Together they crawled up the edge of the pages, which lay in a hundred gentle steps. Kerryd commented how beautiful and inviting the tiny paper steps appeared.

Sister Three had been quite correct. The pages held black marks in neat and orderly lines across their surface. Kerryd stared at them. She traced around several of the marks with her foot and then her left antenna. She walked along the lines of marks one at a time, hoping that perhaps a song might come. But nothing did. She looked to Edwud for help. Edwud looked hard at the marks, moved his face closer, and licked one of them. Kerryd looked at him hopefully. Edwud shook his head. The marks were so neat and orderly and stretched onto page after page that Edwud was overwhelmed when he thought of how many inscriptions there were in just one book, let alone all of the books on all of the shelves. He had an idea: what if the marks were notes, singing notes?

"Do you think they might be?" Kerryd said.

"They could be," Edwud said, becoming excited by the possibility of understanding the book. "One mark may indicate a high note and another a low note," he suggested. Kerryd looked at the marks again.

"Which ones would be which?" she asked. Edwud stared at the black marks and then at Kerryd. The inscriptions looked so complex. If each one was a different note, Edwud thought, perhaps they could try to count the different types of marks. Kerryd watched him run along a line, turn, and run back down the next, counting out loud as he went.

"Twenty-one!" Edwud said triumphantly when he reached the bottom of the page.

"That's too many," Kerryd replied dismally. "There aren't that many notes."

Edwud agreed with the logic, mildly grateful that he didn't have to work out which mark was which note. Edwud retraced in his mind what Sister Three had said about books: "Sometimes when they open them, they sing, and sometimes they speak, and sometimes they just keep star-

ing at the marks on the pages and don't make a sound."
What could it be about the marks that could do this?
Edwud pondered. If *he* stared at something for a long time
without saying anything, it was because he was thinking,
and when Kerryd sang, it was because she had thought of
something or felt something she wanted to tell everyone
about. Edwud's antennae shot up suddenly.

"That's it" he said. Kerryd ran to join him. "That's
what they are. They're thoughts!" Edwud became very
excited and began pacing up and down the lines of black
marks. Kerryd wasn't convinced. Edwud flapped his wings
as his mind raced to try to understand. Perhaps each of the
twenty-one marks was a different part of a thought. He
looked again and noticed how the marks came in clumps—
clumps of different parts of thoughts. When they were put
alongside each other in different order, they made different
thoughts; and different thoughts, Edwud reasoned, when
put alongside others, made for larger and larger thoughts.

Edwud looked at the neat steps the pages made as they
stacked one on top of the other. So many thoughts—in just
one book. He looked around the room, which lit up
momentarily as a road machine passed outside. So many
books, each one crammed thick with pages, each page
stacked with row after row of black marks—Edwud felt
dizzy, imagining there were probably other places where
even more books were kept. Edwud experienced a sensation completely new to him: it was like falling through the
air—something like the time in the Kitchen, only this time
he supplied no energy and the falling kept on; and instead
of the ground becoming closer, it moved farther and far-

ther away. It wasn't a frightening experience, but more one of feeling disconnected to everything in his life that had made him who he was. Kerryd was shaking him.

"Edwud, are you all right?" she asked with a worried expression. Edwud smiled reassuringly at her. "I think we should get back to the others," she said. Edwud was not yet ready to leave the book.

"I'm going to stay here for a while," he said. Kerryd hesitated, looking closely at Edwud to see if a shadow of Lennod might be appearing. Edwud stroked her head with his antennae and waved her to go. "They're probably more hungry for one of your beautiful songs than for a chump," he said. Kerryd smiled through her embarrassment and disappeared over the edge of the table.

Edwud turned to the page in front of him. Like expressions on a face, he thought, that's how the marks might work. He knew it was possible to understand so much of what a collector was thinking by the tiniest change of a mouth, eye, or the position of an antenna. But so much—so many thoughts, Edwud sighed as he scanned the packed shelves. If only he could turn his own thoughts to marks on a page like the one before him, so that others could come to know them, like expressions on a face—and he could come to know theirs.

Edwud let himself imagine how his thoughts, in a book, could outlive him; how they could be recognized and understood by those who had never seen him. He wondered what it would mean—such a capacity to see the thoughts and feelings of others. He wondered how it would be if he could leave marks for the humans who used the books, marks that could get them to understand how it felt to be a collector. He looked at the complex inscriptions methodically stationed across the page waiting to express themselves, and he knew that he would never be able to understand them, and that he would never be able to leave such marks. For a moment Edwud had a vision of collectors as permanently separated from each other as each mark was from every other on the page in front of him.

36

For as long as possible the group stayed near the cool metal box among the rows of musty books. Food was extremely scarce in the old rooms and water or other liquid spills were even more rare. Occasionally one or two of them would venture out onto the street and return with some small find; however, eventually it was considered not worth the risk to stay in the open so long, as each night required a greater distance to be traveled.

For a while Edwud tried to explain to the others the sadness he felt about not being able to understand the marks in the book. He gave his opinion about how good it would be to pass among collectors books with the ideas and thoughts of everyone. A part of his sadness was caused by his growing belief that collectors considered thoughts to be like nimfs: their own being the ones they mostly cared for.

Edwud was the last to leave. As if farewelling a good friend, he waited on the step until the lights from a road machine gave him his final glimpse of the rows of books. Raising his antennae in respect, Edwud nodded to the books, turned, and followed after the others.

Along the streets and gutters, the heat they had avoided for some time among the books now welcomed them back. Down they went into the storm-water channel and along the drains, where the generous side to the increased fumes and foul swills was escape from the relentless heat.

For some reason the drains reminded them of the yard. Perhaps it was the shape of the pipes or the scent of the passing swills that had something familiar to them. Perhaps the yard had become part of their *old* memory—that which returns with greater force and color than the memory of more recent times. They seldom spoke, preferring to meditate in time with their steps and remember the comfort and happiness of their old home.

Edwud thought of Sera—had she become the Reverend Viel's matrimate? Did she think of him, ever? What was it like at the yard, with the Monoocal gone? In Edwud's mind Nolan answered that the yard was probably very comfortable compared with what they had been contending with on their journey—and that he, for one, wouldn't mind going back. Edwud laughed out loud. The others, following along behind, looked up quickly. Edwud knew they were now always on the alert in case he slipped down into the foam again.

He laughed again, although the laugh was at himself. He marveled at how he could choose to do something that he didn't want to do. How was it that he did become sotted? It felt good at first—a warm, liquid sensation flooding through him—but later there was pain and thickheadedness, and a feeling of emptiness. And this Lennod they all told him about, where was he at the times when Edwud was not sotted?

Filip had slowed down considerably since leaving the coolness of the book rooms, and even though Edwud stopped more often, they were waiting longer and longer for him to catch up.

"We'll have to do something," Jinni said.

"We could carry him," Nik suggested.

"He wouldn't like that," said Wulfe. "And I don't blame him."

"We can't keep waiting for him all the time, can we, Edwud?" Sister Three asked. "If we explained how he's holding us up too much . . ."

Wulfe and Jinni glared at Sister Three. "I think it's the fumes," Edwud said. "That's what's slowing him down." The others looked at each other and back down the pipe to see if Filip was in sight.

"Edwud, he's . . . ," Kerryd began to say. "He's become . . . a lot . . . older."

"Of course he has," Edwud agreed.

"He may not be able to . . . to . . . go much farther," Kerryd said quietly. Edwud realized reluctantly that he had been avoiding the obvious truth about Filip for some time, protecting himself, perhaps.

When Filip finally caught up with them, he could sense that they had been talking about him. "You lot just go ahead. I'll catch up . . . I can always catch up," he said. "Actually I'm not as tired as I was. I think these drains get me going." Filip tried to keep the noise of his rapid breathing down to a minimum, which made the words come out in little puffs of air, disjointed from each other.

"Oh, well, I was thinking of getting out of the drains for a while," Edwud said. "I don't think I can stand the smell much longer."

"Or the sound of the swills," Jinni said.

"I don't think the air's very good in here either," Wulfe announced.

Kerryd sang a few high notes. "I'd like to sing in the open. See how it comes bouncing back at me? It's really quite difficult."

Filip stood up and limped off in front of them. He stopped, turned to look at their surprised faces, and gave a loud and enjoyable laugh. "It's my legs that are going," he said. "Not my brain." He walked off up the pipe, laughing to himself as he went. Jinni looked at Wulfe, smiled, and imitated his voice.

"I don't think the air's very good in here either," she mocked. Wulfe laughed at how they had all treated Filip as if the cold had shrunk him to a tiny nimf. The others joked and repeatedly made fun of the silly reasons they had given to spare Filip's feelings.

"Come on, you lot," Filip called back to them. "How will you feel—being led by a blind collector? Mind you, I don't know what good your eyesight seems to do you."

As they came out of the drains, a hot, dry wind was blowing, and although it was much warmer, the air was cleaner and fresher. They followed along behind Edwud for some time as he chose pathways that afforded the most protection from the wind. The roads they crossed were almost free of road machines and the only light came from a full moon watching directly over them. Several times Edwud or one of the others was struck by a rolling leaf or twig and would remain pinned underneath until the weight was lifted off. Progress was slow and frustrating.

At the first reasonably safe-looking shelter, Edwud stopped and beckoned the others around him. Between a large, flat chunk of sandstone and the earth surrounding it lay an abandoned hole that smelled as if it had once held mice long ago. The group gratefully slumped into the old nest out of the wind. The smell of mouse, no matter how old, was unsettling, however, and none of them could fall asleep, except for Filip, who leaned heavily against the sandstone and dozed off with little care about mice teeth or anything else.

In his sleep Filip twitched and jerked, occasionally calling out the name of a collector of whom none of them had heard. Once Edwud had wondered where Filip went in his dreams. He had watched him in sleep before and it never seemed that Filip was back in the Kitchen Wars. From his expression and the tone of his calling out, and the waving of his antennae, Edwud got the clear impression of nimfs playing. If that was where Filip's dreams chose to take him, back to his beginning, then Edwud felt there must be some reason. Surely Filip's life since leaving his nimfhood held greater events to which he would be drawn.

Around the middle of the night, the wind departed, leaving a polished stillness over the surface of the ground. Edwud climbed out of the hole with Jinni. The chunk of sandstone rose in perfect flatness above them high into the air. Climbing up its narrowest side, Edwud and Jinni could see that there were similar chunks of stone pointing rounded tops at the sky all around them. In front of each stone lay a rectangle marked by metal lacing or concrete or neatly placed bricks. Edwud lowered himself down the broad face of the stone and called out to Jinni to follow.

Etched into the face of the stone were marks like those Edwud had found on the pages of the open book. He showed Jinni how they ran in lines, and how they sat in such even spaces from each other. He walked around each of the marks in turn as if their very shape might hold some magic understanding.

From the ground in front of the stone, Edwud looked up, and with Jinni watching closely, he began to copy, with his foot scraping the ground, the marks on the stone:

MATHEW IVERSON
DIED 7/26/1998
AGED 19 YEARS

Jinni and Edwud stared at the marks for a long time. Filip joined them, claiming there was not enough space in the hole to feel comfortable. Edwud had been discussing with Jinni how the rectangles in front of the stone were all about as long as adult humans, and when Filip informed him that he had seen humans put their dead cat into a hole in the ground, Edwud knew immediately that the place they had chosen as a shelter was a burial ground—not one for cats, but for humans. The stones were there to tell about who it was that had been buried there, Edwud decided. He could not see how the marks could say very much about the life of the one who lay underneath. For an unknown reason the small number of marks on the stone, compared to the countless rows in the books, disturbed Edwud. Were these few marks enough to represent the dead one?

"What marks . . . I mean . . . if we did . . . instead of leaving . . . to the ants . . . I mean . . . would you place on my stone, Edwud?" Filip asked quietly. Edwud looked at Jinni and Filip and up to the sandstone reaching above them.

"Filip was a brave fighter . . . a kind collector . . . and a loyal friend," Edwud said. Jinni turned and walked toward the mouse hole, stopped, and called back to them.

"And just like . . . my father . . . I love him," she said, and disappeared into the hole.

"Did she say I was like her father?" Filip asked Edwud.

"You heard perfectly well," Edwud said, smiling at Filip's happy face.

Edwud didn't give any reasons for leaving the burial ground other than saying he wanted to move on. In their minds the others couldn't help wondering, move on where? Edwud led them down into the drains again for several nights and then out into the streets, up winding narrow alleys thick with buildings and road machines. Following the guidance of his own antennae, Edwud balanced the need for food with the need for safety whenever deciding a new direction.

There was one particular scent among the hundreds of city smells that intrigued Edwud: a salty, attractive mix of fragrances that, as he walked in one particular direction, became more dominant. The others noted it too and were quite pleased when Edwud persisted toward it. The ground also began to change in small ways as the smell became stronger, but of much more concern was the increase in the number of birds flying, flapping and screeching overhead.

Eventually the group climbed down a concrete wall and stepped off onto rolling hills of pure, dry sand. Progress was slow as their legs sank into the yellowish grains, and every movement created a sliding avalanche. Edwud quickly led them back to the concrete wall, which they followed as it curved around gradually toward an intermittent thump-crashing sound coming from a distance.

The wall stopped at an area of sand that erupted in pockmarked gray rocks covered with beautifully patterned snail shells, pools of clear water, and bright green trails of slippery weeds. None of them had ever seen or smelled anything like it. The sand between the rocks was sodden and packed, and very easy to walk on. Edwud led them from rock to rock as they marveled at the new sights, sounds and smells, and the enjoyable wetness of everything.

The regular thump and crash was intriguing, and Edwud moved closer. On top of a particularly high rock, Edwud saw in the moonlight the cause of the noise. It moved toward him in a billowing mass that gained strength and height, as if it were reaching like a gigantic animal to swallow the lot of them in one graceful sweep.

"Grip!" Edwud screamed to the others loud enough to tear something in his throat. They were all of them on top of the rock and he knew that if they could hear, then grip the rock they would.

The wave struck the rock stronger than any wind Edwud had ever known; it rolled him backward and into a long strand of weed that streamed after the rush in homage. Edwud clung to the weed, feeling the pressure of not being able to breathe as the water sucked and pulled at every fiber of his body. Even as he clung desperately, he knew that some of the others would not have been able to hold on. The water was salty and carried fine particles of sand and pieces of dead things that Edwud's antennae could not recognize. And then it drained from the rock as quickly as it had appeared.

Edwud looked around for the others. He could see Wulfe and Lolli clinging to the side of a small pool in the rock, which would have lessened the drag of the water. Below him, wedged between two empty snail shells, were Nik and Sister Three, still gripping each other and the shells. Kerryd, Jinni and Filip were nowhere in sight. Edwud looked in the direction from which the wave had come and saw another one gathering.

"Run!" he called. "Run—there's another one coming." He waved the direction to the others and leapt onto the sand. The water was now running back the other way and Edwud was immediately swept up and carried toward the oncoming wave.

"Stay on the rocks," he managed to call out before he disappeared, dragged backward with the water. The other four leapt from rock to rock, avoiding the sand, occasionally looking behind them to see how close the new wave might be. When it struck, it was much weaker than the first, and the four of them held on easily, locking their legs together for extra grip.

Edwud was at the mercy of the water; he tried to remember what Jinni had told him about being able to stay on top of the water. Flap your wings or kick your legs, she had said; Edwud couldn't recall which. He did both, snatching air whenever he could reach the surface.

The next wave turned him again and thrust him toward the rocks with the speed of a road machine. Edwud saw the rocks coming at him as if they were being tossed by some giant malevolent collector. With his wings spread, he managed to stay on the surface of the water until it folded in on itself and drove him from a dreadful height into the sand. Edwud's left antenna struck the sand first and he felt it buckle under the strain. And then followed the water. As if the weight of the sky were falling on him, Edwud felt his plate crushed between his body and the sand. He dug all of his legs into the wet grains as deeply as he could and held on as the water passed, first one way and then the other.

When it stopped he began to run, but his head was spinning and his legs did not seem to work properly. He wasn't sure which way he was running until the surface began to loosen underfoot and he found it more difficult to move forward. It was becoming drier with every step. Edwud realized that the drier it became, the safer he would be from the pounding water. He wanted to reach the sliding yellow-grained hills of sand and never touch water again.

Farther up the dry white sand, in a small hollow, Wulfe, Lolli, Nik and Sister Three slumped against each other, gasping for air. None of them had ever run so fast against such odds before. Wulfe called breathlessly for Jinni, then Kerryd, then Filip. There was no answer. The four of them looked at one another, waiting and hoping for some kind of reassurance from someone.

"They wouldn't have survived that," Nik said, shaking

231

his head and trying to suck more air into his body. "I saw Edwud dragged out . . . out . . ."

Wulfe ignored him and climbed out of the hollow. He swept his antennae slowly and carefully in a full circle around him. The moonlight was strong but allowed shadows to form in lumps and peaks across the sand, so that it was difficult to pick out any dark-colored collectors. The moist, salty air made it impossible to detect light odors at more than fifty leggs.

"We'll have to search for them," Wulfe said. Sister Three, he noticed, was mumbling toward the sky again. Lolli was sobbing in time with her deep gasps for breath. "Lolli, you come with me," Wulfe said as he reached down into the hollow to help her up. Lolli slowed her crying and took hold of Wulfe's outstretched leg. "We'll meet on the wall where we first came onto the sand," he told Nik, as he led Lolli away toward the rocks.

Edwud couldn't get up. It was the strangest feeling he had ever had. Each time he stood, the ground rolled over him and stopped above his head, as if he were trying to walk on the sky. He couldn't seem to establish exactly where the ground was. It moved away from him whenever he thought he had it pinned down, but it moved only if Edwud himself moved. If he remained completely still, then everything returned to its rightful place. His mind functioned perfectly. He couldn't stop it from thinking that not moving was attractive precisely because everything stayed exactly in the same place. In the distance he could hear Wulfe calling out. He attempted another climb but ended on his back. He shouted Wulfe's name a few times

232

and then settled back to wait for the world, which swung like a looping pendulum around his head, to become still.

"Edwud?" Wulfe called. "Are you all right?"

"I don't know," Edwud answered, as Wulfe and Lolli climbed down to him. He saw how they stared at him strangely and looked at each other.

"Your antennae," Wulfe said, glancing at Lolli.

"They're . . . sort of . . . ," Lolli attempted.

"Damaged," said Wulfe. Edwud tried to focus on his antennae and realized with a shock what his problem was: both antennae were bent about halfway down, so that they crossed over in front of him like two large pincers. Edwud remembered the exact moment it had happened—as the water flung him into the sand.

"Can you straighten them?" Wulfe asked. Edwud tried unsuccessfully to remove the kinks. Lolli and Wulfe held one end and forced it to straighten, but as soon as they let go, it swung back into its deformed shape.

"The others?" Edwud asked. "Where are they?"

"Jinni, Filip and Kerryd are missing—Nik and Sister Three are looking for them," Wulfe said. Edwud stood and noticed that the world wasn't spinning as much as before.

"If one of you gets on either side of me, I think I can make it out of this hole," Edwud said.

Nik had found Kerryd on top of a dry rock. She was humming softly to herself and watching the waves tumble in the distance. The legs on her left side had been injured and she could walk only by leaning one side across Nik's back. Getting her off the rock was difficult. Sister Three decided that they could do it with Kerryd placing one side on Nik and one side on herself. As they made it safely to the sand, Nik was so pleased with the fact that Sister Three was helping that he stood and stared at her, smiling so much that Kerryd said he looked the handsomest she had ever seen him.

As daylight approached, they met near the wall and found a safe hyde under a pile of dry stones rolled and polished by the sea long ago. Only slightly giddy when he moved his head quickly, Edwud continued to look for Jinni and Filip. Wulfe headed in the opposite direction, and Edwud held back from remarking that Wulfe wasn't as used to the light as he was and would find it difficult. The look on Wulfe's face told him that he wouldn't listen.

Edwud determined that it wasn't much use calling out, as the noise from the waves as they toppled and smashed into the sand swallowed his voice within a few leggs. Underneath his concern for Jinni and Filip was a growing anger that here, once again, the Lord Maker had attracted him to a dazzling promise—the fresh, salty smell and sound of the water—only to reveal its darker side as he drew near. Perhaps that was what Wulfe did to protect himself: looked for the dark side, the mean side of things, first so that he seldom had to be disappointed. Edwud felt tired in a different way than ever before as he watched the light transform the shadows. He wondered whether it was the mean or the generous side of the night.

Some distance away, on top of a large rock that had a flattened surface with dozens of tiny channels running crisscross, Edwud saw Jinni. He had never before seen her so still, with wings outspread as if she might lift from the rock at any moment. Edwud called out but his voice sank in the air like water on sand. The sky was lifting and tossing bunches of birds that screamed at each other as they gripped and slid along the strengthening breezes in search of food. As he climbed toward Jinni, Edwud was relieved that the birds appeared to be moving farther out to sea.

At the top of the rock Edwud saw that Jinni was leaning over something, that her wings were spread over some object. He couldn't see what it was because Jinni, in a hunched position, completely sealed it from the light. Edwud moved closer slowly, remembering the two sides of everything. Pleased he had found Jinni, he moved quietly to face her, wondering if she would be shocked by his bent antennae. Jinni didn't move. Edwud waited. The salt water had dried on Jinni's wings in small white clumps. Edwud brushed at them with his front legs. Jinni did not respond. She appeared to be part of the rock. Edwud stroked her face with his crooked right antenna.

"Jinni?" he said softly. Edwud could still see in her face the boldness of the nimf who, all by herself, followed after them in the drains. He could see much more now: the questioning that turned boldness to wisdom, and the generous courage that caused the heart to love. Gently he raised the edge of her forewing to see what it was she protected, and as the first light streaked across the water, the Lord Maker revealed another dark side.

37

ilip had been under Jinni's wings for some time. Together with her he had been washed from the rock, through the weeds, and rolled over the sand. The air was squeezed from him and water breathed in. As the wave receded, Jinni had clung to him and dragged him up onto the top of the flat rock. He had asked her to hold him up off the ground, but she didn't have the strength. She said that she wouldn't leave him.

"What a wonderful time I have had, Jinni B," Filip had said. "I felt so many things . . . tasted so many . . . fought so many things . . . learned so . . . little." Filip had coughed and laughed weakly. "I never did seem to . . . to . . . understand much. I had such a wonderful time. Do you think I have . . . a . . . an . . . otherself? Ha ha . . . it must be very small . . . if I do . . . I never gave it much . . . of . . . a . . . a . . . chance. What a wonderful life." And Filip had died.

Edwud led Jinni down from the rock. She said nothing, and Edwud remained silent. There was too much and too little to say. From the sand they could see Filip's body pointing out toward the sea, as if he could see something in the faraway moment where, in a line of endless balance, the sky and the water pressed against each other.

As they headed back toward the others, Edwud knew that something inside him had changed: he wanted to go home. Home was the yard, regardless of all its shortcomings, failures and hypocrisy. He felt, for the first time, the certainty of his own death, which connected him to Filip and Nolan in a new way. More than weariness, the feeling was one of being—out of balance. A balance that he knew intuitively could only come from completion.

Before reaching the wall, Edwud stopped walking and placed his broken antennae around Jinni. It was the final time they would be able to see Filip outlined on the rock. To his surprise, Jinni was smiling.

There was nothing helpful to say to her; like the moon striving for roundness each night, she too had to find her own balance and completion.

*N*ot one objection was raised when Edwud told them he wanted to return to the yard. Nor was there any surprise when he told them they had been on such a course for some time. The announcement to the others of Filip's death brought silence rather than surprise, except from Wulfe, who insisted on being taken to where Filip remained on the rock, and then asked to be left alone there for a while. Edwud was beginning to understand how each collector's "balance and completion" was as different from every other's in the way that the same parts of a face came together to create each different face.

39

The Gerscapheos occupying the shed in the yard were increasing in number. Sneeringly called "scaphs" or "shed lovers" by the yard collectors, they would, from time to time, cross The Strip in search of food, and a fierce battle would ensue. Wings would be torn out, legs broken and bitten off, and terrible facial and bodily injuries inflicted on both sides. Many seriously damaged collectors were carried back to their hydes to die slowly and painfully, and others were left where they fell until the ants came to carry them off in pieces.

Once, in the later days of the conflict, the yard collectors discovered outside the Kitchen door a large piece of bait used within the plastic cave traps. They carefully dragged it near to The Strip and left it for the Gerscapheos, who took it inside the shed at the first opportunity. The number of dead scaphs that resulted from this was never clear to the yard collectors, but body parts were carried out by the ants for many days afterward, and it was considered a victory of superior cleverness.

The water in the Great Sink had changed from the early days when it was clear and had its own peculiar clean smell. It had turned dark green, with a sour odor bubbling through a thick, furry layer that sat on the surface choking the air and light out of it. For some time the Longleys had not been seen in the yard. The lawn was strangled by weeds, and many of the sweet-smelling bushes and shrubs had died as the days and nights became hotter.

All committees and positions except for those of the Director and the Law Stewards had been dissolved. Worik T was named Soldier-in-Chief and used the Law Stewards to command groups of collectors, known as clusters. The Director came out of her hyde only for ceremonial occasions or to show that she was still alive. She was usually informed of decisions long after they had been carried out. It was rumored that her patrimate was living in another hyde with a younger collector, a situation which once would have caused so much gossip and turmoil in the yard that such a thing would not have been permitted to happen. Since the war, nothing seemed to matter other than killing another Gerscapheo, finding a chump that wasn't damaged by the sun, and staying alive.

There were no songs in the yard anymore; no laughter and no satisfying talk between friends. There were no friends in the true sense, for when food was shared with another, it was called a "gathering gift." Such a gift had to be returned, but not in the original size; it was a law now that the original gift would gather in size for every night that it had not been repaid. Those not able to repay were placed on the first line facing The Strip. Some wealthy crests lived entirely off gathering gifts.

When the Reverend Viel lost his prestigious hyde in the

shed to the Gerscapheos, he became an unwanted liability to his former friends, and one by one they deserted him. At the point of desperation he was forced to accept as inheritor the circle of a collector killed in a Gerscapheo raid. To his horror, it was a circle that he himself had allocated so long ago: the circle of Edwud K.

Sera laughed when she realized the irony of the inheritance, and insisted on cleaning and using Edwud's old hyde. The Reverend refused to join her there and lived at the far end of Edwud's old circle, where he could still command a large number of bitter collectors who found that shouting out their hatred and blaming the Gerscapheos drowned out the inner voices whispering to them of their own responsibility.

Without giving any reasons, Sera refused to fight. Normally such a stance would bring the wrath of Worik, and the fight-refuser would be forced to face the next attack at the front of The Strip, but Worik never moved against Sera, and no one ever reminded him that he hadn't.

Sera was left alone to spend her time collecting and thinking. She wondered about life in the yard as it was now: was it worth collecting and eating, collecting and eating— as an end in itself? Collect, eat, and die. Without their otherselves, there was no love, only fear, and there was no point to any of it. And Sera was beginning to realize that they had lost their otherselves as surely as they had lost Edwud and his loyal friends.

40

ithout Filip to slow them down, the group moved at a faster pace. After thirty nights of silence, Jinni finally spoke. She told them that Filip's death had been that of a soldier; that he had had a wonderful life. And then she cried without making even the smallest noise. The group crowded around, offering silent comfort as Kerryd sang softly an old nimf song about the power of standing close. Even Sister Three joined in without once glancing upward. Later she told Edwud that when they stood so close together, when their antennae were touching, it was as if the pain ran like drops of liquid between them, sharing itself out so that no one collector absorbed enough to drown.

The faster walking pace, Edwud believed, also came from the thought of arriving back at the yard sooner. Each night someone would mention something they remembered about the yard: an old friend, the scented wisteria and jasmine, even the tiresome meetings. Stronger than anything else was the difficult-to-describe feeling of belonging to a place—of coming home.

With the yard on their minds, the group of collectors was surprised late one night to come across the largest mix of smells they had ever encountered. There were different kinds of smoke fumes, rotting-food smells, any number of chemical scents and rusting-metal odors.

"I don't think we should go toward whatever it is," Nik said.

"It's coming from such a wide area—it will take ten or more nights if we go around," Edwud told them.

"I don't detect any chlordane," Wulfe said.

"There are more things to worry about than chlordane," Nik challenged.

"We'll take a vote," Edwud announced. The others looked at him with surprise. "I believe we should at least get close enough to see what it is," he said.

"And I think we should go around. Remember what happened back at the ocean—we followed our antennae then," Nik said in a warning tone.

Jinni, Wulfe and Kerryd moved immediately closer to Edwud. Sister Three moved to Nik, while Lolli hesitated between the two.

"It doesn't matter which way you vote," Wulfe told her.

"What?" Lolli said. "Why doesn't my vote matter? Why are you saying that to me? You can't say that . . . that . . . my vote doesn't matter. . . . My vote matters as much as anyone's. . . . Why are you looking at me . . . like that . . . ?" Lolli swung from one group to the other. Kerryd raised her antennae to comfort her.

"He's not saying your vote is worth any less than anyone else's," Kerryd attempted to explain.

"Yes he is . . . ," Lolli continued.

"There are three of us voting with Edwud, and only two with Nik . . . your vote doesn't . . . ," Wulfe tried to explain again.

"Count . . . I know . . . I heard . . ." Lolli's voice trailed off. The situation suddenly became clear to her. She dropped her eyes to the ground in embarrassment. The others wanted to minimize her suffering but they could find no way.

Edwud walked off toward the source of the mixed odors and the others followed. He tried to understand why Lolli immediately assumed that *her* vote would be considered not to matter. The same information presented to Jinni or Wulfe or Kerryd would not have brought such a response. What did Lolli do with information that came to her? Why did she change it to infer something about herself was inadequate, as if she was waiting all along for some kind of confirmation? Confirmation of what she had already decided about herself? He knew that from now on, the others would carefully avoid causing pain to Lolli, as if she had an injured leg that they would nurse, and shield from bearing weight, until one day the leg would fail to support her at all.

As they climbed the last hill, the source of the rotting odors became visible. Originally placed into a gigantic hole cut into the ground, the pile of throwaways soared upward, creating a mountain that stretched for thousands of leggs in every direction. There was rubbish of every kind: road machines, house objects, dead garden shrubs and bushes, spoiled food, bottles, packets and papers, and unknown lumps and pieces of every color and scent. The collectors marveled at the size of the monstrous heap, which smoked and rattled in various parts as if not quite dead.

As they moved closer, the heap blotted out more of the night sky with every step. There were signs and scents of collectors around the edges of the great pile, but the group ignored them until they noticed a broad-backed collector struggling in front of them, half dragging, half carrying a colorful object. The broad collector stopped when he sensed the strange group watching. He dropped the object he was carrying and stared to see if the strangers were about to attack him. None of them moved. Edwud lowered his bent antennae in a friendly gesture and then noticed that the collector had no wings, only an enlarged plate that stretched farther down his body than a yard collector's.

"Ho," Edwud called. The heap collector ignored the greeting, grasped his colored object, and continued dragging it away.

"That wasn't food he was carrying, was it?" Wulfe asked Edwud. Edwud shook his head. "Did you see, he had no wings?" Wulfe said, as he turned to the others to see their reactions.

As they continued farther into the great heap, someone or other would call out or point with his or her antennae toward an object of particular interest. From time to time there was a strong smell of cat and other animals that kept them alert and cautious. The pathway became thicker with throwaways, and progress was slower and more demanding. Edwud decided to skirt the heap rather than climb through its middle, and the others readily agreed. When he found a narrow gap between a thick pile of tins and bottles, Edwud waved the group to follow him.

The gap led to a wider cave, which all of them knew, from the moment they entered, had the scent of collector about it. It was a beautiful hyde that opened up enough to safekeep fifty collectors. Overhead, a number of bottles crisscrossed each other to form a strong roof that allowed enough moonlight in for them to be able to see comfortably. Around the walls and floor was an amazing assemblage of items that glittered, shone, and colored the hyde. Pieces of green and amber glass, chips of hardened and painted clay, plastic circles with holes, silver paper, copper threads and multicolored cloths.

The group had never seen anything like it. This was so different from any hyde they had ever known that they were in awe and spoke in hushed tones out of respect. They moved slowly around the hyde, touching objects gently as they went, and calling each other to come see what they had just discovered. The objects had been placed in some sort of pattern, Edwud decided, that showed them off to their best advantage. Such a collection as this was a lifetime's careful work. In the most barren and neglected-looking corner, Edwud came across the hyde's owner.

After the initial shock of seeing a large, broad-backed collector facing him in the semidark, Edwud recovered enough to see that he was dead, and had been for a very long time. The others gathered around to see what sort of collector would have spent his life accumulating such a hoard. When Edwud touched him, the outer layer of the heap collector crumbled to dust, revealing a hollowness throughout his whole body. Edwud stared at the dead collector, noting how helpful such a broad back would have been in carrying the objects to his hyde.

Leaning closer, he thought he could see tiny protrusions behind his plate. Edwud resisted touching the tiny lumps for fear that they too would collapse inward. They looked as though they could have been the beginnings of forewings or hind wings that never actually matured. Edwud felt an immense sorrow for the long-dead collector, who had clearly spent so much of his life carrying shiny things across his back that he failed to develop wings for his otherself, after death, to fly to Ootheca.

It took seven nights of difficult climbing and walking for the group to reach the other side of the great heap. As they traveled they passed many wingless collectors carrying precious objects toward their hydes. On seeing the yard collectors, the hoarders would stop to see if they were about to be attacked, and as soon as they felt secure, they continued on their way without any attempt at communicating with the group of strangers.

Once, on a cleared stretch of ground, two heap collectors were viciously fighting over a large piece of gold foil paper that still smelled strongly of tobacco. They stopped as Edwud appeared, but neither of them would let go of the gold foil. Edwud spoke to them but received no reply. He stepped closer and they both reared up with their plates tilted toward him. Edwud stopped, indicated he meant no harm, and saw that even under threat neither one of them had let go of the foil.

Moving away from the giant smoldering heap, they all

fell into the rhythm of Kerryd's new song, joining her
loudly and joyfully on the chorus that went:

> *"Tokens and takings and*
> *specklings to guard.*
> *Chippers and wrapplings and*
> *slithers and shards.*
> *Watching the others and*
> *playing a part—*
> *can't fill the hollow that*
> *empties the heart."*

47

The thought of getting closer to the yard encouraged them to walk longer each night. Kerryd's legs had returned to normal and Edwud had adjusted to his bent antennae. They passed through stretches of hard tarred surfaces and large gardens, and in the most dangerous street areas they traveled through the storm-water channels and the drains. Jinni walked with Edwud as often as she could, and Edwud was pleased to see her reach boldly for the truth again rather than mourn silently inward.

"What will you do when you get back to the yard?" she asked Edwud as they walked.

"For ten nights I'm not going to walk or make a single decision," Edwud replied, laughing to himself.

"I'm going to collect for crests until I get my father's circle back," Jinni said, staring ahead resolutely.

"Good for you," Edwud said. He envied her clarity of purpose, for he truly had no idea what he would do when he returned. He had no circle—and certainly no influence, having angered just about everyone in the colony before he left. He knew he was building a false idea of the yard in his mind, but he didn't care: there was nowhere else he wanted to be.

"Will you . . . still want . . . Sera T?" Jinni asked as casually as she could.

"She would have become the Reverend Viel's matrimate . . . long ago," Edwud said.

"Would she?" Jinni said, not having thought of such a possibility. "I don't like him."

"Neither do I," Edwud said, laughing. "But we don't have to."

"He only ever thinks other collectors' thoughts."

"Sensible thing to do—let someone else try them out first," Edwud joked.

"I'm going to find a patrimate," she said.

"You won't have to look far," Edwud said. Jinni concealed her delight with the compliment behind a smile. Edwud glanced behind them at Wulfe, and Jinni realized with dismay that Edwud meant *Wulfe,* and not himself, as the potential patrimate.

"There was a Law Steward who was very . . . interested in me," Jinni said. "After my father . . ." Edwud was surprised, remembering that she had been so young when she left the yard. Jinni watched Edwud closely. "His name was Worik T," Jinni said casually. Edwud stopped walking so suddenly that Jinni bumped into him. Obviously, Edwud thought, she didn't know who it was that had removed her father's head at the Remedial Court. Pleased by Edwud's reaction to her lie about Worik T, Jinni dropped back in the line to walk with Kerryd, leaving Edwud confused about what it was he did feel.

Later, Wulfe joined Edwud at the front of the line. Glancing back at Jinni from time to time, he told Edwud that when they reached the yard, he would want her to be his matrimate. Edwud wondered whether he should tell Wulfe about Jinni's own plans, and her mention of Worik T. If he told him, then Wulfe might give up trying to attract Jinni, or perhaps he would confront her about Worik. Edwud decided that sometimes it was easier to act when there were whole areas of ignorance. He remembered how easy it was for him, when he was a young nimf, to take action: like his freedom in the garden before he found out about the cat; like his belief that collectors need only hear about unfair balances to redress them; like his assumption that everything and everyone dear to him would always be there. Knowing things was another of the Lord Maker's double-sided gifts: on one side, the wisdom giving courage to act; on the other, the knowledge giving fear of its consequences.

The smell of the yard was growing stronger night by night, as each of them recalled more and more incidents from their earlier times: always happy moments, often from nimfhood. Even Sister Three got caught up in the excitement. They talked more openly and honestly with each other than ever before. Something had happened to them, Edwud thought, that had changed them from the collectors that had climbed down into the drains so long ago. He wasn't sure what it was, for in many ways they were also much the same. Perhaps it was how they dealt with each other now. There was less fear that another would do or say something hurtful or damaging to them. Edwud thought about it for a long time. They had once been afraid of what another collector would do or say, *before* he had said or done it. Which meant that what they feared must have been carried around inside them: the fear of others was, in fact, a fear of what they themselves were capable of. Edwud's first glimpse of the fence surrounding the yard came as he realized with a shock that what collectors were afraid of was *themselves*.

42

Memory's prisoners,
reluctant convicteds,
trammeled and hobbled
to otherpast crime,
uncloistered, released
through light-hungry
doorways;
remanded reminders
of time.

DANCING SONG OF VERY OLD COLLECTORS

*A*s the group came nearer to the yard fence, they broke into a run. The thrill of coming home swirled through their bodies in a joyous, nimf-like dance. They laughed as they raced past each other, calling and teasing the stragglers to keep up. And then they were through the fence where the yard that had been building in their minds met the yard that was real.

Bunched together, panting and gasping, they saw what the yard had become: the dead shrubs, the overgrown weeds, the green slime choking the water of the Great Sink, the sense of strange collectors and, worst of all, the smell of dead collectors. With legs suddenly leaden, as if in a nightmare, Edwud led them across the yard searching for a familiar face or feature. It was as if they walked through the dark side of their memory of the yard.

A young collector that none of them recognized accidentally came across the group. He gave a blood-tingling yell and disappeared immediately. The jasmine, the lemon tree and wisteria were all dead—they reached toward the night sky, forgotten skeletons of their former selves. The group stopped at the edge of the Great Sink. The green carpet of slime was so thick that it had collector prints trailing across it in all directions. None of them spoke. Perhaps they believed that if anyone said anything, it would make the scene before them real. Directly ahead of them they could sense that a number of collectors were gathering.

"Is this it—is this the yard?" Sister Three asked with obvious disappointment. No one answered. "You said it was beautiful—with scented flowers . . . and . . . sweet water . . . and fresh chumps . . . and everyone . . . so . . . so . . . friendly?"

There was nothing anyone could think of to say. Edwud noted that, out of sight, they were being slowly surrounded by collectors. He told the others to come closer together and form a circle, with each of them facing outward so that every direction was covered. With wings touching, they calmly lowered themselves to the ground and waited.

"Would you like me to sing something, Edwud?" Kerryd asked. Before he could answer, the collectors surrounding them began to move closer. At first Edwud could recognize none of them, and then familiar faces began to emerge. They had changed so much that Edwud was shocked—more than the folds and leaching of time, his old colony's collectors had eyes that had lost their depth, and mouths that turned down in bitterness.

There was little doubt they were about to attack him and his group of weary travelers.

"Ho!" Edwud cried out. The advancing collectors stopped suddenly. "I'm Edwud K," he said. "I belong here. I . . . I . . . lived here . . . we all did. Some time ago."

"Edwud?" A voice from the rear of the encircling collectors was familiar to Edwud. Worik T stepped forward. "It *is* you. I can't believe it. What . . . what is wrong with your antennae?"

Edwud had forgotten the new pincerlike look of his antennae. "We came back" was the only thing Edwud could think of to say.

"I can see that," Worik said. Turning to those around him, he issued several orders and the collectors disappeared into the night. Edwud heard "The Strip" mentioned several times.

"What has happened here?" he asked Worik. "What is The Strip?"

Worik shook his head. "Ah, so much . . . so much, Edwud . . . . Things are not how they used to be." Worik sighed.

"I'd like to see the Director," Edwud asked firmly.

"I don't think that's a good idea," Worik answered sadly.

As the night slowly faded, the group of travelers listened to Worik tell how the yard had changed, almost exactly after Edwud and the others left; how the Director refused to come out of her hyde; how lawlessness forced him to take strong punitive measures; and finally how the Gerscapheos came and took control of the shed.

Worik arranged for the group to take over the circle of a collector recently killed on The Strip. They asked for no food, and none was given. They went to see The Strip, and Edwud, sensing the death, injury and pain in every legg of

255

the battleground, felt so exhausted he retired to his circle, but not before he went past his old hyde under the now-dead lemon tree. He knew instantly the strong scent of Sera T, and behind it, much lighter, the unmistakable odor of the Reverend Viel. Edwud remained outside his old hyde, and for a while, with his eyes closed, he defied the new reality and enjoyed the past.

The group found separate hydes in various locations within their new circle. Edwud located a spiraling Gerscapheo burrow that fascinated him enough to claim it as his new hyde. He intended to clean out the loose dirt that still lay on the bottom of the burrow at a later date. The burrow was much cooler than most locations on the surface of the ground, and Edwud suspected that perhaps the Gerscapheos had some interesting things to teach the yard collectors.

Edwud was visited on his third night back at the yard by a Law Steward called Cevon, who was in charge of a group of circles called a cluster. As cluster leader, Cevon had to ensure that collectors from his group of circles appeared at The Strip for their three nights of fight duty. Cevon was anxious about approaching Edwud, as he had heard many of the rumors about Edwud's strangeness, but Worik had ordered him not to make an exception of Edwud and the returned group.

"We don't expect an attack," Cevon told Edwud reassuringly. Edwud said nothing. "We can usually tell when they're getting ready for a raid . . . when their food stocks are getting low. . . . They're not such good fighters . . . as they look, you know . . . they're not as quick as we are . . . and we have found a way of . . . getting behind them . . . and taking off one of their back legs . . . and . . ." The Law Steward fell silent for a moment, confused by Edwud's silence. "We tried to . . . to . . . negotiate . . . a way without . . . fighting, but if we gave them the shed, how would we ever know that they wouldn't want more? They're not like us . . . they're not reasonable . . . or . . . or fair."

"I'm not going to fight," Edwud said.

Edwud's comment failed to register with the Law Steward. "Your group will be a big boost for our cluster," he said.

"I won't fight," Edwud said again. This time the message got through.

"But you have to fight . . . we all do . . . it's the law . . . we all have to fight," he said.

Edwud called the group together and told them of the new fight laws and how they were required to fulfill their duty on The Strip. Wulfe and Jinni shook their heads in disbelief. Kerryd began humming to herself, while Nik, Sister Three, and Lolli weren't sure what they thought.

"I've heard what they do," Jinni told them. "They line up along The Strip facing the shed and call out to the Gerscapheos, who line up under the shed door, and then someone from one side rushes forward, and the others immediately follow, yelling and screaming."

"It's what we did as nimfs. you remember, Edwud . . . that game we called 'touch plates'?" Wulfe asked. "Only we didn't leave wings and legs behind us."

"I suppose we will have to do it," Nik said. "Fight-refusers lose their circles, I'm told." Sister Three looked upward to the sky and began mumbling to herself for the first time in many nights. The sight saddened Edwud.

"We've lost our circles before," Jinni said.

"I'm not going back . . . back to that," Nik snapped.

"What are you going to do, Edwud?" Wulfe asked.

"I'm not going to fight," Edwud said. The others looked at the ground, not sure how to respond.

"Well, I'm not going to fight either," Jinni said.

"And neither shall I," Wulfe said firmly.

"They force fight-refusers up to the front of The Strip anyway," Nik said desperately.

"I couldn't . . . do anything to injure another collector," Kerryd said. "I wouldn't be able to sing again." Edwud knew it was true that Kerryd's music came from wanting to add beauty to the lives of others, not damage.

"Perhaps if we all turned up at The Strip for our duty . . . but we kept the . . . the . . . idea . . . er . . . the decision not to fight . . . er . . . to ourselves . . . ?" Lolli suggested.

Edwud thought it wasn't the best solution, but it might give them some time to think more deeply about the question—so long as they didn't suffer a Gerscapheo attack while at The Strip. "What a very good idea, Lolli," Edwud said. Lolli beamed with pleasure. The others agreed, although Edwud could see that Jinni and Wulfe recognized the danger in the plan.

Edwud had avoided meeting Sera since his return. He had heard that although she had not ever appeared for fight duty, she had never lost her circle, nor had she been dragged to the front row of The Strip. He now needed to know why. As he approached his old hyde, a confusing mix of emotions flooded through him. He knew that the Reverend Viel no longer shared the hyde with Sera, and regardless of how he tried to deny it, a rising expectation of the meeting forced him to face again how powerfully he had fallen-in-fantasy with her long ago.

The sight of Sera outside his old hyde struck Edwud almost as violently as the ocean wave on the sand. She had changed hardly at all in appearance, and Edwud was immediately forced to swim among competing emotions. For several moments neither one of them spoke.

"Your antennae—what happened?" Sera asked finally.

"What? Oh, an accident . . . ," Edwud mumbled.

"You look different," Sera said.

"Do I?"

"Yes."

"You look almost exactly the same."

"Do I?" Sera laughed at their stilted conversation, and Edwud joined in. "What was it like—your journey?" she asked.

Edwud sighed and wondered whether he could convey it—whether, in fact, he knew himself what it was like, what it meant to him and the others, and how they had changed. He wanted to tell her; he wanted to make sense of it, to give it a shape, a color, something that could be held outside himself, that could be passed around to others, so that they could immediately understand. She listened as Edwud turned his journey into words.

For most of the night Sera and Edwud talked. She told

him that the Reverend Viel had been swallowed by hate long before the invasion of the Gerscapheos. He rarely came to see her of late, preferring to meet nightly with Worik and the Law Stewards as they considered ways of destroying the invaders.

"I would return your circle to you," Sera said. "But they won't allow it."

"I'm very comfortable—our foreign friends have something to teach us about making cool hydes."

Edwud asked about the Director and was told that she had not been seen for so long that many nimfs had ceased believing she existed.

"I have to see her, soon," Edwud said. "To tell her I've failed."

Edwud felt that Sera misunderstood; that she thought he meant the journey itself. Perhaps he couldn't explain; perhaps she couldn't understand. Suddenly he had only light, superficial things to say to Sera, and he had no interest in saying any of them. They faced each other in silence.

"Edwud," Sera said softly.

"Yes."

"I wish I had gone with you." Edwud wasn't sure how he felt at that moment. He had learned along the journey that the decisions one makes—the actions one takes or doesn't take—describe each collector more clearly than any words. "Did you know you called me by another name tonight?" Sera said.

"Another name? Did I? What other name?" Edwud asked, genuinely puzzled.

"Jinni," Sera said.

43

 dwud realized, after he left Sera, that he never did find out why she had survived as a fight-refuser. At the bottom of his burrow, he began enjoying the physical challenge of cleaning the loose dirt away. He would have enjoyed learning from the Gerscapheos how they did it. There was no doubt they had a more efficient method than Edwud was employing. Digging was the easy part; getting rid of the dirt was something else. By jamming moist lumps between his palps and plate, Edwud could climb out of the hole carrying a reasonable amount.

For a while he could escape the misery that had become part of the yard colony life. He noticed now that when he thought of the long journey he had taken with his friends, it seemed more and more attractive. Edwud laughed at the dishonesty of memory. He thought how Nolan would have reminded him of all the bad moments they had experienced—and how Filip would have hated being a fight-refuser.

As Edwud scraped up the last of the loose dirt, his foot struck something hard.

"Dung!" he called out. It was too dark to see what it was, and as it was embedded deep in the soil, Edwud assumed it was a stone. He touched it again and felt the smooth hardness of metal. He stopped to consider whether he should cover it up or try to dig it out. He scraped around the object with his front feet. Surprisingly it was quite thin. Edwud continued digging on each side, throwing the dirt away from himself and into a pile on the other side of the burrow. The sides were made of glass, he discovered as he felt his way deeper down the object. The metal was thin and ran along the outside of the glass in a beautifully rounded curve. Edwud increased his digging rate, hurling the dirt so quickly that before long he had to climb out of the burrow for fresh air to breathe. He was tired but so excited that he paced around outside, impatient for the dust to settle.

Back in the hole he began digging at a more even pace, stopping regularly to carry out dirt and breathe clean air. He worked on into the night, with his legs and body aching with pain and his feet bleeding from the continual scraping.

The night finished and light began seeping into the burrow. Edwud worked on into the day, with the heat and light making the work more difficult and more dangerous. By the evening, the work was finished.

The object was revealed. It was round—round as the moon—and only slightly larger across than the length of his own body. He could see through it, and everything on one side was larger, but from the other side everything became smaller. Edwud knew he had found the Monoocal. It had never left the yard; it had been here all the time.

With the help of his friends Edwud dug out the

entrance to the burrow to be large enough for the Monoocal to fit through. They lifted and pulled at it, enjoying the feeling of working and being together again with a purpose. When it lay on the ground in the moonlight, the group gathered around its glassy roundness and stared with genuine awe. Carefully they lifted it onto its metal edge and rolled it like a wheel until they could lean it almost upright against the trunk of the lemon tree.

For the rest of the night the group moved from one side of the Monoocal to the other, gasping in amazement at how when they looked through its glass, the collectors on the other side were either smaller or larger. When they stared directly at the surface, Edwud pointed out, they could see, very faintly, their otherselves.

Shaking with excitement, Edwud left the Monoocal with his friends and ran to the Director's hyde under the house. Her patrimate no longer lived with her, Edwud knew, so he called out to her. There was no answer, and Edwud had too much respect for the Director to enter her hyde without welcome. He returned to his friends, who were beginning to depart as daylight warnings issued from the sky. Only Wulfe and Jinni remained behind, as fascinated with the Monoocal as Edwud was. They brushed dirt, which had caught in tiny scratches across the surface, from the glass and polished the Monoocal with their wings and tongues until it shone brilliantly.

"Do you really think it's the Monoocal?" Jinni asked.

"Yes, yes, I'm sure it is." Edwud paced around the glass, admiring it from every angle.

"You said you saw the Monoocal before . . . when you

saw yourself on the white square," Wulfe reminded him.

"Yes, I know . . . I don't understand it. . . . Perhaps the other wasn't the Monoocal; perhaps there are lots of them," Edwud said, looking at how large Wulfe became on the other side of the glass. The light was increasing rapidly, and Edwud enjoyed how he could see the Monoocal more clearly as each moment passed. Jinni and Wulfe were becoming anxious, he noticed, as they repeatedly glanced about as if something might emerge from the light itself.

"I think you should both go. I'm going to stay a little longer," Edwud said.

"What are you going to do with it?" Jinni asked.

"I'm going to return it to where it rightfully belongs . . . with the Director."

"You'll need help," Wulfe said.

"Tonight, come back tonight . . . and we'll all roll it together," Edwud said joyfully.

Wulfe and Jinni left together, both turning occasionally to look back at Edwud and the Monoocal.

The sun had risen to be free of the ground, echoing the roundness of the Monoocal. Like father and nimf, Edwud thought, as he watched a brightening world through the glass. Although his fear of the light had never been conquered completely, he had come to understand during the journey that it was not a product of the viciousness of light itself, but something he created himself and attached to light through ignorance of it: being afraid to understand, Edwud had learned, was what had kept his fear alive.

As he sat, Edwud began to feel a rapid rise in temperature. He moved from behind the glass and immediately noticed that it was cooler. He tested the heat again by moving behind the Monoocal. It was true. The Monoocal was strengthening the light and heat from the sun, just as it made everything larger on one side. Edwud watched in fascination as the Monoocal released a narrow shaft of light, which met at a point about thirty leggs away. Like the white square, Edwud thought, only this one was much smaller and round; the white square that could have been the window into an otherworld for the humans.

As he watched, the light point slowly moved to center on an old leaf fallen from the dead lemon tree. A trail of bluish smoke rose from the exact point of contact. Edwud leapt to his feet. What was happening? He couldn't understand what was happening. The smoke turned white and increased to form a spiral upward.

Edwud moved closer. The leaf, he could see quite clearly, had a perfectly round hole eaten into it; and then without warning, as he watched, the leaf burst into flames. Edwud opened his wings in shock, fanning the flames, which consumed the old leaf. The flames flickered out as quickly as they had arrived, leaving Edwud's mind spinning in confusion. He had seen fire before, but never where it had come from—never had he seen the maker of fire.

The point of light had moved slightly from the ashes of the leaf to the ground closer to the Monoocal. Edwud wondered whether the ground itself could catch fire. A part of him wanted to wait and watch and to know the answer; another part quickly thought through the possible consequences.

He leapt at the Monoocal, reaching as high up its glass

face as he could, and pushed, so that it fell from its upright position to fall flat against the earth. Edwud dragged several fallen leaves to cover the Monoocal and headed off for the Director's hyde.

This time he called out from the entrance, waited a few moments, and then entered. At the bottom of her hyde the Director was curled in sleep. Edwud was shocked at how much she had aged. Her dark color appeared to have been drained, and her once-trim body had become thick and flabby. As she woke and looked at him, with lines of hopelessness streaking her face, Edwud tried to hide his thoughts. She stared at him for a long time before she spoke.

"Not . . . quite . . . the same, am I, Edwud?" she said.

"Er . . . Mem, I . . . have some wonderful news," Edwud said, too excited to be patient with his vast secret.

"You do? Good news? Are you sure, Edwud? This hyde hasn't heard any good news since . . . since . . ."

"Mem, I found it!" Edwud said, almost shouting.

"You found it? You found what, Edwud?"

"I found the Monoocal!"

"The Monoocal?" the Director said, as if she hadn't heard correctly.

"It was here all along—here in the yard. I dug it out . . . out of a Gerscapheo burrow, right here in the colony," Edwud cried triumphantly.

The Director stared at Edwud as if she couldn't quite focus on his face—as if the words didn't quite have a meaning that made sense.

"It's beautiful," Edwud continued. "And I found out something . . . something . . . special about it. . . . As the sun came up this morning, I found out . . ." Edwud paused for the Director to appreciate fully what he was about to say. "I found out that it can make fire."

The Director appeared to be unmoved, and Edwud was disappointed. Hadn't he brought the best news she could ever have expected? Hadn't he turned his failure into a victory? Why wasn't she responding how Edwud imagined she would?

"The Monoocal, you say, Edwud?" the Director asked calmly.

"Yes, Mem, it's round and you can see through it . . . and . . ."

"It's not the Monoocal, Edwud," the Director said.

"Oh, it is, Mem . . . er, Dell . . . I know it is . . ."

"It isn't the Monoocal, Edwud."

"My friends and I will roll it here for you tonight, so that you can . . ."

"It isn't the Monoocal, Edwud, because it can't be." The Director sighed and shifted the weight on her legs.

"I could take you to see it," Edwud said eagerly.

"It can't be the Monoocal, for a very good reason," the Director said solemnly. Edwud could hardly believe how she was behaving.

"But, Mem, it's everything my father and mother told me it was."

"Edwud, there is no Monoocal." The words of the Director spun and echoed around Edwud's mind: "There is no Monoocal, there is no Monoocal."

"But I've . . ." Edwud couldn't finish his thought.

"There never has been a Monoocal. It was a . . . story . . . a . . . fantasy . . . made up . . . so long ago. . . . It was never real," the Director said.

"But I went looking . . . I've . . . My parents . . . I dreamed of it . . ."

"When the last Director was dying, she called me: it was how each Director was appointed—each one was 'given the knowledge.' As long as the colony believed there was a Monoocal . . . it would flourish." The Director looked at Edwud with great sympathy. "I'm sorry, Edwud," she said.

All of Edwud's disappointments, failures and pain seemed to distill into that moment. He had failed again. There was no Monoocal. He looked at the Director and asked quietly, "What is it that *I* have found?"

"I don't know, Edwud," she said sadly, gazing past him out beyond the entrance to her hyde. "But it seems that *I* have found something."

"Have you?" Edwud asked, trying to understand.

"It seems, without intention, I have made my selection," the Director said, smiling at Edwud.

44

dwud went from the Director's hyde straight to the drains. He could smell the soapsud fumes from a distance of a hundred leggs, as if they called him by name. Immediately on entering, he scooped up several mouthfuls of foam and sat back to wait for the effects of losing touch with himself and his failures.

The hollowness of the drains, which no longer held his fellow travelers, gave the suds a bitter taste. Edwud scooped up a large piece of foam and, before placing it into his mouth, looked at it: tiny bubbles, which even as he watched, burst and disappeared. Is this what he wanted? To disappear like the bubbles? Is this what the foam offered? To take away the pain, but also to take away what was Edwud along with it?

Edwud was so tired of pain and disappointment and loss: the loss of Nolan and Filip and Sera. The last bubbles of the soapsud foam burst and disappeared. Edwud looked at the space that once held them. The foam, just like pain, could be outlasted.

It was by pushing against obstacles that one developed strength. If he pushed and struggled against pain, rather than avoided it, then perhaps he would become stronger. Edwud scooped up another chunk of foam. Bringing it close to his face, he said good-bye to Lennod, flung the foam back into the passing swill, and walked out of the drains.

Word of Edwud's find spread through the colony quickly. The Director insisted that it wasn't the Monoocal, that she kept the real Monoocal hidden, as always, in the bottom of her hyde. Rumors persisted that Edwud and his friends had secretly brought the object back with them from some far, unknown place, and that it was probably the Monoocal of another colony, and perhaps it was more powerful than their own. Edwud strenuously denied the rumors, which seemed to many collectors in the yard to confirm their chosen belief: "He denies it too much," they said.

At first it became known as Edwud's Monoocal, and then, after a while, just the Monoocal. Edwud saw how the colony appeared much happier to believe in something they could see, something that could be controlled and that could be used, rather than the never-seen Director's Monoocal.

The Law Stewards and Worik convinced Edwud to show them how the Monoocal could make fire. With great difficulty, they remained outside in the early morning sun long enough for Edwud to set a leaf ablaze. They were amazed. Edwud noticed that the Reverend Viel stood at the back of the group, avoiding any contact with him, and he could not prevent himself from calling out loudly, "Perhaps the Reverend would like to step up to the front to see more clearly."

Reverend Viel glared angrily at Edwud and turned away violently from the group, raising a small puff of dust, as Edwud, watching him through the Monoocal, saw how he appeared to shrink with each step, until he was not much larger than the tiny pile of ash that was once the leaf.

At the end of his demonstration Edwud toppled the Monoocal and covered it with dead leaves, while the others hurried away to their hydes before the light increased.

The night before he was due to report for duty, Edwud visited The Strip. He walked behind the line of yard collectors facing the door of the shed. None of them turned away from their focus on the enemy as he passed. High up on the shed wall, through the one small window, Edwud saw a Gerscapheo watching him and the line of yard collectors below. Without thinking, Edwud gave a wave of his bent antennae. The foreign collector moved closer to the window, as if to see more clearly. Edwud looked to see if anyone was watching, and then gave another wave. The Gerscapheo did not respond but remained watching Edwud closely. Edwud could see that he was hardly much different in appearance from himself: shorter antennae, a larger mouth and a slightly lighter color were the main differences. Edwud raised his bent antennae to the enemy collector in one final, respectful salute and left The Strip as quickly as he had come.

When he arrived back at his hyde, Sera was waiting for him. He was surprised that she had entered his hyde without waiting for permission. Edwud felt the powerful wrench of attraction run through his body as soon as he detected her scent. Even as he struggled to organize his thinking, he wondered why he felt like this about her. She had betrayed his trust and refused to come with him, had chosen to become the Reverend Viel's matrimate; and despite all this, he wanted to join with her.

Sera made no apology for being in his hyde. She said nothing. Edwud thought about all the reasons why he should walk away from her—even as he moved closer. Why was she here now? he could hear Nolan ask inside his head. Had she been attracted by Edwud's recent rise in importance? Filip's old and deep voice insisted, "The heart and the head and the body, Edwud, are not always speaking in the same language."

Edwud raised his left antenna and stroked the full length of Sera's body. She quivered and moved closer to him. Edwud's heart was pounding so loudly, he could hear neither Nolan, Filip nor himself. Sera unfolded her delicate forewings, settling into the hollow in the floor that once held the form of the Monoocal. Above his hyde he could hear movement, but Edwud ignored it. He touched Sera's face with his right antenna.

"Edwud!" the voice above him called. For a moment Edwud thought it was Sera who had called his name. Sera folded her wings back in place and stood up, shaking her antennae to move Edwud backward and away from her.

"Edwud!" The call came again. This time Edwud recognized the voice: it was Jinni's. He picked up her scent, which was quickly beginning to fill the hyde, turned, and climbed out of the burrow.

"I'm sorry, Edwud . . . I know . . . Sera . . . is there with you, but something has happened," Jinni said.

On seeing Jinni, Edwud immediately remembered the rest of Filip's words: "The heart, the head and the body, all connected, Edwud—that's what we always want when we love. But do you know, Edwud, I think you can never have all three with any one person." Jinni had his head, Edwud thought, the part of him that thought clearly and best what was good, but Sera had his body, the powerful flush that carried his thinking away in pounding excitement. And his heart, Edwud wondered, who had that?

"The Monoocal is gone," Jinni said. "I just came past the lemon tree and the leaves have been moved—and the Monoocal is gone."

Edwud and his friends arrived late for duty at The Strip. Cevon, the cluster leader, was about to inform Worik that the group had become fight-refusers when they appeared. They took their places standing alongside each other in the line facing the shed.

"I thought you weren't going to come," Cevon said to Edwud nervously.

"We were looking for the Monoocal," Jinni said rudely. Cevon, grateful that they were all present, held back his annoyance with her insulting tone.

"You needn't have bothered looking at all," he said to Jinni, enjoying the fact that he knew something they didn't.

"What do you mean?" Edwud asked.

"I know where it is," Cevon said, smiling to impress the other collectors around him.

"Where is it?" Jinni demanded.

"You'll see, soon enough," he answered. He nodded and grinned to another Law Steward farther down the line and walked away.

As the night dark deepened, Edwud watched the shed underdoor area, praying that there wouldn't be an attack. He looked along the line of yard collectors and saw how they had hardened their faces by hiding fear and concentrating on a single-minded hatred of their enemy. Looking at the window high up on the shed, Edwud tried to see if the Gerscapheo he had seen the night before was there, but the window was empty.

Just before dawn, as the line of yard collectors was beginning to relax, a shout came from behind them. Edwud heard the voice of Worik and some others calling orders rapidly. As he looked into the graying light, he saw, rolling toward them, the Monoocal.

Edwud watched as the Monoocal was rolled slowly up to the line of collectors facing The Strip and was turned carefully so that its glassy face fronted the shed. Edwud was pleased to see the Monoocal again, and at the same time angry that Worik had obviously taken it without first asking him. A large number of yard collectors followed behind Worik, including the Reverend Viel. In teams of three and four they carried dried leaves and pieces of dead grass. They stopped at the line, and then, after an order from Worik, they crossed The Strip, placing their loads against the door of the shed.

"What are they doing?" Lolli asked.

Jinni looked at Edwud, who was staring fixedly at the Monoocal. "They're going to start a fire, aren't they, Edwud?" she said. Edwud broke away from the line and ran toward Worik. Several collectors in the line mumbled and pointed at Edwud with their antennae: no one had ever broken line before.

"You can't do it!" Edwud called out. Worik turned from waving forward the leaf carriers and spun around to face Edwud.

"Ah, Edwud . . . I'm sorry we didn't really have time to consult with you . . . ," Worik said. Edwud pointed at the leaves with his crooked antennae.

"You can't do this . . . the shed . . . you can't . . . it will . . . the flames will burn . . . ."

"Edwud, it was you who showed us the way," Worik said loudly enough so that most of the front line of collectors could hear. "You found the Monoocal, Edwud. . . . Without you, well, we . . ."

"The Monoocal is part of *my* collection . . . and I forbid it to be used for such a thing," Edwud shouted. Reverend Viel stepped between Worik and Edwud, smiling confidently.

"For the good of the colony, Edwud, the Law Stewards met and decided that the Monoocal, which you named yourself, is the property of the colony, regardless of who found it," the Reverend said.

"It will burn," Edwud said, turning rapidly from Worik to Viel. "The whole shed will burn . . . and the Gerscapheos will . . ."

"Burn along with it!" Worik cried out. The yard collectors gave a wild cheer. The Reverend Viel turned to face them.

"Burn the lot of them!" he shouted. "Burn them, burn them . . . burn!"

"Burn! Burn! Burn!" they all shouted. Edwud looked at his friends. Not one of them was cheering. They looked at Edwud with confusion and sadness. Edwud saw the Gerscapheo of the night before high up on the shed wall, at the window, watching them. In the distance the sun was beginning to rise. Worik continued to wave the leaf carriers forward.

"The Director," Edwud called out to him. "This is a decision for the Director."

Worik ignored him, and the Reverend Viel laughed out loud, moving closer to Edwud to whisper privately.

"You seem to have lost everything, Edwud," the Reverend said, sounding pleased with himself. Without thinking, Edwud struck out at Viel with his front legs and antennae, flipping him over onto his back. The yard collectors nearby stopped what they were doing and gasped in horror. The Reverend Viel scrambled to his feet again, flapping his hind wings as if he could cover his wounded pride. Several young collectors moved aggressively toward Edwud.

"No," the Reverend said to them. "Edwud is upset. I shall pray for him—he has lost . . . everything."

Edwud confronted Worik. "Please don't do this," he asked. Worik turned on him, angrily shaking his antennae.

"You never understand, do you?" he said accusingly. "I am doing this for peace . . . for the good of the colony. . . . Don't you see? It takes great strength to make such hard decisions. . . . If we give in to them . . ."

"What will happen if we give in to them?" Edwud asked.

"They're not like us . . . they wouldn't allow things in the colony to go on in the same way."

"How are things in the colony?" Edwud asked, sweeping his antennae around to take in the whole yard. "Is this how you want things to go on?"

"It was better before they came . . . everything was

better . . . you remember . . . ," Worik insisted.

"I remember that almost no one in the yard was truly happy, long before the Gerscapheos arrived. It was changing—before I left."

"Well, we are going to get it all back," Worik said firmly.

"Don't you see, you can't get it back . . . everything keeps changing . . . only dead things fail to change. . . . If you do this . . . the yard will be a dead thing."

"Then better a dead thing than led by Gerscapheos," Worik said finally, as he turned abruptly. "You don't have to watch—you don't have to help. Take your friends and go." Worik hurried away to supervise.

Edwud noticed for the first time that Jinni, Wulfe, Kerryd, Lolli, Nik and Sister Three were standing close behind him. The feeling of failure that had been with him for so long suddenly seemed to lift. He turned to them and said, "I'm going to warn them—in the shed, the Gerscapheos. I'm going to tell them they have to get out before the flames get too large."

The group looked at Edwud and at the collectors piling leaves against the door of the shed.

"I'm coming with you," Jinni said.

"I'm damned sure I'm not staying here to burn collectors," Wulfe said.

Kerryd, Lolli, Nik and Sister Three all nodded in agreement. "It wouldn't be right, your setting off anywhere without all of us," Kerryd said with a laugh. "We always journey together."

"We can't wait," Edwud said quickly. "The sun's coming." He looked at The Strip and back to his friends. "You know they will probably attack us as soon as we enter."

"Edwud, what if we did something, as soon as we enter the shed, to show them we don't want to fight?" Nik asked. "Like turning onto our backs."

Edwud thought about Nik's suggestion: it could send a message quickly to the Gerscapheos that they were not there to fight; it could also leave them very vulnerable to attack. In that position the thorax was completely exposed. But the Gerscapheos would only have a very short time to escape before the heat from the fire trapped them. There wasn't time to think of a better plan. "Nik, I think it's an excellent plan—we should try it," Edwud agreed. Nik beamed with pride and smiled at Sister Three.

"I don't mind going first," Nik suggested.

"We should all go together, in a line," Edwud said. "Perhaps the Gerscapheos will be so surprised by such a number that we'll have a chance to explain to them."

"Good idea," said Wulfe.

"We will have to get back into the front line, and when I give this signal . . ."—Edwud lifted his crossed antennae high above his head—"we'll run immediately across The Strip and under the door." Edwud stopped talking as a Law Steward moved closer, attempting to listen. Edwud signaled the others not to talk, as he led them back to the line.

Both Worik and Reverend Viel were pleased to see the group return, and they both saluted a welcome. Behind them the sun had almost cleared the earth, and Worik was directing the collectors holding the Monoocal to begin focusing the light onto the large pile of leaves stacked at the door. A slight breeze had come with the rising sun, lift-

278

ing small puffs of dust and shuffling the dead leaves. It carried no perfumes from flowers or shrubs, and Edwud remembered for a moment the yard of old with its rich fragrances. Edwud thought about attempting to knock the Monoocal to the ground, but there were far too many collectors supporting it and Worik. He felt the sun beginning to heat his back, and as he turned to check its progress, he saw and smelled the unmistakable presence of Sera.

The light from the Monoocal was narrowing to a pinpoint on the stack of leaves as Sera walked calmly and surely to where Edwud stood alongside his friends in the front line of The Strip.

"Sera!" Edwud said anxiously. "You shouldn't be here."

"Are you here to fight?" Sera asked.

Both Wulfe and Nik made their views known to Edwud: "Tell her to go," they both said. Edwud saw both Worik and the Reverend Viel register that Sera had for the first time come to The Strip, and that she spoke not to either of them, but to Edwud K. As Edwud looked at the two powerful collectors, he saw in their unguarded faces a mixture of resentment, jealousy and a strange kind of defeat.

"Go away, Sera, now!" Edwud said aggressively.

"I know what they're doing," Sera said with dismay. "I didn't think you would be here . . . helping them . . ."

Edwud's friends glanced nervously at Sera and at the sun rising behind them. The white-hot circle of light was forming on the leaves. Sister Three looked up at the sky, once only, and focused on the shed door. The others watched Edwud's antennae. Edwud turned his back on Sera. A thin film of blue smoke rose from the leaves.

Edwud braced himself as he felt his breathing increase and his heart pound heavily. Sera took hold of his plate, pulling hard to force Edwud to turn to face her. The blue smoke turned to white. Edwud felt the weight of Sera holding him back. He turned to look at her, touched her gently with his left antenna, and then, opening his hind wings quickly, broke her grip. As he turned to his friends, he gave a reassuring smile and raised his crossed antennae above his head.

As one body, the seven of them moved forward from the line as the pile of leaves burst into flames. The Strip suddenly seemed to widen as their feet strained to go fast enough to get to the door before the burning leaves, lifted by the breeze, blocked their entry. A shout of surprise rose from the yard collectors on the line. Edwud knew that for several moments they would not know exactly what was happening.

Without slowing their pace, and with antennae flattened, the group burst under the door of the shed. Aligned in front of them in several rows were dozens of Gerscapheos, who reared backward in shock as the strangers appeared. Edwud immediately rolled over onto his back and the others followed. Viewing the Gerscapheos upside down, Edwud called out loudly, "No attack! No attack! We want to talk! No attack!"

At first the Gerscapheos looked on in amazement, and then, deciding that this was another yard colony trick, they advanced, running with plates down to attack.

s Edwud watched the advancing Gerscapheos, he noticed that one of the yard collectors hadn't rolled over—it was Sera. She had followed him into the shed. Edwud gave her a violent kick with his legs that tumbled her over onto her back.

"We came to warn you!" Edwud called out. "Listen to us, please." The Gerscapheos paused when Edwud spoke: they were obviously very confused to see a yard collector flip one of his own kind over onto her back. When nothing else occurred, the shed collectors attacked.

The first wave leapt for the thoraxes of the supine yard collectors. Edwud felt the weight of his attacker fall heavily onto his legs, which he held above his body for protection. The Gerscapheo's teeth were snapping together at any part of Edwud he could contact. Edwud coiled his legs under the collector and thrust with the energy of fear and anger. The shed collector was flung into the air and backward almost twenty leggs.

Edwud glanced at his friends, realizing that they had automatically reacted in the same way; that the vast nights of walking during their journey had given them unusual strength in their legs. On his other side, Sera had not managed to repel her attacker; she had been bitten on her front legs and palp. Edwud leaned across, feeling his fury rise; he kicked hard at the collector snapping at her. Another line of Gerscapheos was running at them and, even under such threat, Edwud was surprised to feel that he wanted them to come; he wanted to kick and maim and hurt them; he wanted to kill them, all of them; they deserved to die. The force of it consumed him like the fire outside the door consumed the leaves.

"Lo!" A voice rang out through the shed. Edwud looked to see where it came from. The line of attackers stopped immediately. On top of a number of stacked bricks, Edwud recognized the Gerscapheo he had seen the night before, the one who had watched him from the shed window. Edwud rolled off his back and stood up; the others followed. Edwud spoke to the collector standing on the bricks.

"We came to warn you," he said. "The shed is going to burn. You have to leave now, before the door is taken by the heat and flames." Edwud turned to the door behind him and saw how the flames were reaching under the full length of the door, like the tongues of hungry nimfs.

A roar of amazement rose from the Gerscapheos as the heat drove the yard collectors forward toward them. The collector on the bricks said something to Edwud that he could not understand. Edwud watched him cross his antennae above his head, and realized that it was his bent antennae that the collector had recognized. Perhaps he had been watching from the window when Edwud disagreed with Worik and Reverend Viel.

The flames under the door leapt higher and Edwud was forced to move farther into the shed to avoid the heat. Pointing to the fire, he suddenly realized that it was too late to escape under the door, and the heat was so intense he had to keep moving farther into the shed every moment. The Gerscapheos backed away as the yard collectors advanced.

The walls on either side of the door released thick smoke, which darkened the inside of the shed. The leading collector had climbed down from the bricks and was trying to understand what Edwud was attempting to do for them. Edwud saw that Sera's injuries were not serious; the other members of his group were looking from the fire to the surrounding foreign collectors. There was no way out of the shed. Every gap, hole and possible exit had been blocked by the yard collectors long ago.

Edwud pointed with his antennae toward the ceiling of the shed. The heat was becoming intense and both groups of collectors crowded together as far as possible from the blistering walls. Edwud raced to the rough timber beams that ran up the rear wall, and began climbing to the top. The yard collectors were the first to follow and then came the Gerscapheos.

High up, the smoke was thicker but the heat was less intense. Edwud searched the window frame and the ceiling battens for an opening or a crack of any kind that might offer an escape. There was none.

The collectors crowded across the ceiling, gasping and choking, as Edwud dragged and pushed his friends to take up safe positions on the windowsill. Underneath them, half of the wall was engulfed in flames, and Edwud saw the beams twist slightly with the weight of the roof pressing down. There was no way out: he had led them all to a fiery death.

As the heat increased, Edwud looked at his friends with love. He thought of Filip's words to Jinni: "What a wonderful time I have had." Edwud thought that he too had had a wonderful time with his friends, as they struggled to understand what it was they could do that would bring harmony to the colony and to themselves. And there had never been any easy answers, as every step forward moved them closer to more change. Perhaps that was what he and his friends had come to know that made them different—that the important thing was to try, to keep trying to understand, to think, to act, to forgive others for what is in yourself.

Several of the Gerscapheos clinging to the ceiling succumbed to the heat and fell unconscious into the fire below. Edwud spread his wings to shield some of the heat from Jinni, who had collapsed alongside him, barely breathing. As he lifted her up off the windowsill and saw her look at him and smile, he felt and heard a loud cracking sound from the window.

The wall underneath the window had shifted, splitting the glass and leaving a gap the entire length of the window, through which smoke eagerly poured out. Edwud called out loudly and waved to the collectors he could see.

"A gap! Follow the smoke!" he called. He pushed Jinni through the gap and ran to tell the others. The message spread quickly as the collectors jostled and clambered their way through the streaming smoke between the broken glass. On the outside of the shed it was impossible to climb down the walls; the fire had spread and was burning fiercely on all sides below. Edwud led them upward, across the gutters and onto the tiled roof. The air was hot but mostly free of fumes. The collectors spread out across the tiles, breathing deeply, grateful to be still alive.

Edwud knew it would not be long before the walls gave way and the roof collapsed. He could hear the ceiling begin to burn beneath him and could feel the rapid rise in temperature of the roof tiles under his feet. He saw his friends circled around him, and realized that it was Jinni he had helped through the glass first. She was alongside him. Edwud moved closer to her and saw that she was now breathing normally.

On the ground below them Edwud could see the yard collectors watching in awe the monster they had unleashed. He looked for the Monoocal, which was not in the position used to start the fire. Edwud thought it must have been abandoned by those holding it when the fire flared up, and then he saw where it had rolled toward the shed and fallen so close to the flames that the metal around its edge had melted and the smooth round glass had cracked into small pieces.

The heat rising from underneath lifted Edwud's wings and reminded him of the Kitchen so long ago, and Nolan's terrified face, and. . . . The front wall suddenly gave way, causing the roof to sag on one side. The collectors on the ground gasped as they saw those clinging on the roof in the midst of the fire.

Edwud opened his wings and began flapping them up

285

and down. The others around him watched, fascinated that Edwud would be doing such a thing in such heat. Edwud closed his eyes and worked both forewings and hind wings as hard as he could. With his wings in perfect harmony, he rose upward above the roof. Another wall collapsed, sending the roof lurching to the other side.

Edwud called to the collectors on the roof, "Fly! Use your wings and fly!"

Edwud's friends immediately opened their wings and fanned them up and down in the heated air.

The yard collectors on the ground cried out in both shock and fear as they watched the group of collectors on the roof rise high into the air above the burning shed.

The Gerscapheos tried, but their wings, from lack of use, had never developed enough to carry such great weight. They wrenched them up and down desperately, watching Edwud as if his wings might lift them all.

Among the Gerscapheos was Sera. As she flapped her carefully unused hind wings, she lifted a few leggs from the roof but then flopped awkwardly down again. Clearly Sera had none of the strength the travelers had gained as they resisted and defeated the pain and difficulty of their long journey.

Edwud folded his wings from beating and floated down toward her. He placed his forewing under her body and encouraged her to try to rise again while he lifted her weight. She flapped both wings earnestly as Edwud lifted with all his strength.

The roof of the shed collapsed and a burst of flame and hot air shot upward, lifting the collectors effortlessly skyward. Edwud watched the world beneath him shrink slowly as he rose among his fellow travelers, their wings beating in harmony.

The Gerscapheos had, for a short moment, moved upward on the rush of hot air, and then rapidly disappeared into the flames. Edwud had lost contact with Sera as they lifted. There was nothing he could do.

Below them Edwud saw the yard collectors as if they had been nailed to the ground. Many of them appeared to be praying. Edwud could hear them crying, not to be left behind, pleading to be taken upward to Ootheca with Edwud and his friends.

Higher and higher the flying collectors rose in the warm air, with the world below dropping away like a stone in a pool. The collectors on the ground merging into one another; the yard blending with other yards; the city streets uniting with the country fields; the earth and the water losing their separateness.

With wings in harmony, Edwud and his friends continued rising. Edwud saw that he could, at that moment, be flying to what the Lord Maker promised: he could be flying to Ootheca. He thought of his life: it *was* what the Lord Maker promised—rich and filled with love and pain; a world of light and dark; of failure and success; of loss and gain; of unknowable mystery; of journey and homecoming.

Edwud turned to his friends about him, their wing tips brushing, and saw their hopeful faces.

The air was cooling; the heat was giving up its strength as it always did. The rise of the collectors was slowing.

Below him the world was beautifully round—a circle

that became itself, that was itself, that included itself and returned to its beginning, which was its end.

And then they were all headed for the beautiful, round circle. Edwud began to flap his wings to speed his progress: a moment of perfect floating fayth, as together they returned in afterflight to Ootheca.